THE GIRL WHO STOLE THE QUEEN'S EYES

THE GIRL WHO STOLE THE QUEEN'S EYES

MARILIZE LOXTON

ZENITH PUBLISHING

CONTENTS

Prologue   1
Chapter 1   7
Chapter 2   21
Chapter 3   31
Chapter 4   44
Chapter 5   53
Chapter 6   62
Chapter 7   75
Chapter 8   86
Chapter 9   95
Chapter 10   106
Chapter 11   121
Chapter 12   131
Chapter 13   144
Chapter 14   156
Chapter 15   170
Chapter 16   182
Chapter 17   199
Chapter 18   210
Chapter 19   221
Chapter 20   231
Chapter 21   241
Chapter 22   252
Chapter 23   264
Chapter 24   274
Chapter 25   285
Chapter 26   295
Chapter 27   308

Thank You For Reading   319
Other ZENITH Titles You May Enjoy   321
About the Author   323
About The Publisher   325

PROLOGUE

The air in Madame Spicebrook's teashop had a dryness to it. It smelled earthy—slightly of grass but mostly of black tea. A kettle hissed over a fire in the corner, billowing steam across the room. This revived even more scents. Cinnamon. Jasmine. The roasted rice of genmaicha green tea.

Pearl resisted a sneeze. The bridge of her nose prickled and her eyes watered, but she couldn't leave. Not after she had braved the dark, guard-infested streets to get there. Not after she had risked so much already, and this on the night before her sister's coronation.

"You all right?" asked Finn. He had his hand on her lower back, each of his fingertips burning through her cloak and onto her skin. His hazel eyes were barely visible under his hood.

"Yes," Pearl said and nodded. "As long as we get what we came here for."

"Are you sure? I mean, if you'd rather want to do this another night—"

"I'm not leaving here without an answer, Finn."

"Very well." Finn took his hand off her back, the absence of his touch causing chills to ripple across her skin. She watched him lower the latch on the door, locking them both in. And anyone else out.

The kettle's hissing amplified to a screech, its lid rattling, threatening to shoot off if not tended to.

"Alright, hold ye horses," came a woman's raspy voice from the back of the teashop. Her figure soon followed, short, stumpy, and with a waddle to her walk. "I'm coming ye lousy—"

The woman's words stilled in her mouth the moment she saw Pearl and Finn by the teashop's entrance. Her eyes, golden by the firelight, swerved across their cloaks, their hoods.

"The teashop's closed at night," she said and reached for the tea towel on a hook above the fireplace. Her hand was riddled with blemishes and her forehead and chin with wrinkles. She removed the kettle from the fire, and its screeching ceased, casting the shop in silence.

"We haven't come for tea," said Finn. He glanced behind him through the teashop's front window, his eyes scanning the moonlit street outside.

No one. Nothing. A village fast asleep.

The woman's expression relaxed. "Have ye got money?"

"We do." Pearl revealed a bag of coins under her cloak. It jingled as she held it up, music to the woman's ears.

"And we've got more. Please, they say you can tell from a single touch."

Seconds passed in which the woman studied Pearl, from her concealed face, all the way down to her stomach. She expelled a breath and said, "I'll do it. And don't worry about more money. I'm not really the rob-every-desperate-soul-in-sight type of sorceress." She waddled around a shelf to a cot in the corner, the floorboards creaking under her weight.

"Thank you so much," said Pearl, close to sobbing. She and Finn shared a look, then he beckoned her further into the teashop around some shelves and beyond a curtain of beads to the cot.

The woman held out her hand. "Ahem," she cleared her throat.

Pearl dropped the bag of coins into her puffy, short-fingered hand. Only then could she sit down.

"You *are* Madame Spicebrook, aren't you?" queried Finn while the woman counted the money. The fire reflected off the coins, almost as though setting fire to each one, adorned with the face of a man. The late king. He had a chiseled chin, long nose, and even longer beard.

"That depends on who's asking," she replied. Once satisfied with her payment, she popped the bag in her apron pocket and turned to Pearl. "I take it the two of ye share in a forbidden love?"

"That depends on who's asking," Finn imitated her.

Madame Spicebrook didn't take kindly to this. She raised a brow at him, then shouldered him out of the way.

A snort escaped her lips. "Right, unbutton ye corset, dearie."

Pearl glanced at Finn, who nodded at her.

"Go ahead," he said. "I'll be right here if you need me."

Pearl swallowed. Her fingers trembled across the buttons, her skin rippling with bumps when exposed to the teashop's air. She only unbuttoned the bottom of her corset, solely to reveal her stomach. Madame Spicebrook told her to lay on her back, and Pearl obeyed.

"Are you comfortable?" Finn wanted to know.

Pearl opened her mouth to say something when Madame Spicebrook's cold, fleshy hands made contact with her skin, and a yelp escaped her lips. Her heartbeat sped up as the woman murmured under her breath, her eyes shut and her voice low, hollow almost.

"Am I—" Pearl began, but Madame Spicebrook suddenly jerked and stumbled back, right into a shelf.

A jar of green tea crashed to the floor, scattering crumpled leaves and their residue throughout the teashop. It no longer smelled of cinnamon and jasmine, but grass—an entire prairie.

"Madame Spicebrook?" asked Finn, having stepped in front of Pearl. She raced to button up her corset.

The woman plucked a handkerchief from her apron and dabbed across her forehead. She clutched it to her heart as she said, "My apologies. I just had a wee bit of a fright."

A pause.

"Yes, dearie, ye are with child."

Pearl and Finn shared another look. This time, instead of relief, concern clouded their faces.

Madame Spicebrook hesitantly approached. When she spoke, her voice had lost its crackle. "Ye're Princess Pearl, aren't ye? Second-born daughter to late King Lancelot Allessien?"

Pearl gasped. Finn put his arm in front of her, half protecting her, but the woman raised her hands.

"Don't fret," she said. "Yer secret's safe with me."

But Finn didn't believe her. His eyes set ablaze as he asked, "What do you want from us? More money?"

"Finn, don't," Pearl began, though Madame Spicebrook interrupted her.

"Finn Rawd? Captain of the royal guard? My oh my, ye really are sharing in the most forbidden love."

Finn's face turned crimson. He sneered, but Pearl held him back again. She wept now, tears gushing down her cheeks. "Finn, stop it. She knows about us. And about our baby."

"What do you plan on doing now that you know? Hand us over to the royal guard?" he snapped at Madame Spicebrook.

"Escanian law dictates that I do," she replied. "But I won't."

Pearl got up from the cot. "Why not?"

Madame Spicebrook's eyes swerved to her belly. "That child of yers possesses immense power." She paused. "But ye both already knew that before ye came here, didn't ye?"

No reply.

"Ye knew that as the firstborn of the next Allessien

5

generation, he or she will inherit the family's power. The power that keeps this kingdom hidden from the outside world. The power currently in possession of yer older sister, Extine. The future queen."

Pearl burst into sobs. Her shoulders shook to such an extent that Finn had to gather her in his arms. He kissed the top of her head and whispered, "Pearl, you didn't mean for this to happen. Neither did I. But you know what you have to do. We have no other choice."

"Finn, I can't."

"You have to. If your sister finds out we stole her first-born's inheritance, she'll have our child killed."

Madame Spicebrook nodded. "The captain's right, dearie. Ye broke the law. Yer a fugitive now."

Finn raised Pearl's chin and met her eyes. A moment of silence passed between them. Tense. Thick with sorrow. He pressed his forehead against hers, their lips nearly touching. He took her necklace into his hand, a heart-shaped charm with the kingdom's crest on it.

The only gift he had ever given her. And on the night they had declared their love for each other.

"Finn—"

"I know this is difficult, Pearl," he chimed in. A single tear dripped from his chin as he added, "I don't know how I'll be able to carry on. But you've got to flee the kingdom."

A pause.

"Tonight."

CHAPTER ONE
CAMILLA

*C*amilla opened the cubicle door. She tucked her blouse into her skirt inch by inch until it puffed just right, then walked to the basins by the wall. She pumped some soap from the dispenser, twisted open the tap, and let the water foam up her hands. As she scrubbed, she studied her reflection in the waxy, restroom mirror. Light-brown hair, olive skin, and...

"What beautiful blue eyes you have, my dear," said an old woman by the basin next to her.

"Oh, thanks," replied Camilla, almost automatically. She lowered her head, rinsed her hands, and took a paper towel from the dispenser on the wall. It crunched between her fingers.

"I bet young men are just lining up for your attention, eh?"

"No, not really—"

The woman spoke over her. "I have a grandson about your age, you know. He's just the most darling young man. And, wouldn't you know it, he goes to school right here in town!"

"That's really nice, ma'am, but I'm afraid I'm in no rush to start dating. Thanks anyway." Camilla rounded the woman and slipped out the restroom door. She briefly glanced back as it closed. The woman waved at her, an almost deranged smile across her face.

Camilla sighed to herself.

No matter where she went, people constantly commented on her eyes. *Her beautiful blue eyes.* No one ever said anything hurtful, but their comments weren't exactly authentic either. Personally, Camilla had no idea what the fuss was about. Plenty of people had just as pretty eyes, if not prettier. Emerald green was her personal favorite.

Like her mother's eyes.

"Oh, I recognize that look," said Pearl as Camilla slid into their booth. Hidden in a corner by the restrooms, far from the kitchens, and with a view of the parking lot, it proved the most private booth of all. *Their* booth. "Why do you look like you just saw a ghost in there?"

The seat whistled under Camilla. She tossed back her head and studied the ceiling, counting the water stains. One. Three. Seven. She allowed the sounds of the diner to surround her. Clattering plates and utensils. The scents. Butter, coffee, and lemon disinfectant.

"Maybe because I did," she huffed.

"Is the ghost of your beautiful blue eyes haunting you again?" teased Pearl. She smiled, but her dimples didn't show. Her hair was flecked with what Camilla guessed were scrambled eggs, and ketchup stained her apron, still glossy. Her mother had worked at the Bunbun Diner for as long as she remembered, yet she never quite fit the part of a waitress. There was something in her eyes, in her skin and voice and posture, that almost made her seem... princess-like.

"They're a part of you, Camilla," said Pearl. "You only get one set of eyes. Why not embrace them?"

"I know," Camilla replied. "But sometimes I feel like no one really notices me. The real me." She sat upright as another waitress, Hannah, arrived with their order. Two large waffles.

Pearl's had only ice cream and syrup on top, whereas hers modelled a mound of berries and whipping cream. She licked her lips, and Pearl gestured for her to clear away her phone.

"Here you go," said Hannah with a smile. She attempted a wink, but the size of her false eyelash rendered it impossible. "Happy birthday, pet. You've grown into a fair young lady."

"Thanks, Han."

"Enjoy." With this, Hannah left and Camilla rotated her plate. The waffle's sweet aroma tickled her nose, and her stomach rumbled. At last, breakfast was served. She reached for a knife and fork, but Pearl leaned across the table, her hands wrapped around a tiny, black box.

"I know I've said this a thousand times today, but happy birthday," she said, smiling wonkily. Her upper lip twitched and tears pooled in her eyes, but she kept it together. Mostly.

Camilla struggled to think of a response. "Mom, you know you didn't have to buy me a present—"

"Don't worry," Pearl chimed in, "I didn't buy it. Someone gave this to me a long time ago."

"Oh."

A pause.

"And you didn't like it, so you're regifting it to me?" Camilla raised a brow. She nonetheless took the box and undid the crimson ribbon around it. She removed the lid, followed by a film of cream-colored tissue paper and gasped at the necklace inside.

"Do you like it?" Pearl wanted to know.

Camilla took the heart-shaped charm in her hand. This was no trinket from an arcade or a pawn shop. This was real gold, or the closest thing to it, engraved with a crest of some sort. She tilted it to the light. An eye in the center of a crown, encircled by rays of light.

"I love it," she said, letting it hang. The charm spun on the chain. "Mom, who gave this to you?"

Pearl made no reply. She unwrapped a knife and fork, then dug into her waffle. A moment passed in which Camilla merely sat there, watching her eat. It appeared her mother had no intention of answering. No intention of even acknowledging Camilla's question.

"Mom," she repeated, more persistent, "why didn't you sell this? It must be worth a lot of money."

Pearl's cutlery rang against the plate. She chewed, swallowed, and dabbed her mouth with a napkin. She put it down and said, "Everything's not always about money, Cam."

"Isn't it, though?"

Camilla met her mother's eyes, wishing, hoping, pleading for her to answer truthfully for once. She never admitted any of their money problems and always declined when Camilla offered to get a part-time job or sell some of her stuff—like the necklace, for instance.

"Alright," Pearl yielded, almost as if Camilla had spoken out loud. "If you really have to know. I didn't sell the necklace, because…" She paused. "Because it was a gift from your father."

Camilla choked. "My father?"

"Yes. He gave it to me before he—"

"Died in the car crash?" Camilla bit her tongue. After saying it in so many words, she was no longer hungry. She shoved aside her waffle and examined the necklace. The chain wound around her fingers, molding with the creases of her skin. She closed her palm around it.

The mere thought that her father had once touched it, held it, filled her chest with a terrible weight.

"Yes." Pearl wiped under her eyes. She reached out and wrapped her hands around Camilla's, squeezing. Her skin was rough and dry, the result of washing dishes and carrying hot plates for a living. "He wanted me to give it to you once you were old enough."

Pearl's eyes waxed over, shining with tears. She hardly ever talked about Camilla's father, but she always wept when she did. The sight of it hurt Camilla in a way she never thought possible. Deeply. Infinitely. As though she had a splinter lodged under her nail.

She swallowed hard.

"Mom," she began, but Pearl cut her off.

"His name is Finn," she said.

Camilla gasped. *Finn*. After eighteen years, she could finally put a name to the face in her mind.

To the father she never knew.

"What was he like?" she dared to ask.

"Well, your father was a wonderful man. I couldn't believe how lucky I was. He was just the most handsome, caring, and courageous person. I see him in you every time I look at you, especially now you're all grown up. Oh, how I wish he could've known you."

Camilla tightened her grip on the necklace. "I wish I could've known him too. But he sees us, Mom, I know it." She reached across the table, about to take her mother's hand when a stack of files dropped in front of them.

The plates bounced, and ice cream spilled onto the chequered tablecloth from their plummet.

Karen Bunbun, the owner, stared down at them, her hands on her hips and her left foot tapping on the floor. "Pearl," she sneered. "What have I said about taking breaks outside of lunch?"

Pearl scrambled out of the booth. She smoothed her apron and pushed back her fringe as she straightened. Next to Karen, who was dressed trimly in a pantsuit with smoothed-back, chin-length hair and designer shoes, she looked much less princess-like than before.

"Karen, I'm so sorry. It's my daughter's eighteenth birthday today, and I just wanted to—"

"Oh, spare me the details!" Karen slapped her hand on the stack of files. "Little things like these are setting back the diner, Pearl. I know you've been working here for almost two decades, but I'm starting to doubt whether you're still a fit for this establishment."

Pearl's cheeks flushed tomato red. Her eyes swerved to Camilla, though only for a second. When she saw her staring, she curved her shoulders, almost as if she was embarrassed.

Camilla couldn't stand seeing her mother so degraded. Not only did she give her best years to this place, but she worked her fingers to the bone. She couldn't stop herself. She slid out of the booth and said, "Not a fit anymore? Is this because she took one little break?"

"No," replied Karen, lingering a moment on Camilla's face, on her eyes. She picked up the files and held them out. "There are ten dollars missing in the books. And since last time was your turn to do the admin, Pearl, I'm curious to know where the missing money went."

"Ten dollars?" Camilla blurted out. "That's why you're angry with her?"

"Camilla, please," hissed Pearl, then turned to Karen. "Listen, there has to be a mistake. I assure you I didn't steal any money. Yes, things are less than perfect at home, but I'm not a thief."

Karen studied Pearl, from her messy bun to her stained sneakers. She pressed the files against her chest and pulled up her shoulders. Her bottom lip furrowed as she said, "I'm sorry, Pearl. But, as the owner of this diner, I have to set an example. I'm letting you go."

"Y—You're firing me?"

"I'm afraid so." Karen tilted her chin and placed a hand

on Pearl's shoulder. "I'll be sure to write you a great recommendation, though." She let go and was just about to walk off when—

"Karen, *wait*," said Camilla, perhaps too desperately.

Karen turned, slowly, stiffly. She raised her brows and parted her lips, but the moment their eyes locked, her brows smoothed and her mouth shut. She uttered a low "Mmm?"

Camilla tensed. She had just called Karen by her first name, and she didn't seem to care. Instead, her shoulders dropped, her face went blank, and the files slipped from her grip.

A strange calmness washed over Camilla, a type of poise she had never experienced before.

She blinked, and Karen blinked.

She frowned, and Karen frowned.

It was as if... as if she was in control of her. A tingle raced up Camilla's spine, right into her eyes.

It swirled and sputtered and sparked.

"You can't fire my mom," she said-half-commanded. "You said it yourself, didn't you? She's been working here for two decades. She's given absolutely everything to the diner."

"She's given absolutely everything to the diner," Karen repeated.

Camilla frowned at this. She searched for signs of falsity in Karen's face but couldn't find any. She was seriously, honestly out of it. And that made her feel good, powerful almost. She spoke on, "I don't know what happened to that money, but my mom didn't steal it." A brief glance at Pearl, who merely stood there, stunned. "She's not that type of person."

"Right, of course she isn't," Karen agreed with sincerity.

And suddenly, Camilla didn't feel as powerful anymore. This was all getting too strange.

Karen ought to have banned her from the diner by now, ought to have chased her mother off. The tingle in her eyes faded, and she rolled her tongue, unsure of what followed next. But when Karen said nothing—did nothing —Camilla added, "She's not fired, then?"

Karen shook her head. "I guess not."

"That's great!" Camilla cheered and wrapped her arms around her mother. "Isn't this great, Mom?"

No answer.

Camilla peeled away. "Mom?"

Her mother stared at her, less ecstatically than she had hoped. Instead of gratitude and amazement, a sort of concern glazed her eyes. A fear that went deeper than one would expect.

This unsettled Camilla, and she stepped back.

"Alright," snapped Karen, all of a sudden awake again. Her voice chirped. "Off to work!" She turned on her heels and walked off without a fuss. She swayed a little as she strode and didn't respond when Hannah asked her something about the new coffee suppliers.

"Mom, what's wrong?" asked Camilla once they were alone.

Only now did Pearl reply, her voice thunderous, "Don't ever do that again, do you hear me?"

"Do what?"

"Don't try and persuade people like that. You might not understand this right now, but controlling people is dangerous." Pearl pushed past Camilla, then started to clear their table. They had hardly touched their waffles, and the ice cream lay in a puddle on Pearl's plate.

"Controlling people? Dangerous?" Camilla scoffed. "Mom, what are you talking about?"

"You felt the power, Camilla. I know you did."

"Power? What power? I just saved you from getting fired!"

"We can't talk about this here. Not now." Pearl turned her head. "Go home. We'll discuss this later."

Camilla licked across her front teeth. What was going on? Did her mother know what just happened?

"Mom—"

"I said go."

Camilla deliberated whether she should pry some more, but decided not to. Her mother rarely got upset, which meant she probably had a good reason. A reason which she'd find out later. At home. When it was *safe*, and when her mother couldn't brush her off.

"Fine, I'll leave," she said, then grabbed her jacket off the seat and made a line for the front door. Her mother sighed in her wake, but she refused to look back. She refused to apologize for something she didn't do. For something she didn't even know she did.

The bell on the front door chimed as she pushed it open and stepped outside. The summer air hit her in the face, adding even more heat to her already scalding cheeks. Camilla tied her jacket around her waist. She stormed down the parking lot to the bike racks.

What a wonderful birthday. Eighteen years of life. Eighteen years of being treated like a child—

"Watch out!" someone shouted.

The next moment, Camilla was yanked out of the way of a reversing car. She stumbled, falling against her savior's chest. Her head fit snuggly under his chin, nestled against his collarbone. He smelt of aftershave—pine and mint—and a hint of sweat. She pressed away from him, but he kept holding on to her, his fingers latched around her wrists.

Once he noticed this, he let go and scratched behind his head.

"Oh, L—Logan, it's you," stuttered Camilla, tilting her head to meet his gaze. Her mouth was parched, and she struggled to swallow. "Thanks for, uh, well, saving my life just now."

Logan Wheeler. Tall, dark, and handsome. The son of the owner of a paper factory, a champion kayaker, and one of the most popular guys at Crystalvale High. His family's tree farms surrounded Crystalvale, and their factory provided most of the townsfolk's jobs.

Camilla had gone to school with him all her life. And they used to be friends, too, before his shoulders had broadened and his voice had deepened. Before he had made her heart pound.

"No worries. Just another day in the life of a super-hero." Two symmetric dimples dented his cheeks as he rubbed across his head. "Although, you should watch where you're going."

"Yeah, I know. I'm sorry," she said, unsure of where to look. She wanted to keep staring into his eyes—his dark, dreamy eyes—but that only made her palms clammy and caused her words to slur. "It's just this thing with my mom. I wanted to help her, but she…"

"I understand, trust me," Logan interrupted her. He put a hand on her shoulder and leaned in close, whispering, "You know, I'm also here because of my mom. She wants me to spend more time with my nan, so she's forcing me to share a milkshake with her every Friday."

"Your nan?" asked Camilla, sort of grinning. "I think I might've run into her in the restroom just now."

"You don't say?"

"Yep." Camilla bit her lower lip. "You know, she actually wanted to set me up with you."

Logan's mouth pulled into a smile. His hand slid down her shoulder to her upper arm, then to the nook of her elbow. "That wouldn't be too awful, would it?" he asked, his voice raspy.

Camilla started. She jerked away and tightened her jacket around her waist. She struggled to form an answer, once again swallowing. "I, uh, have to go. Good luck with your nan."

"Hey, wait," said Logan before she spun. "Isn't it your birthday today?"

"Y—You actually remembered?" asked Camilla, brushing a strand of hair behind her left ear. It immediately slipped free again, which prompted her to repeat the movement.

Logan parted his lips, a smile coiled around his mouth. He took his phone from his pocket and held it up. "I could lie and say I did, but... you know, Facebook helped a little."

"Ah, I see."

"Yep. So, happy birthday."

"Thanks. I appreciate it." Camilla slipped on her helmet before Logan could lean in for a hug. If he even wanted to. She unchained her bike and hopped on. Just as she was about to pedal off, Logan stepped in front of her. He scratched behind his head, and his shirt raised a little.

Camilla's eyes flicked to his bare flesh, to the V-shaped lines that cut across his skin into his jeans.

"You know, Camilla," he said, "I was wondering, well... I have this kayaking tournament at the lake tomorrow and... would you maybe want to come and watch me compete?"

Camilla's eyes widened. She combed her thoughts for an excuse, any reason not to go, but none came to mind. Of course, she'd like to go. She had, after all, known him her whole life.

"Sure," she said, barely exhaling, "what time?"

"The race starts at noon," he replied. "Thanks, Camilla. I'll be sure to look out for you." He leaned in again, too fast for her to move away this time, although not to hug her. Instead, he whispered, "Oh, and don't mind my nan. You know how old ladies can be."

His breath tickled the tip of her nose.

"Y—Yeah, okay."

"See you tomorrow, then," he said and stepped out of her way.

"Tomorrow—see you," she stammered. With this, Camilla pedaled off. She tried to withhold herself from looking back, but, unlike in the diner, she failed to do so. She nearly swerved off the road when she caught him staring. He waved, but she didn't wave back.

Not because she didn't want to, but because she if she did, her heart might've burst through her chest.

CHAPTER TWO
EXTINE

"No, that's not right either. Move it to the opposite side, but not against the wall," ordered Extine, flicking her long, skinny finger from the one side of the throne room to the other. Her head lay in her palm, and her left leg swayed to the rhythm of the clock in the corner.

Tick. Tock. Tick. Tock.

"Right away, Your Majesty." The servants heaved as they raised the fern, fully-grown, hefty, and mounted in a ceramic pot. They waddled to where she pointed, blinded by leaves.

"How's this, my queen?" asked one of the servants.

The other plucked a handkerchief from his waistcoat pocket and dabbed across his forehead.

Extine framed the pot with her fingers. She sat back in her throne, alternating her eyes. "You know what," she said after a moment of thought, "it looked better on the other side."

"E-Excuse me?"

"That means move it, you imbecile," she snapped. "I don't pay you to question my every decision."

"Of course not, Your Majesty. My apologies."

The servants slouched, but nonetheless obeyed. They muttered something amongst themselves, then proceeded to lift the pot. They barely managed it this time, moving a fair bit slower than before. A line of soil trailed behind them, dirtying the royal blue carpet. The queen rolled her eyes, regarding them as utterly pathetic.

Extine rapped her fingers on the throne's armrests.

Rap. Rap. Rap.

Servants these days were useless, especially when it came to physical, nitty-gritty work. Her husband, Finn, could do better in his sleep. In fact, he'd lift the plant with one arm.

"How about now, Your Majesty? Perfect, right?" the servant dared to ask once they had put down the pot. He slurred on his words, and sweat dribbled down his line-streaked forehead. The other servant offered him his handkerchief, although he motioned it away.

"Well," Extine began, sitting back again. She raised her hands to frame the fern when a spark ran up her spine. And not just any spark. The same spark she felt whenever she used her eyes and their power. Yet something was different this time, terribly different.

She winced when she looked through her hands. The fern was but a fuzzy blob of green and brown.

"Well?" the servant repeated.

Extine blinked, again and again. She turned her hands

around and studied her palms. Even they were blurry. Their bends, their creases. She couldn't so much as point out a vein.

She was just about blind.

"Is everything all right, Your Majesty?"

"Yes, uh, no," Extine stuttered. She got to her feet and stumbled down the carpet to the throne room doors. One of the servants approached her, though she couldn't distinguish which one. He reached out to her and she pushed past him, staggering into the fern.

"Your Majesty!" exclaimed the second servant.

"Don't follow me, either of you." Extine struggled around the plant and out of the throne room. She felt along the wall as she walked, brick by brick—cold and brittle and sharp. Her fingers easily slid into the gaps, guiding her around the corner. She yanked on a pair of curtains, tossed aside a set of armor, and followed the windowsills down the corridor.

"No, no, no," she said to herself. "This can't be happening. It's impossible. There's no way." Extine looked at the sun in one of the windows. Her eyes refused to focus, even as they seared from its brightness. She blinked vigorously, and her breathing quickened.

A mix of grey and black and white. That's all she could see. A fuzziness, waxiness, fogginess.

And then, as quickly as it had gone, her sight was back.

"Remy! Milo!" she shouted, reclaiming her balance. She blinked a couple of times and looked around. Her sight had returned, although not quite to the same clarity as before. *Come on.* She reeled up her dress and set off down the corridor. "For goodness sake, where are you?"

"Mom, what's wrong?" Remy and Milo, her two children, rounded the corner into the corridor.

Remy, at seventeen, had bright blue eyes, though not as bright as Extine's, and her father's reddish-brown hair. Milo, at sixteen, looked the spitting image of Extine, save for his eyes. While he inherited her platinum tresses, the windows to his soul were grey.

Extine grabbed her daughter's wrist. "Remy, did something happen today with your eyes?"

"Mom, you're hurting me," Remy argued, trying to wrench away, but this only made Extine squeeze harder. Her nails pierced into her flesh, almost to the point of bleeding.

"Your powers, Remy," she clarified. "Did they come in today?"

"What? No. My eighteenth birthday isn't for another few months. Why, is something wrong?"

Extine didn't answer. She let go of Remy's wrist and paced along the carpet, her eyes still blurring a little. "Something's wrong. Something's terribly, horribly wrong," she muttered.

"Sh—Should we get Dad?" asked Milo.

Still no reply.

"Seriously, Mom?" Remy set after Extine down the carpet. She grabbed her wrist, pulled her back, and jumped in front of her. The hoop through her nose glittered in the sun. "You can't just call out to us in hysterics, then refuse to say anything. Tell me what's wrong."

24

Extine scanned Remy's face. She had no reason to lie about her powers coming in, but she must've. There was no other explanation. As her firstborn, the Allessien eyes could only pass on to her. Unless something else, something much more sinister, was going on.

"Don't bother with your father," she said. "Summon the most powerful sorceress in Escana."

EXTINE MARCHED down the corridor into the foyer. She upped the grand staircase to the first landing, where she turned left down another, slightly darker corridor. She strolled to the very end, to the large cedarwood doors that led into the library and barged through them.

The space inside was quiet, abandoned, save for a single woman. Her skin was as dark as night, and her eyes shimmered golden by the candlelight. Her hair hung to the ground in thinly braided rods, and she wore a sheet-style dress, held together by a broach in the shape of a tooth. All the curtains were drawn, and the room had a staleness to it—a murk that was only intensified by the ring of candles on the table in front of the sorceress.

Extine crossed the threshold.

She shut the library doors, turned the key in the lock, and whirled around. She pressed her back against the wood and breathed for a moment, blinking vigorously again, struggling to distinguish sorceress from bookshelf. She shut her eyes and counted to ten.

"Struggling to see, are we?" asked the sorceress, calmly and collectedly, almost eerily in the silence.

"It comes and goes," answered Extine, still with closed eyes. She waited until she could at least make out the sorceress's face before she approached. "Sorceress Juniper, is that correct?"

"The one and only." Sorceress Juniper twirled her hands through the air, though her face remained vacant of any expression. She tilted her head, revealing at least five earrings on each earlobe. "I presume Your Majesty's eyes are the reason for my summoning, then?"

Extine placed both hands on the table. It creaked under her weight, so she lessened it. She watched the withering candles, breathing in their smoky aroma. Not even fire hurt her eyes.

Not anymore, at least.

"How much will it cost for you to help me?"

"I have no need for money. The sight of the great Allessien eyes is payment enough." A pause in which she hummed under her breath. "Might I add, they're even more mystical in person."

Extine pushed back off the table. She had no time for games, or chitchat. Her eyes were at stake. Her power was diminishing. She had to get to the bottom of things. "Tell me, then, Sorceress Juniper, what's happening to my eyes?"

"Why, isn't it obvious?"

"Not particularly, no." Extine grimaced.

Sorceress Juniper seemed little bothered by her reaction. She flexed her long, bony fingers, curled them around one of the flames, and made her hand into a fist. Extine waited for her to wrench away in pain, but she didn't. She moved her palm sideways and hovered it over an unlit candle. When she opened it, the flame dropped and the candle ignited.

"The power in Your Majesty's eyes has been passed on."

"Passed on?"

"Handed over."

Extine instinctively blew out the candle. She grabbed it, dug her nails into the wax, and tossed it across the room. It hit one of the bookshelves, and a stack of books toppled over. "Impossible!" she declared. "If you're trying to make a fool out of me, I won't fall for it."

Sorceress Juniper hardly twitched a brow. Her eyes shifted from the candle on the ground to the pile of books around it, and then to Extine. She focused on the queen's lips, smart enough not to look her in the eyes. "Believe me, Your Majesty, I'm not the kidding type."

Extine rubbed her forehead with her thumbs and shook her head. "No. Absolutely not. The Allessien power couldn't have been passed on. Neither of my children has come of age yet."

"What about Your Majesty's sister?"

"What about her?"

Over eighteen years had passed since Princess Pearl's disappearance. Over eighteen years since she had gone to see Madame Spicebrook. Sorceress Juniper blew out one of the candles. A trail of smoke rose to the ceiling, swirling and shaping into something—a baby.

Extine fanned it away. "You can't possibly be suggesting that she..." Extine trailed off. "No, Pearl would never break the most sacred Escanian law." She briefly considered it. "I refuse to believe it!"

Sorceress Juniper kept a straight face.

Extine wanted to scowl, but her sight blurred again, and she was forced to support herself on the table. She lowered her head and closed her eyes, trying to process what the sorceress was suggesting. There had always been rumors about Pearl sneaking out to see Madame Spice-brook. But rumors as they were, she never paid much attention to them.

Perhaps if she did, this wouldn't have happened.

"I know this must be difficult to hear, Your Majesty," said Sorceress Juniper. "I too would never have expected the younger princess to be capable of such an act of treason."

"What do you suggest we do?" asked Extine.

Sorceress Juniper hesitated.

"What is it? Tell me!"

"Well, the child has come of age, which means he or she will soon be fully in control of the Allessien power. And even though Princess Pearl broke Escanian law, her child has done nothing wrong." Another moment of hesitation. "He or she is the true heir to the throne."

"No, stop talking."

"Your Majesty—"

"I said, *stop talking!*" Extine swept her hand across the table, knocking over the circle of candles.

Sorceress Juniper curled her fingers. She followed each candle with her eyes as it rolled off the table. Extine waited for the carpet to catch on fire. The flames lapped hungrily at the threads, yet nothing happened. Nothing except for a dulling in the library's lighting.

"That child—that *illegitimate* child—is not the heir to the throne!" she hissed through her teeth. She motioned to the doors. "I have two strong children, two worthy children. Both of whom would make twice a better ruler than whoever possesses my eyes!"

"Your Majesty's family's eyes," the Sorceress corrected her.

Extine would have dismissed her, had she not still required her help. She approached the table and leaned across it, making sure to stare Sorceress Juniper in the eyes this time. They might not be at full power, but the queen's eyes still ought to do something.

Anything.

"What'll happen to Escana if we don't crown Pearl's child? What'll happen if I remain queen?"

"As the child ages, their eyes will only increase in power. It's only a matter of time until Your Majesty goes entirely blind, and the kingdom of Escana is revealed to the outside world."

The word "blind" hit Extine harder than she expected. She stumbled back, grabbed her hair, and cursed under her breath. She paced down the length of the table while Sorceress Juniper merely sat there, surrounded by fallen candles and books. She watched her, perhaps judged her.

Minutes passed, and after three more blind spells, Extine finally got an idea. She set her jaw as she said, "You wanted to know why I summoned you to the castle, didn't you?"

"I did."

"Well, you're the most powerful sorceress in Escana. And my request is somewhat of a stretch."

"If my power allows it, it shouldn't pose a problem."

"Give me my eyes back."

Sorceress Juniper, for the first time, raised an eyebrow. She got to her feet, adjusted the sheet across her shoulder, and said, "Your Majesty, the greatness, the difficulty, of this request . . ."

"If you're not able to do it, just tell me. I'll find someone else. I'm sure there are plenty of other sorcerers in Escana who'd be more than willing to give me what I want."

Sorceress Juniper thought about it for a moment.

"So?" pressed Extine. "Can I depend on you?"

The sorceress sat down again. She rolled back her shoulders and regained her composure. "I can do it, but I have to warn Your Majesty beforehand. This is a dark type of magic." A pause. Her voice turned solemn. "And it might come with a great price to pay."

Extine locked her elbows by her sides and gritted on her teeth. She said, "I don't care about the price. I'm the rightful Queen of Escana, and I will have my eyes back no matter what."

CHAPTER THREE
CAMILLA

*A*round noon on Saturday, Camilla cycled to the lake. Instead of only a couple vendors, she arrived at an ocean of pavilions and booths—more than what had been at any previous kayaking tournament hosted in Crystalvale. The trailers of athletes from across the state filled the parking lot, each with at least three kayaks strapped on top.

A metal fence had been pitched around the shore all the way from the one side of the forest, across the length of the parking lot, to the other side. Two ambulances were parked near the entrance, and a line of people trailed almost to the road. Camilla fell in at the back of it.

Nearly fifteen minutes passed in which she checked her phone for messages, searched for Logan amidst the crowd, and endured various compliments regarding her eyes.

"That'd be five dollars," declared the booth attendant when she finally reached the front of the line.

Camilla rifled in her bag for the money. The last thing she'd expected was paying an entrance fee, and thus had left her wallet at home. All she had in her bag were sketchbooks, stationery, and gum. Perhaps she had cash in her pencil bag? She zipped it open and searched inside.

Nothing.

"Five dollars, please," the booth attendant repeated.

"Sorry, I don't have any money with me," she said softly, trying hard to keep this information a secret from the people behind her. The last thing she wanted was someone taking pity on her. In fact, it was already humiliating enough holding up the line like this.

"No money, no entry," said the attendant.

"But—"

"Listen, doll, I don't get paid enough to deal with this." The attendant parted his lips, just about to call for the next person in line when he met Camilla's eyes—which had started to tingle again. His pupils dilated, and his face dissolved into a wonky grin. His glasses slid to the tip of his nose, at the brink of falling off, but he simply stood there.

Entranced.

"You go to Crystalvale High, right?" asked Camilla without intending to. She focused on the tingles, on the adrenaline in her veins. "Is it okay if I pay you back at school on Monday?"

The attendant swayed on his heels. Camilla frowned at this, and he snapped back to life. He removed his glasses, wiped the lenses with the end of his shirt, and shook his head at her.

"Pay me back later?" he said. "Not a chance."

Camilla's cheeks warmed. How silly of her, thinking her *charms* would work a second time. But she had to try. There was just something in Karen's reaction at the diner —in the look on her face and the tone in her voice—that had convinced her she could do it again.

As usual, though, she was in over her head.

Camilla adjusted the bag over her shoulder. She turned and was just about to step out of line when—

"You don't have to pay me back at all. Go right ahead." The booth attendant's entire demeanor had changed. He didn't even put his glasses back on. "Enjoy the tournament."

"Really? Are you sure?" asked Camilla. She extended her hand and the booth attendant stamped it.

"Yep."

"Uh, thanks." Camilla was free to enter. She walked inside with hesitation, a part of her wondering whether he was pulling her leg. But as she glanced back, he had already helped the next person in line. Did she really do it again? Did she really . . . do what, exactly?

Camilla recalled her mother's words. She had persuaded him like she had persuaded Karen. Her mother had made it sound like a bad thing, but how could something that felt so good, be bad? Her eyes buzzed with electricity, almost as though she had reached out and grabbed the booth attendant's soul, shaking him into submission.

Camilla shivered. She pushed aside the incident and focused on finding a place to sit. Three pavilions overlooked the lake, all of which crawled with onlookers. She made for the nearest one, then strolled along its length, browsing the bottom steps for an opening.

Nothing.

"Do you want my seat?" asked someone in front of her, and she winced. It was a young man, possibly in his twenties, at the bottom of the pavilion. He looked, stared, gaped at her.

"Excuse me?" asked Camilla.

"I asked, do you want my seat?"

Camilla, still surprised, replied, "Don't worry about it, really. You don't have to get up for me."

"No, no, I insist." The man gathered his things. His movements were frantic and unorganized, as if unintended. He stuffed a camera under his arm, rolled up the blanket he was sitting on, and downed his last bit of coffee. "A girl with such pretty eyes can't possibly stand."

This made Camilla cringe.

She wanted to decline his offer, but he was up and out of the way before she so much as opened her mouth. He gestured for her to sit down, the same, ever-unsettling smile around his mouth. Then, he tipped his hat at her and strolled to the adjoining pavilion.

"Th—Thank you!" she called after him, alas to no response.

Camilla sat down with her bag in her lap. She had a perfect view of the lake: a dark blue expanse of water surrounded by thick forestry. She spotted Logan, slightly to her right, in what resembled the warmup area. He lay on the ground, stretching, surrounded by girls.

They swooned and laughed and touched him every

available chance. He did nothing to lead them on, but he nonetheless seemed to enjoy the attention, often returning a smile.

"I'm rooting for you, Logan," said one girl. "After the race, how about we celebrate together?"

"*We?*"

"Yeah, just you and me."

Logan choked. "I—I'll have to pass on that one, Beck. But thanks, maybe some other time?"

"Oh, yeah. Sure."

Camilla almost felt bad for Beck. She watched as more girls threw themselves at him. One of them removed a black-and-green wristband from her pocket and offered it as a gift.

"I braided it myself," she said.

Logan smiled as he let her put it on him. She giggled and, quite daringly, pecked him on the cheek.

Camilla sighed and looked away. Of course, he didn't invite her because he wanted to see her. As a serious competitor, Logan sought as many people present to support him as possible. She was just one of many, another pair of hands to applaud him. To call out his name.

She opened her bag and took out her sketchbook, a tattered-looking thing with crinkled pages and water-color stains across it. Next, she unzipped her pencil bag, chose the sharpest pencil, and scanned the lake for something to sketch. A light breeze brushed the water, swaying the trees and bobbing the buoys that marked the tournament route.

The whole scene, while perfectly serene, seemed somewhat artificial to her, almost manufactured. The pine trees were planted in perfect rows, and the buoys were tied exact measurements across and apart from each other. Perfectly calculated. Flawlessly executed.

Camilla stroked the blank page. She made to shut her sketchbook when something on the lake caught her eye.

Not on the lake, exactly, nor behind or in front of it either. It was just there, in the air, in the middle of nowhere. She only distinguished a wall at first, but the longer she stared at it, the clearer, the more solid the picture became. Beyond the wall was a building, a castle. It sported quite a few towers, all with fluttering flags, and its bricks glittered off the sun.

A blend of soft purple and light pink.

Coral, almost.

Camilla squinted at the crest on the flags. It seemed terribly familiar, yet she couldn't place where she had seen it before. She sat back and glanced around her. People cheered, chatted, and worked on their phones. None of them noticed the castle. Not even the little boy next to her, who held out his toy boat while pretending it sailed on the lake.

"Hey, don't you see that?" she blurted out.

The boy turned his head without lowering his boat. "See what?" he asked, clearly oblivious.

"That . . . There . . . On the lake!"

"Oh, those orange, floaty things?" the boy wanted to know. "Aren't they great? I love everything about sailing and boats! Boy, I wonder if they'd let me keep one once this is over."

Camilla pursed her lips. Orange floaty things? The boy had no idea what she was talking about.

Like everyone else, he didn't see a thing.

"They might if you ask them," she sighed, giving up on the castle. "I like your boat, by the way."

"Thanks, it's the newest model. My mommy gave it to me for my birthday. It takes batteries and everything..." The boy rambled on, but Camilla only half listened to what he said.

As avidly as she tried, and she really did, she couldn't ignore the structure in front of her.

Either she was going crazy, or this too had something to do with her eyes. Except they weren't tingling. And she wasn't persuading anyone.

Camilla's hand began to draw, almost on its own. If no one else saw the castle, she'd have to make them see. She sketched the lake, the walls, and the towers, exactly as they floated on the water. And with every line she drew, every shade she colored in, the apparition solidified before her. It became clearer, more realistic, almost taking full shape when—

"What are you drawing?" asked a voice.

Camilla started, and the tip of her pencil broke. She looked up, nearly jerking when coming face to face with Logan. He stood in front of her, dressed in a wetsuit that stretched around his upper body and thighs. His hair was wet already, water skidding down his temples.

"Sorry, I didn't mean to scare you," he chuckled.

"Oh, no, you didn't. I just—wasn't expecting you to stand there." Camilla put her pencil behind her ear. She tried to shut her sketchpad, but Logan helped himself to it before she could.

"Nice," he praised, turning the page around. A frown split between his brows, but he paired it with a grin. "A castle? On the lake? You've got quite the vivid imagination."

"Who, me?" She gulped. "It's just something I came up with. It's not even that good." Camilla stood up and reached for her sketchpad, but Logan yanked it out of her reach.

He turned and held it up to the lake, aligning it with the water. "Wow, it's almost as though the castle's really there!" He paused. "But I have to agree with you, it's not that good."

"Oh, well—"

"It's amazing."

Camilla blushed.

"You've got a real talent," Logan praised her, still facing away. "Why don't you enter competitions and stuff? You shouldn't hide your drawings. Not while they're this good."

"Oh, I don't know."

Seconds passed, and when he still hadn't returned her book, Camilla got on her toes and reached for it. She lengthened herself, just about grazing the bottom left corner when Logan spun and tipped her over. She fell right into him, onto him, with her hands around his neck.

"Whoa!" he exclaimed as his arms found their way

around her waist. "If you wanted to make a move on me, Camilla, you could've just asked me out. There's no need to throw yourself at me." He waited before he let her go, his palms shaping to the curve of her back.

"I wasn't throwing myself at you," Camilla insisted. She pried herself away from him and yanked back her sketchbook. "I was but redeeming my stolen property. There's a difference."

Logan cocked his head at her. "Stolen property?" He smirked. "But seriously, that's really good."

Camilla reclaimed her seat on the pavilion. "Thanks" was all she managed. Her cheeks properly seared, and her palms stuck to the sketchpad. She hid her face behind her hair.

"I actually came over to say I'm glad you're here." Logan exhaled, and his abs tightened.

Camilla swooned internally. "No problem. What are friends for, right?"

"Friends," Logan agreed and scratched his elbow. "Right." Before he could add anything else, a siren blared from the side of the lake, calling all competitors to prepare their kayaks.

"I guess that's my cue."

"Good luck."

"Thanks." Logan flashed her a tight smile. "See you around, Camilla." Then, he spun and returned to the warmup area.

One by one, the competitors dragged their kayaks along the shore. Once in the water, they rowed out to the dock where a ribbon suspended across the lake—the starting point.

"Ladies and gentlemen," announced a man on the dock. He had a microphone in one hand and a horn in the other. He wore a fancy suit with gumboots and a floppy hat, with sunscreen slathered across his nose. "Welcome to this year's kayaking state championship!"

The crowd whistled and cheered.

Camilla applauded, although she had no idea what the man was saying. Her eyes scanned the lake, searching for the castle. For the towers and flags and walls. It had all vanished, and nothing but a manufactured puddle lay before her. A lake with orange floaty things.

"Twenty competitors from across the state have travelled here today with one thing on their minds: to win a spot at nationals." More cheers. "Only the first two competitors will achieve this, though, so it truly is a battle to the death. Now, on the very end, we have Logan Wheeler from Crystalvale High . . ." The man went on to introduce all the competitors, each of whom received a generous amount of applause from their supporters.

Once he was done and had gone over the course, he raised his horn in the air and blasted it.

The kayaks set off, each one faster and more eager to win than the next. Camilla found it terrible to watch, as she really wanted Logan to win. She had been wrong about him before. He didn't just invite her to fill up the stands, and had actually made the time to come and talk to her. He was a good friend. One who looked quite hot in a wetsuit.

Camilla scolded herself for her thoughts.

Logan was her friend, and that was all they'd ever be. Not only was she nowhere near as pretty as Beck and his other fangirls, but he had a way too big personality for them to match. He liked to talk, and she didn't. He loved to go out and party, and all she wanted to do was stay in and draw. The only possible thing they had in common was cycling.

And school, of course.

"The Morris brothers from Leonasville High have taken an early lead, although it seems Logan Wheeler from Crystalvale High is catching up to them!" The man ran up and down the dock, relaying whatever was happening to the crowd. "Oh, and what's this? The wind has suddenly taken up!"

Camilla scoured the lake. He was right. The waves were now much, much bigger than before. And not only did the wind take up, but an ominous bank of clouds had covered the lake. The sky rumbled and groaned, expelling flashes of light that lit the darkened sky.

The crowd reacted accordingly. With each flash, each rumble and strike, they gasped, some even whimpered.

"Look at that! We have two kayakers overboard!" shouted the man over the microphone. The speakers pitched, adding to the already ominous atmosphere. "And three more! They're tipping over one after the other!" A pause. A gasp. "Look at that monster of a wave!"

Camilla, like the rest of the crowd, got to her feet.

"Oh, my goodness!"

"What a sight!"

A gigantic wave had risen from the other side of the lake and was rolling, gushing, tumbling towards the shore. Towards *them*. People across the pavilions wrestled to climb down. They gathered their children, shouted at the competitors, and fled for their vehicles.

"Look! It seems the Morris brothers are still at it! They're not giving up; they're simply not giving up! And what's this? Logan Wheeler's still on their tails . . . He sees the wave, he's sizing it up . . . He's decided to abandon ship! Logan Wheeler has tipped over his own kayak!"

Camilla let out a deep breath. Good. He shouldn't risk it. The wave would swallow him whole.

"Will the Morris brothers turn around?" asked the man, mostly to himself. He ran down the dock, across the shore, and into the tree line. His breathing echoed over the speakers, along with the rustling of his clothes in the wind. "No, they're heading right into the wave!"

"Don't do it!" cried someone.

"Turn around!" added another.

Camilla found herself frozen in place in the pavilion. She knew she had to move, had to flee, but something kept her there. Something made her stare at the water, right into the heart of the wave. She gave a couple of rapid blinks, and the castle began to take shape again.

The monster of a wave surrounded it, almost as though the castle was the source of its power. She searched for Logan and spotted him a bit off the shore, swimming as fast as his arms allowed. He might've bailed out, but the Morris brothers were determined to win.

They were going at it, trying to surpass the wave

before it reached them. And for a moment, a short, mere one at that, it looked as though they were going to make it.

Then a strike of lightning hit the water.

Logan rolled onto the shore just in time, whereas the Morris brothers were trampled by the wave, engulfed whole. The moment they disappeared, the wave collapsed, the thunder died down, the clouds cleared, and the wind stilled. A silence roamed over the lake.

"W—What just happened?" Camilla rubbed her eyes. The castle had vanished again, but that was not the only thing. The Morris brothers didn't resurface. Their kayaks were gone.

Their oars were gone.

They were gone.

CHAPTER FOUR
EXTINE

*E*xtine reached for the hand mirror on the table next to her throne. She briefly caught her reflection in a jug of water and looked away. Contorted as it was, she saw enough to give her chills. Her fingers curled around the mirror's handle, her lungs filling with air. She flipped it and raised it to her face, afraid to look. One. Two. Three. She opened her eyes.

Alright.

Not too bad.

Sorceress Juniper had done everything possible to fix Extine's sight, although her power still lacked in places. The inside of her eyes had turned a rosy color, and a shade of faded black encircled them. Her eyes tingled, itched, and seared every time she blinked.

Extine brought the mirror closer. She placed a finger under her left eye, hesitantly, tenderly. She was just about to press down a little when the throne room doors burst open and her husband, Finn, stormed inside. She winced, stuffing the mirror under the cushions.

"Extine, here you are," he said.

"Here I am? Well, where else would I be?"

Finn huffed as he ran down the carpet to her throne. The buckles on his boots clanged, and his leather vest crunched as he moved. A moment passed in which he looked at her—at her eyes—then he shook his head and said, "Can you tell me what's going on?"

"What do you mean?"

"There's something wrong with the Escanian borders."

Extine sat up, the mirror pressing into her side. "What kind of something?"

"I don't know how to explain it, but they're all—"

A pause.

"Flickering," he finished. "And on top of that, the lake's been uneasy since this morning. You know what this means, don't you?" Finn absently grabbed at the sword on his belt. He took another, much larger step forward, upon which Extine leapt from her throne.

"It means the borders are failing," she agreed with her head lowered and her hands on her hips.

"Which is why I need you to tell me what's going on."

Extine turned and paced to the far end of the throne room. The last thing she wanted was for Finn to see her without her eyes. She wasn't in full control of her power anymore, even under Sorceress Juniper's magic. There was no telling what effect that might have on him. How he might feel about her now that she couldn't control him anymore.

Finn combed his fingers through his beard, a brownish thing with a white streak in the middle. He remained in position with perfect posture. After more than eighteen years of marriage, he still acted towards her like the captain of the royal guard: formal and detached. He hardly ever touched her and solely confessed his love when she compelled him to.

Only now that she had lost her eyes—her power—she feared she might never hear those words again. Never feel the touch of his lips against her cheek or his hand around her waist.

"Extine, just speak to me already," Finn pressed. "You haven't looked at me since I came in here."

Extine froze. She clenched her fists, rolled back her shoulders, and turned on her heels. She kept her head down as she approached him, hoping, wishing, praying that her eyes didn't look as bad as they had in the mirror. Red and puffy was hardly their normal appearance.

"It's not you," she half whispered as she reached Finn. She waited for him to take her hands, but when he didn't, she took his instead. He squeezed them slightly, then let go again.

Finn tilted her chin and pushed a strand of hair behind her ear. "Extine, please, look at me."

"I—I can't."

"Why? Did I do something wrong?"

"No, of course not." Extine pursed her lips. She swallowed a final time and forced her eyes open.

"Extine!" he yelped, getting a good look at her for the first time. "What happened to you?"

Extine briefly thought about acting surprised, as if she too had no idea, but her emotions suddenly took over, and she blurted out, "Do you know why my sister ran away, Finn?"

"Pearl? N—No, why?"

Extine turned her head away from him. She walked sideways to the windows and stopped when she spoke. "I always thought she was jealous of me. That she wanted to be queen. I thought when I was crowned, she couldn't handle it. I always wondered what I could've done to make her stay. But no. She ran away, Finn . . . because she was having a baby."

Finn stumbled back. He tripped over a loop in the carpet but managed to reclaim his balance. His eyes bopped about the throne room, and his jaw worked, yet no words emerged from his mouth.

"I know," she went on, "I couldn't believe it myself." Extine let her hair drape over her eyes again, hiding them, shielding them from the light that entered through a slit in the curtains.

"That was over eighteen years ago," she added.

Finn's face became alive when she said this. "Eighteen years? Well, doesn't that mean—"

"Yes, it does. As the firstborn child of the next Allessien generation, Pearl's baby is the heir to the throne. He or she has taken my eyes from me and has stolen our daughter's legacy."

"Extine—"

"Remy was supposed to be crowned Queen of Escana!"

Silence.

"Pearl broke Escanian law, Finn. She knew the power of my eyes would fade once the firstborn of the next generation comes of age. She also knew *I* was supposed to give birth to said child. She could've gotten rid of it, but she didn't care. She only thought of herself."

"It's a *baby*, Extine, not an *it*."

"Are you defending her, Finn?"

His face drained of color. "N—No. I'm just saying, you don't know what her circumstances were."

"I know she was seeing someone behind my back."

Finn choked.

"Probably someone from the outside who knows nothing about Escanian law," she went on. "She ran away because she knew her child would've been killed once he or she was born, and I know said child likely knows nothing about our world. Ha! If he or she is crowned, we might very well take down the borders and merge with the outside right now!"

"Would that really be such a bad thing?"

"Yes! The child simply cannot be crowned, Finn!" Extine spat. She lost herself for a moment, then inhaled deeply and wiped her mouth with her sleeve. She adjusted her upper bodice.

Silence.

"The only thing I don't know is her whereabouts."

"She?"

"Pearl, of course."

"Oh, right. But if you don't know where she is, how did you find out about this in the first place?" Finn ran a hand through his hair for the thousandth time. He kept gazing to and from the throne room doors, almost as if he had somewhere more important to be.

"Sorceress Juniper told me."

"A sorceress? Have you lost your mind?" Finn snapped. A blue vein swelled in the center of his forehead. "You can't seek help from a sorceress! They can't be trusted, you know this!"

Extine couldn't hold herself back anymore. How dare he speak to her, the Queen of Escana, this way. Her dress flared behind her, sailing through the air as she charged down the carpet.

"Do you think I don't know that?" Her fingers spasmed as she balled them into fists, wielding them at Finn. "I am going blind! The kingdom is at stake, and I had to do something!"

"So, you thought toying with dark magic was the best solution to your—our—problem?"

"The borders are still up, aren't they?"

Finn marched towards the windows. He yanked on a golden cord, and the heavy velvet curtains peeled apart. Extine winced at the sun. She could barely tolerate standard indoor lighting, never mind the light from outside. But she couldn't let Finn know about any of the dark magic's side effects. She stood up straight and opened her eyes wide.

"Do you see your kingdom?" asked Finn.

Extine nodded. "I do." But she didn't—not really. "I've seen it every single day since I was born. I'm prepared to do anything to save it, Finn, even if that means trusting a sorceress."

Finn nonetheless went on. "Escana has thrived for centuries and all because of your family's eyes. The Allessiens have been hiding us from the outside world, generation after generation. The borders might still be up right now, but I'm not sure for how long anymore."

Extine stepped further into the light. It burned so terribly, almost as though her eyeballs were laced with needles, but she endured it, faked it, and forced the illusion of confidence.

"We can't trust a sorceress," declared Finn. "Not when the lives of your subjects are at stake."

"You know, *husband dear,*" said Extine after a moment of silence. "I think I liked you better when you kept to yourself." She barely had the chance to witness Finn's reaction when a pain even sharper than the effect of sunlight shot through her head and into her eyes.

Extine screamed. She fell on her knees, covered her eyes with her palms, and shuddered at the trill—the screech—in her ears. Her head spun, throbbing with absolute pain.

"Extine!" exclaimed Finn. He ran towards her, but the ground suddenly began to shake, and he fell over. He skidded on his knees across the carpet, crawling to her side on all fours.

Cries echoed down the corridor beyond the doors, and the windows rattled to such an extent, Extine thought they might shatter. She buried her head between her knees, cupping her eyes.

"Make it stop," she muttered. "Just make this horrible pain stop!"

Finn picked her up and carried her to the center of the throne room, away from the rattling windows. He laid her on the carpet, removed her palms from her eyes, and looked them over.

"Does it hurt?" he asked.

"It hurts, yes. I can't . . . I feel like I'm dying."

Finn frowned when he looked at her.

Extine had no idea what he saw, but whatever it was, it made him grab the jug of water by her throne and dip his hands in it. Then, he hunched over her, wetting her eyes. The moment the water hit her irises, her head throbbed less, and the pain subsided. She could've sworn she heard her eyeballs hiss, though that would be impossible.

"How's that?" he wanted to know.

"Much better." Extine dried her eyes. They returned to normal, or the closest thing to it, and the ground stopped shaking. The trill was replaced with a whistle, a continuous peep.

"How did you know to do that?" she asked, still lying on her back. She studied the patterned ceiling, testing her sight one eye at a time. Left. Right. They were fine now.

Still tingly, still scratchy, but fine.

Finn sat back, out of breath. "I didn't. Not really. I just thought your eyes looked like—"

"Like what?"

"Like they were *smoking*." A pause in which he chuckled. "I must've just imagined it." Then, he grabbed the jug of water and took a large swig. He lowered it onto the carpet next to her and straightened his legs. Just then, the throne room doors burst open again.

Remy and Milo stumbled inside, each fighting to be in front. Their faces had little color, even less than usual, and they pointed outside in rapid jerks. They didn't even notice the empty jug of water, the wet carpet, or both their parents sprawled on the ground.

Remy shouted, "Get up! You have to come!"

"Yes, quickly!" added Milo.

"Don't worry, children, everything's fine," Finn began, but Milo cut him off before he finished.

"No, it's not," he declared.

Remy bopped her head. "There was a storm . . . and the borders . . . followed by a giant wave . . ."

"Two outsiders!" yelled Milo.

"Please, slow down." Finn got to his feet. He raised his hands at them, gesturing for them to breathe, to re-collect themselves. "What are you two talking about? Two outsiders?"

"Two men," Remy affirmed, less frantic now. "They crossed the border. Washed up on the castle walls."

"Washed up?" asked Finn.

"On the castle walls?" repeated Extine.

"Yep, and they're both in kayaks."

CHAPTER FIVE
CAMILLA

*C*amilla stood by the edge of the lake. The water lapped at her toes, wetting her sandals, but she hardly even noticed. Another thing she didn't notice was the time. The sun had settled on the horizon already. She scoured the lake. Three rescue boats crawled across it, slowly, diligently and with men hanging overboard, wielding flashlights.

Every few minutes, a diver or two surfaced for a rest, each with the same hopeless shake of the head.

"No sign of them yet?" she heard someone ask one of the divers.

"Nope. Not even so much as a strand of hair, I'm afraid," the diver replied before he dove back in.

Nearly six hours had gone since the Morris brothers vanished without a trace. The newsflash remained the same, though: their kayaks nor their oars have been found. It was as if that wave had truly swallowed them, as if they'd been transported to another world.

Camilla was one of the very few people who had stayed behind after the incident. She partly stayed because she wanted to check up on Logan, but also because something compelled her to.

"Did you know the missing fellas?" a policeman had asked her shortly after the lake had settled. He had two bloodhounds on a leash, both of which popped their noses in Camilla's bag.

"No, I didn't," she had answered.

"You need a lift home, then?"

"No thanks, I came here on my bike. I think I'll sit here for a few more minutes if that's all right?"

The policeman had reeled in the bloodhounds. He had pursed his lips and glanced across his shoulder. "I don't think that'll be"—his eyes locked with hers—"*a big problem.*"

"Really?"

"Sure, why not. Just don't go near the water, all right?" And with that, the policeman had set off again.

That was about three hours ago.

Camilla had gotten so entranced again, that a few minutes had turned into a few hours. The yellow police tape that surrounded the lake fluttered in the breeze, reminding her of flags.

Of the castle's flags.

At five o'clock, the first search boat had arrived. It belonged to Logan's father but was manned by the Morris brothers' family. The Crystalvale police had broadcasted a plea for every boat owner and diver to lend a hand, although thus far, only three boats and ten divers had responded.

Camilla scanned the lake from left to right. She had no idea what she was looking for, but she knew she was looking for something—anything to explain the castle and the unexpected storm that had somehow died down the moment the Morris brothers disappeared.

"Where are you?" she mouthed to herself.

But no matter how ardently she looked, there was no castle and nothing she could link to it.

Camilla sighed. She gazed down at the sketchpad in her hand with the detailed drawing of the lake. Had it been an illusion? Was she finally, after years of being a loner, losing her mind?

"Camilla!" cried a voice behind her, followed by shoes sloshing across the wet soil of the shore.

Camilla made to turn around, but the person grabbed her by the shoulders and yanked her towards them. It was her mother. Her hair hung in dangles, and her eyes were filled with the type of tears that threatened to spill over at any moment.

Tears of frustration, anger, and absolute horror.

"Mom."

"Are you okay?" asked Pearl, violently rubbing up and down Camilla's arms, checking her wrists, face, and eyes. "Have you been here all day? Have you eaten anything?"

"Mom!"

Pearl ignored her. She added, more seriously, "What on earth are you doing here in the first place?"

Camilla pried herself away from her mother. "I was

here to watch the kayaking tournament." A pause in which she recollected herself. "Mom, shouldn't you be at work right now?"

"I got Hannah to cover the rest of my shift. I came over here the moment I saw what had happened."

"What do you mean, you *saw*?"

"It's all over the news! Two kayakers swallowed by a wave!" Pearl approached the water. She looked up and down the length of the lake, lingering a moment on a certain spot, an empty spot, in the center. She went on, "Did anything happen? I mean, did anything happen *to you*?"

Camilla raised a brow. "I'm fine, Mom. Why would anything have happened to me? I was right here on the pavilion the whole time. But, how did you even know I was here?"

"I, well—"

"You what?"

"I don't know. I had a feeling—" Pearl's eyes swerved to the drawing in Camilla's hand, and she stalled midsentence. She grabbed it and held it out, her chest pumping up and down.

"Mom!"

"What is this?" Pearl demanded to know.

"A castle?" replied Camilla with a shrug.

"W—Where did you see this? Why did you draw it?"

Camilla reached for her sketchpad, but her mother was even quicker to yank it away than Logan. "It's just something I came up with. It's silly, really, and it's not even real."

"That's right. It's not real," Pearl insisted. She ripped the drawing from the sketchpad, glanced at it a final time, then crumpled it in one hand. The paper rustled and crunched.

Her art.

Her masterpiece.

"Mom!" shouted Camilla with an unusual shrillness to her voice. She managed to grab her sketchpad, but not the crumpled drawing. "You have no right to do that! It's my drawing!"

"Is it? Last I checked, I paid for all of your supplies." Pearl drew back, then tossed it in the lake.

It wilted almost instantly.

Camilla thought about diving in after it, but she decided it wasn't worth it. She could always draw the castle again later at a time and place her mother couldn't confiscate it.

"Camilla," Pearl went on.

"What?"

"Don't you ever draw something resembling that again. Ever. Do I make myself clear?" Pearl spoke in jerks, articulating each syllable. Her nails pressed into Camilla's right wrist.

"Ouch, you're hurting me!" Camilla wrenched away. She checked around her wrist for any bruises, but, luckily, there were none. "What's the big deal anyway? It's just a stupid castle."

"It's not about *what* it is, Camilla," said Pearl, matter-of-factly. "It's about *where* you had drawn it," she emphasized, pointing at the lake. "And *why* you had decided to draw it in the first place."

"Mom, have you seen the castle before?"

Pearl was taken aback. "What? No, it's just a drawing. Why would you even ask me such a thing?"

"Because of that!" Camilla pointed to the spot where the drawing had disappeared into the water. "First, you warn me against *persuading* people, and now you're against drawing castles?"

"We're not discussing this now, Camilla."

"That's what you said yesterday at the diner. And then you avoided me all night at home. When will you tell me what's going on with me? If there's something wrong . . . if I'm sick . . ."

"You're not sick."

"What is it, then?"

The wind yanked Pearl's hair from her braid. For a moment, it seemed as though she might open up, but then her eyes swerved across the lake again, and she sucked the inside of her cheek. "Don't worry about it. I'm sure if we ignore it, everything will go back to normal."

A pause.

"Come, we're going home. It's not safe for you to be here."

"Mom, just tell me!" Camilla argued, but Pearl grabbed her hand and dragged her past the pavilions to the parking lot. She kept looking around, combing, scanning, searching for something.

They passed by an ambulance just outside the entrance, at the back of which Logan was being patched up. He hadn't been too badly hurt on the lake but had suffered several scrapes and bruises when he washed up. He had a scuff mark on his neck that reached under his armpit. The paramedics had to take off the top of his wetsuit to have it treated.

This was the first time Camilla had seen him without a shirt on since his growth spurt. She looked away as they passed, but her eyes involuntarily focused on his lean upper body. He lay sideways at the back of the ambulance, his abs bulging as he supported himself.

Logan smiled when he saw her, and Camilla tensed. She thought she might actually die.

There he was, leaning alluringly with a paramedic treating his wounds, while she was being hauled off to an old Chevy hatchback by her mother, who was still in her waitress uniform, no less.

Logan knew about Pearl's job, of course, though Camilla preferred not to remind him. His family practically owned the entire town, which meant she had little to impress him with.

In fact, she still rode the same bicycle she had gotten at thirteen, and her phone was a hand-me-down from her mother. She had nothing to offer and preferred he didn't know that.

Logan paired his grin with a wave. He frowned when she did nothing to respond and made to get up, but the paramedic forced him back down. Camilla looked away at this point. While she wanted to wave back, it'd be better if he thought she wasn't interested.

"Mom, what about my bike?" she asked.

"I'll have Bob from across the street drop it off later. He's got a boat in the water right now."

"Okay, but can you please let go of me?" Camilla wriggled herself free as they got to the car. She rubbed her wrist, which still throbbed from earlier. "I can walk by myself, thanks."

Pearl surveyed their surroundings. "Get in." She yanked open the Chevy door and hopped inside.

The passenger door was locked, though, so Camilla made gestures through the window. She gazed back at the ambulance a final time, almost regretting not having waved back.

Almost.

The door unlocked, and she swung it open. She slid inside just as the Chevy roared to life.

"Why are you in such a hurry to get home?" asked Camilla, half annoyed, half confused still.

"I told you, it's not safe here."

"Well, sorry if I don't believe you. Maybe if you told me why you keep looking around like a maniac."

"Camilla, please, just drop it," snapped Pearl. She seemed somewhere far away as she switched the Chevy into reverse. The engine rumbled, and she jerked on the gears to get it into drive.

Camilla didn't pry any further. All she wanted right then was silence. She wanted to steep in her own thoughts, forget about the castle, and get Logan out of her mind. She turned sideways in her seat, propped her head on her palm, and stared out the window. They turned down a bend, and her view of the lake was replaced with one of the forest. Everything looked the same at first. Trees were trees and rocks were rocks, but then—

Someone emerged from the foliage.

A dark figure.

A man.

Camilla squinted but couldn't see his features, only that he had a brown beard with a white streak in the center. His head followed them as they drove off, his eyes fixed on Pearl behind the wheel. She waited for him to go on about his business, but he didn't.

"M—Mom," she said hoarsely.

"Yes, darling?"

"Do you see that man—" Camilla pointed in between the trees, though the man was no longer there.

"Do I see who?"

"Oh, uh, no one."

"Are you sure?" asked Pearl.

Camilla forced herself to nod. She skimmed the forest a final time, then sighed, reclined in her seat, and focused on the road ahead. Castles on the lake and strangers in the woods? She had doubted it at first, but not anymore: she was losing her mind for sure.

CHAPTER SIX
EXTINE

*E*xtine quickly zipped upstairs to wash her face and drape a veil over it before she hurried underground to the dungeons. Her children didn't know about her eyes yet, and she'd rather not tell them until absolutely necessary. Or unless they were to see it for themselves.

Which, hopefully, they wouldn't.

Finn was already down there when she arrived, along with Remy and Milo and a castle guard. The two outsiders lay fast asleep in the nearest cell to the entrance. Their kayaks were stacked against the wall beside the stairs, both of which were tattered and cracked.

"They're just boys," she acknowledged when she saw them by the light.

"Boys or not, they're outsiders," declared Remy. "How could something like this have happened?"

Extine didn't answer. She looked the boys over, from their strange clothes to their floppy haircuts. They were only boys, yes, but the fact that they had gotten past the borders...

Next time, it might not be *only boys*.

"How long have they been out?" asked Finn, stepping into the cell. He poked one of the outsiders with his foot.

The boy wriggled his toes.

"No clue," said Milo. He crossed his arms and shrugged. "They were awake when they got here but passed out soon afterwards. They must've hit their heads real hard during the storm."

"They're asleep now, at least," noted Finn. "But I don't know what we're going to do with them once they wake up. We have no idea what they might remember about this place."

"Eh, Mom," said Remy as Extine stepped into the light. Her brows contorted, and her voice twisted into one of judgement. "What exactly are you wearing? Is that a *veil* over your face?"

Extine barely saw anything through the netting, though she'd rather endure a couple seconds of blindness than have her children find out about her eyes. About what she had done to them and what her sister had done to her. She harvested every ounce of confidence, of persuasion, she had left and strutted over to Finn in the cell's threshold.

"Just a precaution, dear," she said in the sweetest, least paranoid-sounding tone she could manage. "We don't want outsiders to see the queen's face if they were to wake up right now."

"Okay. But why?" Remy pressed on, cocking her head. "It's not like they're armed or anything."

Extine pondered this for a moment.

When no answer came to mind, she looked to Finn, who merely brushed his fingers through his beard.

"Fine, don't tell me," said Remy and crossed her arms. She stepped inside the cell, crouched to the ground, and picked up one of the boys by his hair. She pried his eyes open with her fingers and raised his face to the torchlight. She repeated this with the second boy.

"What in Escana are you doing?" asked Extine.

"I'm trying to guess how long it'll be until they wake up." Remy let go of the boy's hair, and his head fell back on the concrete. She dusted off her hands, stood, and walked right up to Extine. "From the response in his pupils, I'm thinking we don't have much time left."

Extine peered past her daughter at the boys.

They were from the outside all right, dressed in tight-fitting wetsuits and with fitness trackers on their wrists. She could tell they were related: not twins but definitely brothers.

On some level, she felt sorry for them. Whether or not they remembered anything about what happened, as soon as they regained consciousness, they'd be dealt with one way or another.

"Hey, I got it!" said Remy and clapped her hands together.

"What is it?" asked Finn and Milo together.

"Mom, can't you just use your eyes to make them forget? I mean, we can slap them awake right now."

Finn and Extine exchanged a look.

"What was that?" asked Remy. She turned to Milo by the stairs. His arms were still crossed over his chest, and his head was tilted so it rested against the wall. "You saw that too, right?"

Milo nodded.

"S—Saw what?" stuttered Finn.

"That look you two just shared," Remy went on. She took two steps towards Extine, who thought about bounding back, but stayed in place for the sake of her composure, her secret.

"Don't be foolish, Remy. We didn't share a look," she insisted. "Did we share a look, Finn?"

"Nope, no looks from me."

"You guys definitely shared a look!" Remy placed her hands on her hips and pursed her lips. She was serious now, stubborn and persistent—the one quality Extine never wanted either of her children to inherit. "What's going on here? First, we find the two of you on the ground in the throne room, and then Mom comes down with a veil over her face?"

No answer.

Remy scoffed. "See, you can't even lie properly!" She lunged forward and yanked off the veil.

At first, she didn't react. But then the torch on the wall sputtered, and light spilled across Extine's face. Remy gasped. Her eyes widened, and she dropped the veil, retreating.

"Remy, darling—"

"Yuck! W—What have you done to yourself? Your eyes look like they're—like they're *rotting!*" she shrieked.

Milo peeled himself off the wall and shuffled closer. He stopped a little short of his sister, also with raised brows. His were much thicker than hers, so they didn't rise as far up his forehead.

"What makes you think I did something?" asked Extine. Her feet itched to turn around and storm off, but the rest of her body forced her to stay, to face the wrath of her eldest child.

Of her supposed heir.

"I don't know. Maybe because they weren't like this *yesterday!*" Remy tossed her hands in the air. She paced down the line of cells, every now and then looking at Extine and suppressing a gag.

Extine thought about lying, but Finn came up to her and placed a hand on her shoulder—a touch out of his own will. He whispered, "Don't make matters worse than they already are."

"But what do I say?"

"I think you should tell them the truth."

"The truth?"

Finn was right. He was always right. Remy was about to turn eighteen, and as the firstborn, she expected to inherit Extine's eyes. Her power. She had been practicing her persuasion skills ever since she had found out about her birthright, which was no longer hers.

Extine always had, on some level, sensed something was off. While her daughter did possess her eyes, they were never quite as blue, never as quite clear, and never quite as enchanting.

"What do you mean by that? What truth?" asked Remy. She stomped on top of the veil, pressing it into the ground with her left heel. Her gaze was cold, stern.

"I—I lost my eyes," Extine admitted. The moment the words passed her lips, a switch flipped in her mind. She really did lose them. The only things that made her special, powerful.

Her children and the guard all gasped. Their reactions made her wish she had phrased it differently.

"What do you mean, *you lost your eyes?*" Remy spoke slowly, carefully. She snorted and the ring in her nose glinted off the torchlight. "Did someone steal them or something?" Her voice amplified. "It was that Sorceress Juniper, wasn't it? She took your power for herself!"

Remy bashed her fist against the bars of one of the cells. The entire confinement rattled, echoing into the walls and ceiling. Numerous prisoners groaned, which made her curse at them.

"Shut up, you bunch of slugs!" she shouted.

Finn stepped in and lowered her fist. She tried to yank away, but his grip was too strong. "Calm down," he soothed her, "it's not what you think. Sorceress Juniper didn't do anything."

"Well," Extine wheezed, "she did aid me in a way." She blinked, and her eyes tingled again.

Sizzled, almost.

"What happened?" Remy freed herself from Finn's grip. She rolled her wrist and flicked her claw-like nails.

"Is it the Allessien legacy?" she asked, slightly more vulnerable now.

Extine gave a tiny nod.

"But, how can that be? I haven't turned eighteen yet."

"That was my first thought as well," said Extine. She tried to comfort Remy, who refused to be touched.

"You lost my birthright?" she wheezed, clenching her fists again. She made for the nearest cell, but Finn stopped her from using any more force. She nonetheless kept on punching and jerking.

"Remy," Finn began, although he couldn't finish.

Remy thumped him in the chest to get away. She charged at Extine, though halted several paces off. "How's that possible?" Her voice broke. "Do you have a child we don't know about?"

"Not me. My coward of a sister."

"Pearl?"

"Yes, Pearl. She had a child. Your cousin. I also only found out yesterday," Extine went on.

Remy stared at her as if she had just delivered the worst news in the world—as if she had taken away everything she ever thought she had and left her with nothing except questions.

Extine knew exactly how she felt: robbed and defied. She had felt the same way when she lost her sight. In fact, it still hurt, which made it all the more difficult to feel sorry for Remy.

"Someone else has my power?" Saliva shot from Remy's lips as she spoke through clenched teeth. "Mom,

I'm still the heir to the throne, right? I'll still be crowned Queen of Escana, right?"

Silence.

"I—I'm not the heir to the throne anymore?"

"Darling, you have to understand—"

But Remy wasn't done. "First my eyes are stolen from me, and now my right to the throne? Who does this peasant think they are?" She kicked the veil across the ground, and when that didn't make her feel better, she entered the cell and punched one of the boys in the gut.

"Remy!" shouted Finn. He rushed in to yank her away. "Stop that! They did nothing to harm you."

Remy writhed and kicked and shrieked. She most likely would have bitten Finn had Extine not intervened. She used what little power she had left to compel Remy to calm down.

"Shut your mouth," she tried to soothe her. "And listen for a moment."

Remy, still with a scowl between her eyebrows, ceased her scuffling and went limp in Finn's arms.

"As I was about to say," said Extine. "Pearl's child might have my eyes, but he or she has no right to the throne."

"What about Escana? Won't we be exposed to the outside?" Milo asked, having settled against the wall again. His face was shadowed, his neck and chest visible in the torchlight.

"Sorceress Juniper managed to restore a little of my power. That's why I didn't want anyone in the library with me the other day. I wasn't sure whether she'd be able to do it or—"

"Whether it would actually work?" Milo finished for her.

"Honestly, I'm not so sure she *did* succeed . . ." mumbled Remy, still with Finn's arms wrapped around her. She snorted at Extine's face. "Have you seen your eyes recently?"

"Remy!" snapped Finn.

"What, Dad? What can you possibly say to rectify the situation?" Finn didn't answer, so she went on. "Do the two of you realize that outsiders managed to infiltrate the kingdom?"

Extine had nothing to say to that.

Two men—boys, nonetheless—had crossed the border by accident. Her eyes had made the entirety of Escana quake, and if it hadn't been for Finn, things might have ended quite differently.

"You're right, Remy," she said after a while.

Remy and Finn looked up at the same time. Finn, in particular, seemed astonished by her answer.

"I don't think my eyes will work for much longer, even under Sorceress Juniper's magic. The kingdom of Escana is at stake, and if saving it means we have to hand over the throne to someone—someone who knows next to nothing about our world—well, so be it."

"What? No!" Remy regained some of her vigor. She writhed again. "There has to be another way."

"I'm afraid, there isn't."

"That's where Your Majesty's wrong," said a low, monotone, almost bewitched, voice from the stairway.

Everyone turned to see two women, both of whom

seemed to shimmer even in the dark, descend down the stairs. The first and somewhat older of the two was Sorceress Juniper. She wore a dark green tunic and strings of jewels around her neck. The second was dressed in a plain frock that reached just below her knees. She had dark, chin-length hair, and the only formidable thing about her was her yellow—almost gold—eyes.

"Sorceress Juniper," said Extine, trying not to sound as surprised. "I thought you had gone home?"

"I did," said the sorceress. "And once there, I decided to page through some of my old spellbooks."

"Did you find anything?"

"As I said, there's another way to save the kingdom."

Finn let go of Remy, who at once bounded forward, almost to her knees, in front of the sorceress.

"Another way?" She paused. "No, we can't trust you. Look at what you did to my mother's eyes!"

Sorceress Juniper shrugged, and her earrings jingled. "Queen Extine knew very well what side effects the spell might entail. It was either my magic or being rendered blind and powerless."

Remy made to snap something back at her, but Extine forestalled her. "I chose my eyes—my power—Remy. And while it's not as painless as I'd have hoped, I'd make the same choice again." She approached Sorceress Juniper. "Is it true, sorceress? Did you find another way?"

"I did. A transfer spell."

"A transfer spell?"

"We extract the energy—the lifeforce—from one person's eyes and transfer it to another."

"In other words, we can take back my power?"

Finn gasped. "Wait a moment. You're planning on stealing an innocent child's eyes? Won't they go blind?"

"There's no other way, Finn," said Extine. She thought about Pearl and her illegal child. About how she hated said child, even though she had only learned about them the previous day. What a hindrance. A thief and an intruder. They didn't deserve a face in her mind.

Not even a name.

"Oh, who are we kidding? We should forget it. It'll never work," she added with her head lowered.

The sorceress frowned. "How so?"

"We have no idea where the little thief is."

"Actually, we do," said the girl behind Sorceress Juniper. She held out a paper, wilted and dripping with water.

"Who's this?" asked Extine.

"This is my daughter, Fleur."

Extine grabbed the paper, flattened it as best she could, and studied the smudged scribbles. It was a sketch of the lake.

Of the walls.

Of the castle.

"Where did you get this?" she asked.

"I fished it out of the lake by our cottage. It must have flushed through the border with the outsiders."

"How did you know about the outs—" Extine began, but just by meeting Sorceress Juniper's eyes, she knew she shouldn't ask. The sorceress had, after all, known about her sister's child when no one else did. It'd only be fitting she knew about the kayakers as well.

"Only someone with the Allessien eyes can see Escana from the outside." Sorceress Juniper took back the drawing. "Such a person drew this sketch, which means he or she is nearby."

"In Crystalvale?" asked Finn in a somewhat throaty voice.

"Yes. I'll bet my mother's spellbook on it."

"Great! Then let's go and get them!" Remy declared as she smacked her fists together. "Milo and I'll infiltrate the town, find this thief of a cousin, and make friends with him or her. We'll lure them to Escana and extract their power, then make do with them once and for all."

Finn gulped.

"Remy, no. It's too dangerous," warned Extine.

"Dangerous?" she sneered. "What's more dangerous than failing borders? This is the only way."

"The princess is right," the sorceress agreed. She extended a bony hand to her daughter. "But I want Fleur to go along. As a Sorceress in training, she'll make a great addition to the team."

Extine thought about it for a moment. Finn shook his head at her—mouthing all sorts of reasons as to why she should reject their plan, but she ignored him. "Fine, let's do it."

Remy jumped, her ponytail whipping against her back. "We won't fail you, Mom, that's a promise." Her face darkened, and her voice husked. "And once the power has been extracted, I'll finally receive my birthright. I'll take my place as the rightful heir to the throne."

"Your birthright?"

"The eyes," Remy explained. "They belong to me, don't they?"

"Oh, that birthright," mumbled Extine.

Then, Remy and Milo ran up the stairs. Remy motioned at the guard. "Guard, watch over the prisoners and alert me the moment they regain consciousness!"

Fleur and Finn were short on their heels. Once they were far away enough, Sorceress Juniper said, "*One often burns when playing with fire.*"

"E—Excuse me?" said Extine.

"The Allessien eyes."

"Yes? What about them?"

"Young Princess Remy seems to think the power will be returned to her. But it won't, will it?"

"I—I don't know what you're talking about."

Sorceress Juniper narrowed her eyes. "Your Majesty forgets. I see everything. Smell everything. And if I could be so blunt, the queen reeks of betrayal. Sour. Bitter. Spicy like a pepper."

"Interesting. I'm impressed, Sorceress Juniper," Extine admitted, reaching for her ever-throbbing eyelids. "No, the power won't go to her. The eyes are mine, and I will have them for myself."

CHAPTER SEVEN
CAMILLA

"You didn't have to drive me to school, Mom," Camilla insisted. She crossed her arms and sat back in the seat, watching as they drove from neighborhood to neighborhood to the center of Crystalvale. "I've cycled to school every day since I was ten years old."

"I know, I know. I just wanted to make sure you're safe," said Pearl, rapping her fingers on the steering wheel. She was already dressed for work, wearing the diner's mustard-colored, button-up dress complete with a striped, red-and-white apron and a messy bun.

"Safe? Seriously? Unless a giant wave floods the town, I think I'm in little danger," Camilla muttered. She thought back to Saturday night. Bob from across the street had returned her bike, all wet and sweaty, and with no good news regarding the missing boys.

"They're gone," he had said, rubbing his balding head.

"Both the fellas and their kayaks. It's quite mysterious, don't you reckon? Certainly, too mysterious for this little town of ours."

"Yes, it is strange. Thanks for coming over, Bob" Pearl had thanked him and sent him off with a plate of leftover scones from the diner. Camilla's bike had gone straight into the garage, and she was forbidden from cycling to school until things had cooled down. When Camilla had wanted to talk everything out, Pearl, as usual, fled to her room.

Camilla rubbed her eyes. She didn't sleep a wink the entire weekend as castles, waves, and kayaks had ruled her dreams. She was haunted by the look on her mother's face when she had seen her sketch and by the idea that it could easily have been Logan out there. If he hadn't bailed out when he did, there might've been three boys missing instead of two.

Camilla sank under the dashboard as they rounded the corner and her school came into view.

"Don't make jokes, Cam. Those missing boys . . . it's a real tragedy." Pearl stepped on the brake pedal, and the Chevy squealed to a stop. They parked next to the pavement behind a large, yellow school bus and directly in line with the entrance to Crystalvale High. "Here we are, and with ten minutes to spare. Isn't this much faster than riding your bike?"

Camilla didn't reply. She stayed slouched, bravely sneaking a glance outside. There were students every-where—on the steps, in the parking lot, surrounding the bicycle racks. Several more spilled from the bus, most of whom thronged together on the pavement.

Great.

An audience to witness her humiliation.

"Out you go," Pearl hustled her. She tapped the face of her wristwatch. "I have to get to work."

"Do I have to?"

"What do you mean? Of course you do!"

Camilla glanced out the window. Amidst the sea of students, only one really mattered to her.

Logan Wheeler.

She spotted him chaining his bike to the rack. His movements were stiff and uneasy looking, but he otherwise seemed all right. His friends bombarded him—"Hey, man, saw you nearly drowned on Saturday! What a wicked wave, eh?"—then ushered him up the front steps.

"Fine," Camilla yielded once he was gone. She opened the Chevy door, slipped out, and looped her backpack over her shoulder. "Two people went missing on a lake, Mom, they weren't murdered. Can you please stop treating me like I'm a fragile doll about to break?"

Then, without so much as a goodbye, Camilla turned and shut the door. Part of her wanted to slam it with force, but she decided against it. The door might just fall off if she did.

And that would attract even more attention.

The Chevy roared to life, accidentally died, then roared to life again. Camilla kept on walking, wishing she had worn a hoodie to hide her face under. Shame gushed over her—not the same type she felt for the Chevy, but the type that filled her with guilt, with regret.

It wasn't her mother's fault they couldn't afford nice things. She worked twelve-hour shifts day after day just so they could have a small house and a small car in a small town.

Camilla, despite her scalding cheeks, glanced over her shoulder. She raised her hand in a wave, parted her lips to mouth a goodbye, but the Chevy was already halfway down Main Street. Dark smoke puffed from the exhaust, clouding the rear-view mirror.

Damn.

Now she just felt bad.

Camilla adjusted her backpack, pushed a strand of hair behind her ear, and walked up the steps to the entrance. She swiveled by a couple making out in the doorway and walked down the hallway to her locker. Students thronged all around, laughing, chatting, and gossiping.

"I heard the Morris brothers were flushed out to sea!"

"Nah, my brother says he thinks they staged it. Ran away to escape their power-hungry parents."

Camilla smirked.

If only it was that simple of an explanation.

She entered her combination—2 0 0 3—and the lock clicked open. She unhooked it, opened her locker, took out her physics books, and popped them in her bag. Then, still half listening to the group behind her, she shut the door, fastened the lock, and zipped her bag close.

She jerked when she turned around.

Logan leaned against the locker next to hers, a slight smile coiled around the edges of his mouth.

"Hey," he said.

Camilla huffed. "Why do you always do that?"

"Do what?"

"Sneak up on me when I'm in thought. Can't you approach me like a normal person for once?"

Logan laughed. "A normal person?"

No answer.

"Fine," he said with his hands raised. Then, he spun and wove through the crowd to the entrance. He waited a couple of seconds, then walked back up to her, a swing in his stride.

Camilla toyed with the frayed strap on her backpack. How ridiculous. People were starting to stare.

For the third time that morning, warmth flooded her cheeks. Only this time, she didn't exactly hate it.

"So, Ward, have a good weekend?" asked Logan in a voice that made him sound less cool than intended. He pursed his lips and creased his brows, running his hands across his head.

"*Ward*?" Camilla smirked.

"What? I thought it sounded cool." Logan put his thumbs in his pockets. "Anyway, happy now?"

"Very."

Logan seemed pleased by this. "I didn't see you bike to school today. Took another route or something?"

"No, my mom just drove me."

"Does it have anything to do with what happened at the lake on Saturday? She seemed pretty upset."

Camilla yanked on a piece of thread and the strap unraveled even more. It tickled the inside of her armpit, the type that morphed into an itch. "Y—You saw that?"

"Well, it was difficult not to." Logan's chocolate-brown cheeks took on a shade of crimson. "And you walked right past me. Without waving back, I have to add. I'm hurt, by the way."

"Oh . . . yeah," said Camilla, guiltily. "Sorry about that."

"You should be." Logan frowned playfully and crossed his arms. "That, along with ditching me on your way to school today, I'm beginning to think you don't like me, Camilla Ward."

"*L—Like you?*" Camilla blurted out. "I, uh, don't dislike you, if that's what you were thinking."

Logan smiled, but only with one side of his mouth. He watched her squirm a little, then went on. "Don't worry, I'll let you off the hook this one time. But remember, you owe me."

"Owe you?"

Logan bounced his eyebrows at her.

"Alright," Camilla yielded. "Just stop doing *that*, please." She paused. "Are you, you know, okay?"

Logan straightened and his smile widened. "My left shoulder's a bit sore, but other than that, I'm fighting fit. Thanks again for swinging by the tournament, I really liked having you—" He was interrupted by the intercom starting up, and the principal's voice blaring at them.

"ATTENTION STUDENTS OF CRYSTALVALE HIGH. IN LIGHT OF RECENT EVENTS, TODAY'S SCHEDULE WILL BE SLIGHTLY DIFFERENT.

PLEASE HURRY TO THE THEATRE FOR AN EMER-
GENCY SCHOOL ASSEMBLY. I REPEAT, ALL
STUDENTS, PLEASE HURRY TO THE THEATRE FOR
AN EMERGENCY SCHOOL ASSEMBLY."

"This has Saturday's tournament written all over it,"
said Logan. Then, without asking, he took Camilla's bag
and tossed it over his shoulder. "Come on, we better get
to the theatre."

Camilla hesitated before she followed. There was no
clear reason for him to carry her backpack. They weren't
exactly friends, and they certainly weren't in a relationship. She nonetheless walked with him to the theatre,
where, instead of with his friends, he sat next to her.

"Did you want to sit at the front or in the back?" he
asked, leading her down the center aisle.

"Uh—I think here's fine," said Camilla.

"Ah, smart."

"It is?"

"Yea, we're still close enough to hear, but not too close
to smell the principal's breath." Logan gave a gentlemanly
bow, then rolled a hand in front of him. "Ladies first."

"Oh, okay. Thanks a lot." Camilla dried her palms on
her jeans and waddled into the row.

The same group that had surrounded Logan at the lake
sat behind him. They whispered to each other, "Did you
guys see that? I can't believe he's sitting with her."

"Who is she anyway?"

"Just some girl. I think we might have geography
together."

But Camilla didn't have geography. She shifted in her

seat, tuning them out. She didn't blame them for what they said, as, like them, she too had no idea why Logan sat with her. It was one thing for her to silently, secretly, fawn over him, but a whole other—and totally terrifying—thing for him to fawn back. Nothing like this had ever happened before.

"Is your seat okay?" asked Logan, looking somewhat tense.

"Aren't they all equally as uncomfortable?" Camilla twisted around to prove her point, and the seat groaned. The sound was louder, coarser than she expected, and she blushed.

Logan laughed at her. "Yeah, I suppose you're right."

While the rest of their exchange was cringeworthy, to say the least, nothing she could've said or done differently would've changed that. She kept her hands in her lap, once or twice casting an eye over to his, both of which were curled around the seat's armrests.

The third time she glanced over, Logan looked up.

Camilla swerved her eyes to the stage, where, luckily, the principal was preparing to speak.

"Good morning, students of Crystalvale High!" he said with a microphone to his lips. "I suppose you've all guessed why I called this emergency assembly. It regards the disappearance of two boys Saturday on the lake. One of our own students, Logan Wheeler, also participated in the kayaking tournament and fortunately managed to escape unharmed."

The students clapped for Logan, who briefly stood up and showed everyone a thumbs up.

"The two missing boys are yet to be found, so I'd like to request everyone to steer clear of the lake until we've received word from the authorities. I know the lake's a frequent location for bonfires, but I'm sure you lot can hold off on partying for a couple of weeks."

This time, no one clapped, and nearly everyone groaned.

The principal paid no attention to this. His voice chirped as he went on. "In other news, we've got quite some exciting people joining us today! Transfer students from a little town upstate, called Escana"—two girls and a guy walked on stage—"did I get that right?"

One of the girls nodded. She wore quite an interesting outfit: a black tight-fitting skirt and matching stockings with combat boots and chains as a belt. The other girl wore a plain T-shirt and jeans, and the guy wore a black leather jacket and white pants that matched his hair.

They were transfer students all right, not at all matching the Crystalvale style of half beachy, half prep.

"Escana?" asked Logan. His breath wafted against Camilla's cheek. "Ever heard of it before?"

"Never," Camilla replied, barely managing an answer.

"They'll be joining our senior class for the remainder of the year," the principal continued. "So I'll be needing someone to show them around the school. Do I see any senior volunteers?"

The theatre went so quiet, the principal's breathing rustled over the speakers. He wheezed a little.

Camilla and Logan, like all the other seniors, shrank in their seats. Even the girl who always volunteered for everything, Ling Cho, was nowhere to be seen. She was likely as much scared off by the goth girl as everyone else, and Camilla couldn't blame her for it.

The principal gave them several minutes, but when no one put their hand up, he said, "Alright, since none of you'd like to volunteer, I'll allow our new students to choose a guide."

More groans.

"Hush now! Don't be like that!" the principal snapped. He pulled at his blazer, adjusted his tie, and turned to the transfer students. The girl with the boots stepped forward. "Take a minute to size them up and choose whoever you'd like to show you the ropes."

The girl with the boots wasted no time in doing so. She took the microphone from the principal, strutted to the edge of the stage, and surveyed the sea of students in front of her.

Left, right, left, right.

Row by row.

Person by person.

Every few moments, she paused on someone's face with narrowed eyes, then shortly moved on. It went like this all the way from the back until she came to Camilla and paused again.

Only this time, she paused a little longer.

A lot longer.

Camilla wanted to slide further down in her seat, but she was glued in place, cemented by something inside of her—a feeling of familiarity, a connection of some sort.

She managed to blink, and the spell between them broke. The girl also blinked, her lips thinning.

Camilla half expected her to move on to Logan, but she didn't. She held up the microphone, pointed her finger straight ahead, and said, "Her. We want that girl to show us around."

CHAPTER EIGHT
EXTINE

*E*xtine stood on the southern wing of the castle walls, looking out across the lake. The wind brushed through her hair, each ripple like a finger smoothing, sometimes tangling, her platinum locks. She held her hand over her eyes to protect them from the dawning sun. Not even the spray from the uneasy waves cooled her off. She stared at the lake, at the numerous search boats that sped up and down, over and over without stopping.

It had been that way the entire night.

Every time one of the boats made off, another showed up only to comb the lake all over again.

Those damn kayakers.

They just had to slip through the border.

Extine suppressed a yawn. She got very little sleep last night, having constantly worried about her eyes—the ones she had left—and how much power they still contained. A series of horrifying scenarios had played and replayed in her mind: what if one of the speedboats got through? What if she had another seizure, and Finn couldn't help her out?

The thought of Finn made her sigh.

When she had rolled over in bed that morning, his spot was empty and the mattress already cold. He wasn't at breakfast in the dining room, and none of the guards knew where he went. She had hoped to find him out here on the wall, surveying the search boats, but . . .

Extine hugged herself.

Perhaps things were better this way. The less they saw of each other, the less she'd witness her power wear off on him. Even Sorceress Juniper's magic couldn't make him love her.

Not like her eyes could.

Last night, Extine had invited Finn for a walk about the castle grounds. He had agreed but said nothing the entire time. He *did* speak, but only about the borders, her eyes, and the kingdom. She had tried to flirt with him— subtly pressed her arm against his—but to no reaction. The only reason he had kissed her was because she had compelled him to.

And not even that made her feel better.

Extine winced as one of the search boats whizzed past the wall. Water splashed all over her, wetting her shoes, gown, and chest. She wiped herself off and cursed under her breath.

"Blasted outsiders," she huffed.

When she looked up, she stared at another, slightly larger, search boat right in the face. It was heading her way at a terrible speed, but she didn't flinch, and she didn't step aside. She stood her ground, knowing, hoping, trusting that it would pass right through her.

And it did.

Water splashed everywhere—over the wall, down the pathway to the gates, and through the first-floor windows of the castle. A maid screamed, not in panic, but in frustration.

Extine's mouth filled with bile. Nothing like this had ever happened before. Escana was supposed to be resistant to the outside. The water—like the boat—should've passed right through.

Things couldn't go on like this.

Heck, she could've been demolished just now!

Extine dried herself off again. She turned away from the sun and caught a man emerging from the forest left of the lake. He wore outsider attire—a pair of washed-out jeans and a light grey hoodie—though hardly appeared lost. In fact, she recognized him.

Yes.

It was Finn.

As soon as he saw Extine, he turned in the way of someone about to run off. She waved at him before he did, though, and knew he couldn't refuse. The queen had summoned him.

Finn cleared his throat, drew back his shoulders, and approached. He unzipped his hoodie and pushed his sleeves up to his elbows. The morning heat glazed his face, though it remained emotionless, guiltless all the same. He sloshed through a puddle of water.

"Good morning," said Extine.

"Yes. Quite sunny, I'd say."

"Where are you coming from?" she asked before he could even think of changing the subject.

Finn ran his fingers through his hair. His cheeks flushed, and watery beads gathered on his forehead. Three horizontal lines ran across it, tarnishing his once smooth brow line. "I just, eh, went into town for a bit," he said, gesturing to Crystalvale beyond the pine trees.

The old colonial church tower, barely visible above the treetops, chimed in the distance.

Nine o'clock.

"Headed into town? For what reason?"

"Just some errands. You know."

"No, I don't." Extine narrowed her eyes at him. "But anyway, you left quite early this morning. Not even the guards saw you go. Those must've been some important errands?"

"What are you asking me, Extine?"

Extine scanned his attire. She made no secret of her disgust, as she wanted him to squirm. To give in. "I'm asking why you left at the crack of dawn. What were you doing in Crystalvale?"

"I was securing Escana's safety," Finn replied, raising his voice a little. "I wanted to find out exactly what the outsiders knew. I wanted to hear what they thought had happened to those two kayakers. But if you'd rather we sit around and wait for someone else—"

"No, I believe you." Extine raised her hands in defense. "Relax, I wasn't trying to interrogate you."

"It felt like you were."

"Well, that's not how I meant it."

A moment passed in which neither of them spoke.

Then, Extine crossed her arms. She broke the silence by asking, in a somewhat softer voice, "So, what did you find out? Do the people in town have any idea what might've happened?"

"Not that I could tell. There were a couple of posters up at the diner and post office, but other than that, everyone reckons it was a freak accident. My only concern is that they're bringing in more search boats this afternoon. And some folks are talking about getting the news involved."

"The news?"

"Yeah, apparently national coverage."

"We can't let that happen." Extine worked her jaw, imagining everything that could go wrong: the castle appearing on camera or one of the reporters passing through the barrier. A chill ran down her spine all the way into her fingers. She balled her fists so her nails pierced her skin.

The pain distracted her from the burn, the feeling of fire ants crawling across her irises. She spoke on, "And it won't happen. Escana's safety won't pose a problem for much longer." She twirled her finger at Finn. "And you won't have to dress up like *this* ever again."

Finn put his hands in his pockets and shrugged. "I guess—wait, why won't it pose a problem anymore?"

"Remy and Milo," Extine explained. "Today's their first day as transfer students at Crystalvale High. It's a shame you didn't see them this morning. They looked utterly ridiculous!"

"What? They already went after Pearl's child?"

"Of course, Finn. I want my eyes back. Besides, the kingdom is at stake. We have little time to waste."

Finn chewed this over. He glanced at Crystalvale, then lowered his head and rubbed his brows. Even they were streaked with grey, with the slightest hint of silver and white. When he looked up, his mood had changed. Darkened almost. He stepped towards her.

"I thought we were still discussing the plan, Extine?" he said. "We don't know who this child even is or what he or she knows about their powers. We can't just send our children into the outside world with only a sketch as information! It's much too reckless."

Extine tossed her head back. The sun properly beamed now, and the moment she opened her eyes, she winced. Another search boat whizzed by, yet no water splashed their way.

Good.

As it should be.

"But it's not reckless, Finn," she replied. "They have Sorceress Juniper's daughter with them."

"Yes, which makes it even more reckless! What do we even know about this *Sorceress Juniper*? Just look at what she did to you!" Finn yanked Extine's hand from her eyes, and she grimaced, almost yelping aloud in pain. "You can hardly tolerate sunlight anymore!"

Extine slapped away his hand. "What's the matter with you? Why are you reacting so bizarre?"

No answer.

"You know," she went on, forcing her eyes open. She had to look at him, had to see his reaction when she said, "You've been acting awfully strange ever since we found out about this." A pause in which Finn merely blinked at her. "Did you know about Pearl's child?"

"No, of course not."

"Don't lie to me, Finn."

"I said I didn't know, Extine."

"Are you sure?"

Something inside of Finn snapped. He lurched forward, grabbed her forearms, and pulled her closer. He looked her in the eyes—first the left, then the right. "I'm just really worried about you. I know I've been acting stranger than usual, but that's only because I'm afraid."

"A—Afraid?"

"Yes."

"Of what?"

Finn pulled her several inches closer. "Every time I look at you, I can't bear to see you in pain. I don't want you to live this way, and I certainly don't want to risk anything before knowing that you, and our children, will be all right." His voice softened with each word. When he finished, he leaned in to kiss her, but Extine pulled away at the last moment.

"Y—You better not be lying to me, Finn," she said under her breath.

Pulling away from his kiss was one of the hardest things she had ever done. She wanted him to kiss her, of course, but not like this. Not when trying to persuade her of his innocence. There was no doubt about it. He was up to something. Despite his kind words, and despite his attempts to woo her, he was still dressed like an outsider, and he still knew more than he let on.

"I'm not lying to you, Extine." Finn didn't let go of her. "Have I ever lied to you before?"

Extine chose not to answer. Not because she didn't want to, but because she couldn't. The truth was, she had never allowed him to lie to her. He had been under the power of her eyes ever since their wedding day. Might he still be? She had no idea.

"Alright," Finn yielded. He stepped back and rubbed his hands together. He reversed, motioning to the castle with his right thumb. "I guess I should go check on the kayakers."

Extine bit her lip as she watched him turn and walk off. Her mind told her to let him go, but her heart said otherwise. She squeezed her eyes and blurted out, "You won't find them . . ."

"Excuse me?"

"In their cell. They're not there."

Finn tilted his chin. "What? Why not?"

"Sorceress Juniper and I took care of them this morning. The kayakers no longer pose a threat to us."

All color vanished from Finn's face. He asked, "What do you mean, *you took care of them?*"

"You weren't here, Finn. I had to do something." Extine took a moment to calm her shaky breath. The expression on Finn's face already said more than what she wanted to hear. He knew what she had done, even before she had said it. "I did what I had to do to assure Escana's safety . . ."

CHAPTER NINE
CAMILLA

*C*amilla braided through the students in the hallway. Her cheeks sizzled, and her whole body crawled with chills. Groups of students were gathered by their lockers, tracking her with their eyes as she passed. Sure, she was used to people staring at her, but not everyone at once.

"There they go," jeered someone.

"Yeah, Dracula's spawns!" added another. The person's friends burst into laughter next to him.

They weren't exactly looking at Camilla but rather at the transfer students behind her. Ever since she had met up with them by the theatre's entrance, they had received several insults, a whole lot of sideways glances, and the occasional scoff or two.

And as rude or immature as it was, Camilla couldn't fault any of the received reactions.

When she had first introduced herself to the transfer

students, the girl with the boots had merely pulled up her nose and snorted.

"Remy," she had said.

Camilla had extended her hand at her, who once again scoffed in her face. "Oh, all right. Nice to, uh, meet you, Remy." She lowered her hand and turned. "And you two?"

"Fleur," the slightly quieter girl had said.

And the guy said, "Milo." He was Remy's younger brother and had skipped a couple of grades.

"I guess I'm just smart that way," he said.

They took off through the school, upon which Camilla showed them the cafeteria, gymnasium, and outside area. She had thought about showing them the sports grounds but decided against it. It was too far from the main building and none of them seemed the sporty type.

"You think we're Dracula's spawns, eh?" shouted Remy at the two guys who had insulted them. She balled her fists and launched at them, but Milo held her back. The two boys fell against their lockers, rattling the entire line. "Want me to suck your blood?"

"Freak!" they shouted back.

Camilla's cheeks warmed even more. She ushered the transfer students away, quicker now.

"Dracula's spawns my ass," mumbled Remy through gritted teeth. She stomped her feet and punched at the air. "I ought to rip out their tongues for saying something like that."

Milo massaged her shoulders, keeping her a bay. "Don't listen to them, Remy, they're beneath you."

"Damn right they are!" Remy shouted over her shoulder.

Camilla internally shriveled. Out of everyone, they just had to pick her. The one girl who never draws attention to herself. The one girl with an inability to raise her voice in public.

She quickly changed the subject and asked, "Why, uh, did you choose me to show you around?"

"Eh, I don't know," Remy replied, somewhat calmer. She rolled her jaw. "There was just something about you —about your eyes—that intrigued us. Isn't that right, you guys?"

Milo and Fleur agreed.

"So, you come from a town named Escana?"

Remy nodded. "Ever heard of it before?"

Camilla shook her head. She absently pulled at the straps of her backpack. "Nope, never in my life."

Remy hardly seemed surprised by this.

"You'd actually be surprised at how little people know about Escana," said Fleur in her place. Remy glanced at her, but she went on anyway, "It's sort of . . . hidden from the world."

"So to speak, of course," Milo quickly added. He swiped his fringe from his face, revealing a set of grey eyes. While they weren't blue like Remy's, they sure packed the same punch.

And boy, what a punch that was.

Whenever either of them looked at Camilla, her skin rippled with chills. It wasn't their eyes that unsettled her, but rather the number of times she caught them staring at her, scrutinizing her with shadowy expressions. Remy often lingered longer than her brother.

Like in that very moment, for instance.

"So, we've already seen the cafeteria, the gym, and the theatre, obviously," said Camilla, stopping in the middle of the hallway with no idea where to go next.

Nearly everyone had gone to class already, and the only students still wandering around were the slackers and hall monitor. He leaned against the water fountain, ogling them from a distance. His pencil rapped against his pad, as did his foot against the floor.

"How about—" Camilla began, but just then, Logan rounded the corner ahead of them, and she released a deep breath. Sweet relief. He had been summoned to the principal's office after the assembly and didn't look particularly happy right then. When he saw Camilla, his face brightened, and he approached. He briefly glanced at the transfer students.

"Hi, I'm Logan." He raised his hand, but when none of them reacted, he lowered it again.

"This is Remy, Milo, and Fleur," Camilla introduced them.

Still no response.

Logan grinned without any teeth, then turned to face Camilla. "Still busy with the tour, are you?"

"Yep." Camilla tried to hide her dismay, but a tiny sigh slipped out. She didn't regret missing physics class but was tired of making chitchat. "Why did the principal want to see you?"

"According to him, I'm in serious need of therapy. You know, after the incident at the lake."

"Therapy?"

Logan nodded. "The ol' man assigned me a therapist. Can you believe it? They're forcing me to undergo ten sessions before I can compete again!" He fiddled with the zipper of his hoodie. It had the Crystalvale High emblem across it—a symbol of his contribution to the school.

"Can they even do that?" asked Camilla.

"I compete under the school's name," Logan admitted. "And I guess since he's the principal, he can."

The disappointment in his eyes was real.

Camilla looked at his hand, at his fingers, still around the zipper. She wanted to grab his palm, squeeze it, and assure him it wasn't as bad as it seemed, but she lacked the courage to do so.

Instead, she said, "We, uh, actually have to get on with the tour."

"Oh, right," said Logan, almost as though he had forgotten the transfer students were even there.

He added, "See you later?"

"M—Maybe," was all Camilla could manage.

Logan winked at her, then set off. He turned left into the first classroom—physics class—and for the first time since he had rounded the corner, she managed to breathe properly again.

"Who the heck was that hunk of handsomeness?" asked Remy. She licked her lips, which unsettled Camilla.

"*Him?*" She almost spat the word. The twist in her gut surprised her, as did the fire in her chest. "That's, uh,

Logan Wheeler. He was with the Morris brothers when they disappeared."

The transfer students all raised their brows.

Remy glanced back to where Logan had disappeared off to. A crafty grin tickled around her mouth as she said, "Interesting. Interesting indeed. And, well, the two of you? Are you—"

"No!" Camilla swallowed hard. She recomposed herself and waited for her heartbeat to slow down before she went on, "We're just friends. Yes. Friends. I've known him since I was little."

Remy studied her for a moment, then renewed her grin. "If you say so. Now, does this place have a music room?"

"Actually, yes." Camilla was grateful for the change of topic. "Right this way." She walked briskly, keeping a far enough distance between her and the transfer students so they didn't have to talk. If forced to answer any more questions about Logan, she might just throw up.

They turned a corner and upped a flight of steps. The music room was on the second floor at the very end, just above the theatre. It often served as a waiting room for the actors before they went on stage and had a flight of stairs that led down to the dressing rooms.

It was abandoned.

Camilla put her hand on the door. "Here we are. The music room. Do all of you play instruments?"

Remy parted her lips, but before she could answer, Milo pushed past her. He pressed his left hand to Camilla's chest and bulldozed her inside. His fringe covered his eyes again, but the lines around his mouth and nose gave away the look of revulsion on his face.

"Milo, what are you doing?" hissed Fleur. "It's not time yet! We haven't found out enough!"

"Oh, well. I guess we'll find out everything we need to know right now," he snapped back.

Camilla yelped out of surprise and stumbled back. Remy and Fleur entered the music room behind them.

"Close the door!" ordered Milo.

Fleur obeyed, and Remy approached.

Camilla retreated in between the instruments. She accidentally walked into the drum set and almost toppled a cello. She reached the line of windows at the back of the room—the end of the line and with nowhere to go. Remy was still walking towards her, her face shadowed by the trees outside. Trickles of sunlight passed through the leaves, setting fire to her eyes.

"W—We haven't finished the tour yet," stuttered Camilla. "And the principal only gave us the first period off."

"No worries," Remy hummed. She came so close to Camilla, her breath wafted in her face. "We've seen enough to find our way around. What we really want is to know more about you."

"M—Me?" Camilla tried hard not to wince. Fleur was on her left and Milo on her right. She had no idea what they were doing, but whatever it was they had to trap her to do it.

"Yes, we want to know all about you, *Camilla Ward.*" Remy said her name as if there was something wrong with it—as if she didn't really trust it. As if it was something filthy.

"W—Why me?"

"Didn't you hear what I said earlier?" Remy replied, tracing her nails along the side of Camilla's face, all the way under her eyes. Each nail was sharper than the first, all five of them painted black. "There's something *enchanting* about your eyes. Has anyone ever told you that?"

"Yeah, I hear it all the time."

Remy laughed. "I'm not surprised." Her voice lowered to a husk. "Say, where were you born?"

Camilla had never felt as uncomfortable as she did right then. It wasn't the question itself, but rather how Remy had asked it. It was the same as when she had said her name.

"E—Excuse me?"

"It's just a question," said Milo.

"Answer it," insisted Fleur.

Camilla looked at them through the corners of her eyes. They stood with crossed arms and creased foreheads. Remy was possibly the most terrifying of all, not only due to her appearance, but also because her nails practically stabbed at Camilla's right eye socket.

"Were you born right here in Crystalvale?" Remy repeated, and all Camilla could do was nod.

"Why do you want to know where I was born?"

Remy sidestepped her question with another one of her own, "What's your mother's name?"

"P—Pearl."

"Oh, wow!" Milo squealed with delight. "Did you hear that, Remy? Her mother's name is Pearl."

Remy hissed through her teeth at him. "Of course I heard, you idiot! Tone down the excitement, will you? We haven't found out anything yet." She waited for Milo to obey, then returned to a wide-eyed, terribly confused Camilla. "Where exactly did she grow up?"

"Who?"

"Your mother, Pearl!"

"Why do you want to know all these things? What does it matter?" Camilla bounded forward, but Milo pushed her back again. Her breath was knocked right out of her.

Still no answer.

Remy just went on with her interrogation. "Fine, next question. What's your father's name?"

Camilla hesitated this time. Her mother had told her his name at the diner, but she couldn't bring herself to say it out loud, especially not to someone else. He had, after all, died a long time ago and had been nameless for eighteen years. And what would it matter to some transfer students anyway? They didn't know him, and they didn't know her.

"My father died when I was born," said Camilla.

"How absolutely tragic," Remy cooed, hardly sounding concerned. She traced a nail down Camilla's cheek. "Do you know his name? Was his surname Ward? Was he from Crystalvale too?"

"I don't know anything," Camilla lied. Whatever game they were playing, she wasn't about to cave in.

Remy's nail reached the soft flesh under Camilla's chin. It made its way down, down, down to her neck, where it hooked around her necklace—the one her mother gave her on her birthday.

The one from her father.

"Interesting necklace," noted Milo.

"Interesting indeed," Remy concurred. She held onto it. "And this crest . . . it looks familiar."

"Very familiar," said Milo.

"Where did you get it?" Remy wrapped her hand around the heart-shaped charm, then pushed Camilla back against the wall, against the window. Her head bashed against the glass, almost shattering it. The pivots rattled all the way to the other side of the room.

"Let go of me!" Camilla cried. She tried to push Remy off, but she was too strong, too firm in her stance. "The bell's about to ring, and we're not supposed to be in here without permission."

But Remy didn't budge.

"We're not going anywhere," she declared. "Not before you tell us where you got this necklace."

Warmth rose in Camilla's chest. It flooded to her face, collecting, amassing, gathering in her eyes.

They began to tingle—not in a painful way—and the words escaped her mouth as if automatically, "I said step aside! All of you!" She was frightened by the amount of authority in her voice and even more so when, without question, the transfer students complied.

Remy let go of her and retreated, though her facial expression differed greatly from her actions. Her eyes practically exploded with anger, and her fists stayed clenched by her sides.

Strange. Really strange.

Still, Camilla didn't linger around. Without so much as questioning a thing, she wove through the instruments and left the music room. The bell rang and students piled into the hallway.

"Hey, where are you going? You can't leave us here with nowhere to go; you're supposed to be our guide!" Remy shouted after her, but Camilla walked on without looking back. She did, however, look down at her necklace and wrap her hand around it.

Finn.

Her father's name was Finn, and he had given her the necklace through her mother, a token of his love.

Why that mattered to some transfer students, she had no idea. At least they were right about one thing: the crest on the necklace was interesting indeed. An eye in the center of a crown, encircled by rays of light. The same crest bore by the flags of the castle in her sketch.

Of the castle on the lake.

CHAPTER TEN
CAMILLA

*C*amilla tried and tried but couldn't recall the castle vividly enough to re-create her sketch. She had spent two entire, and incredibly long, nights recalling and dreaming up the apparition on the lake. The walls, the towers, the flags. The way the forest seemed to have grown around it as if it had been there longer than Crystalvale itself.

When morning came on the third day, she still had nothing to show. Nothing save for a single tower with a flag and a pile of crumpled papers so big she had lost her slippers under it.

"What were you doing all night?" asked Pearl at breakfast. She stood by the stove, wielding a spatula as she spoke. "When I went to bed at eleven, I saw your light was still on."

"I just finished some schoolwork," Camilla fibbed through a mouthful of cornflakes. The cereal was stale and the milk slightly tart, but she was so hungry she didn't even care.

"Anything important?" Pearl pressed on. She shook the pan with her left hand and flipped the egg with the spatula in her right. It hissed in the pan and butter splattered on her apron.

"No, not too important. It was mostly art homework. You know, stills and stuff like that." Camilla stood, cleared her bowl and cutlery from the table, and walked over to the sink.

"Okay, but you shouldn't work too hard. Remember to have fun. As long as it's at home, that is."

Camilla nodded and walked off to brush her teeth. Fighting with her mother was futile, as she hardly ever gave in. She also didn't mention the incident in the music room, fearing that Pearl would've gone to the school and demanded the transfer students were dealt with.

That day, she avoided the three of them entirely. Whenever she saw them, she turned the other way, blending with the crowd. Whoever they were and wherever they came from, they were the strangest people. The last thing she wanted was to be alone with them again.

"Is this seat taken?" asked Camilla.

"Yep, sorry," said the girl and placed her backpack on the seat. She waved at her friend by the door. "There's a whole table open over there, though."

It was lunchtime, and the cafeteria buzzed with students. Camilla tried to get there early, but her art teacher had summoned her after class to discuss the eight half drawn pictures of castles on her easel. She had brushed it off as painter's block.

"No, no, it's fine." Camilla squeezed down on her tray and turned. She searched for any other available seats—any way in which she could be amongst people instead of alone. Exposed. Vulnerable. Alas, the open table was her only option. She walked over and sat down.

No transfer students.

She picked up a carton of milk, tore it open, and took a drink.

No transfer students.

She wiped her mouth and put it down.

Boots squeaked across the floor, and leather crunched as someone pulled at their jacket.

Transfer students.

Three figures approached. They towered over the table for a second then flopped down opposite her.

Camilla looked up slowly.

"Hey, Cam," said Remy as though they were the best of friends—or as though they didn't just trap her in a room, push her up against a window, and threaten her the previous day.

A pause.

"I *can* call you Cam, can't I?" she added.

"You don't have to worry, I didn't tell anyone about what happened yesterday," muttered Camilla, hoping perhaps that'd make them go away. She swigged another sip of milk.

"No greeting, then?"

Camilla made no response.

"Fair enough." Remy grinned and sat back in her chair. Her teeth were surprisingly pearly, and there was something about the shape of her face—about the dimples in her cheeks—that reminded Camilla of someone. "Listen. About that. We might've come on a little strong."

Camilla choked on her milk. She grabbed a napkin from her tray and dabbed around her mouth.

"A little?" she scoffed.

"Okay, a lot. But you have to understand, we don't really know how things work around here."

"How things work around here?" Camilla tore the napkin in half. "So, pushing people up against windows, interrogating them, and threatening them are how things are done in Escana?"

Remy pulled up her shoulders.

"That's really weird, you know. Really messed up." Camilla crumpled the shredded napkin, put it aside, and unwrapped the plastic around her sandwich. It was tuna mayonnaise, the cheapest item on the menu. Luckily, it was also one of her favorites.

"Yeah, well, what's normal to some people can be strange to others. Like magic, for instance."

"Magic?" asked Camilla.

The transfer students shared a look. Then, they watched, not hungrily, but fascinated, as Camilla took the first bite of her sandwich. Crumbs fell onto her tray and lettuce crunched between her teeth. She wiped her mouth, put down the sandwich, and frowned at them.

"Why are you all watching me eat?" she asked.

Remy paused before she spoke. "I like you, Camilla. We like her, don't we?" she asked Milo and Fleur.

They both nodded, and Remy continued, "And we wanted to, you know, apologize. We can get a little too excited sometimes, and we forget we don't know you well enough to joke around. I know it might take a while, but would you perhaps . . . forgive us?"

Camilla said nothing at first. She wrapped her leftover sandwich in plastic, since she wasn't about to finish it in front of an audience, and pushed the tray across the table. No one had ever apologized to her for anything before, thus she had no idea how to react.

Should she give them another chance? Were they really as out of control as she recalled?

"What do you say, Camilla?" asked Fleur. "Friends?" She reached her hand across the table. It was coarse and bony, not at all like Remy's, whose was smooth like porcelain.

Camilla didn't take it.

"Don't worry, you'll come around. They always do." Remy swept Fleur's hand aside. Her gaze flicked down to Camilla's collarbone. To her necklace. "You don't have to say yes, but might I have another look at that? I was just really fascinated by it yesterday."

Camilla didn't want to at first. She didn't trust them. Not really. They had the temperament of an autumn day: sometimes hot and sometimes cold. Most of the time unpredictable.

"Please?" Remy pleaded. Her bottom lip folded over. "If you do this, we'll leave you alone . . ."

What a tempting offer.

"Fine, but I'm not taking it off."

Remy leaned in across the table, took it in her hand, and turned it over. She raised it to the light, moving it from side to side as she studied the crest. Her eyes sparkled, and her mouth twitched.

"Do you know what it is?" asked Camilla.

"Wait, you mean you *don't*?"

"I've got no idea."

For the first time, Remy actually seemed surprised. She let go of the necklace, grinned, and got up.

Milo and Fleur followed in her lead.

"What a bummer," she said. "I've never seen it either. It's wicked, though. You should hold on to that."

And Camilla did. She wrapped her hand around it, feeling her heart pound in her chest as she watched them walk away. They truly were strange, even more so than yesterday.

Remy paused by the cafeteria's entrance. She twisted around, raised her hand, and waved at Camilla. Not a full wave, but the kind that only involved her fingers and palm. Camilla shuddered at the sight of it. She thought about waving back but decided against it.

They had apologized, sure, but how long would it be until they pushed her up against a wall again? How long until they came up to her and yanked the necklace right off her neck?

She tried not to think about it.

They were, after all, the only people who had ever expressed an interest in anything other than her eyes.

Their interest might be in her father's necklace—a simple piece of factory-forged gold—but it was something new. Something different. Something that might not be all that bad.

THAT AFTERNOON, Camilla cycled to the lake. Pearl got off work at seven, which meant she had a good four hours to sit by the water and draw. The ride to the lake was slightly longer since she had to go around to the opposite side. Her usual spot—the tournament location—had been taped off by the police, and there were still several search boats on the water.

Three days had gone by, and there was still no sign of the Morris brothers. Neither them nor their kayaks.

Maybe some of the rumors were true. Maybe they really did stage their deaths to run away.

The summer sun seared hot on Camilla's back. She parked her bike under a tree and sat in the shade with her feet in the water. Birds chirped around her, and the air smelled of pine.

She breathed it in and shut her eyes, hoping, wishing, expecting to see the castle when she opened them.

But she didn't.

Camilla began to draw. She sketched the trees, the ground, and a pinecone that bobbed with the waves on the water. Its sides were wilted, and some kind of algae stuck to it. She drew the edges of the dock, then colored in the darker side of the lake.

Still no castle.

Not even a flag.

Time ticked by, and half an hour later, when she had sketched the entire lake, she huffed and tore the paper from the sketchpad. She scrunched it into a ball and was about to toss it away when she heard a splashing sound— several splashing sounds, to be precise.

Camilla stuffed the paper into her bag and looked up. A kayak paddled down the lake towards her. She thought it might be a diver at first or an officer who came over to tell her she shouldn't be there, but as soon as she saw his wetsuit, pearly rows of teeth, and unkempt eyebrows, she relaxed. Not really relaxed, but felt slightly more at ease than before.

"Drawing castles on the lake again?" asked Logan. He put away his oar and zipped down his wetsuit, so his upper body showed. He dove into the water and came up with a smile.

"Nope, no castles today." Camilla pushed the balled-up paper deeper into her bag to make room for her sketchpad and pencils. She sat back, paddling with her feet in the water.

Logan dragged his kayak onto the shore, dripping wet.

"What a shame," he said, tying the sleeves of his wetsuit around his waist. A trail of hair reached up to his bellybutton. "I actually thought it was a cool idea, you know. A castle on the water. Except, how does it stay there? Does it float, or is it supported with beams?"

Camilla only smiled at that.

"What are you doing on the lake?" she asked. "I thought it was off-limits until the police had cleared it?"

"Not this side of the lake. Since it's a part of my father's land, the police can't forbid me from doing anything." He raised an eyebrow. "Come to think of it, you're actually trespassing."

Camilla's face warmed a little. She knew he made a joke, but still, he was right. She was trespassing. "I'm sorry," she apologized, and he outright laughed at her. She nonetheless explained on. "It's just, the other side was entirely sectioned off with police tape, and—"

"Relax, Camilla!" Logan chimed in, touching her forearm. "You're always welcome on this side."

Camilla looked down, afraid he might catch her blushing. He most likely did, for he suddenly let go of her and scratched behind his head. His bicep bulged as he did so, and Camilla couldn't help but stare at it. Her breath thinned and she almost hiccupped.

"Besides, I should be the one saying sorry to you," he went on.

"What? Why?"

"Because you got stuck with those weird transfer students." Logan hauled the kayak upright, so it leaned against his shoulder. "I can't believe they chose *you* out of everyone."

"What's that supposed to mean?" asked Camilla, hugging her knees. She wiggled her toes as she spoke.

"Well, you know, you're kind of . . ."

"Kind of what?"

"A loner."

Camilla didn't know what to say to this. She tried not to seem too offended, but she must've, for his brows immediately contorted, and his cheeks turned rosy. His eyes darted across her face as he said, "Oh, I didn't mean for it to sound like—I just meant that, well, you—"

"It's okay," Camilla forestalled him. "It's true, and it's certainly not a secret. I like being alone."

"Yeah, I noticed. Why is that, by the way?"

"It's hard to explain, really. Whenever I meet new people, especially in the last few years, they're always, well, too nice to me. I know that sounds crazy, and I don't really know how to phrase it"—Camilla swallowed—"but I never feel like anybody sees the me behind my eyes."

"Hold on a second, you have eyes?"

Camilla laughed.

"I'm serious, I've never noticed them. Well, I've noticed them, and they're actually quite nice looking. So blue and glossy, but—he shook his head—"my point is, I see you, Camilla Ward." Logan readjusted the kayak, so his one hand was free. Then, he reached out with his palm facing the sky. She hesitated, so he grabbed her hand and dragged her to the water.

"What are you doing?" she screeched.

"Today, instead of sketching the lake, you'll be experiencing it," said Logan, all philosophical. He pushed the kayak into the water. "In other words, I'm teaching you to kayak."

"Me? Kayak?" asked Camilla.

"Yeah, it'll be fun."

Camilla gnawed her lower lip. While she had never thought about learning to kayak, the moment Logan said it, kayaking was all she wanted to do. She kicked off her sandals and followed him, somewhat warily, into the lake. Water pooled around her, soaking her shorts.

She slipped on a stone, though Logan caught her before she fell.

"Th—Thanks," she stuttered.

"Yeah, no problem." He held her around the waist, guiding her in deeper. Then, he helped her onto the kayak, stabilized her, and got on himself. The kayak was actually only big enough for one person, so they squeezed up against each other with Camilla practically in his lap.

"Here," he said, handing her the oar. "How about you row us to that line of trees over there?"

Camilla accepted the oar even though she had no idea how to hold it. It was made of wood, but felt like plastic, and was much lighter than she imagined. She attempted a few strokes, trying her best to imitate the competitors at the tournament, but they barely moved at all.

"I think you've got the technique down," said Logan after a while. "So how about we *move* now, eh?"

"Hey, don't mock me! I'm new at this . . ."

Logan laughed at her so hard that the kayak bobbed up and down. She nudged him in the stomach with her elbow, surprised at how solid his abs felt. He yielded and leaned forward.

"Here, let me help you," he said, pressing up against her. They were both sopping wet, and a warmth built between them. He breathed into her neck, wrapping his hands over hers around the oar. He began to row with her. "Left. Right. Left. Now we're getting somewhere!"

Camilla couldn't tell whether she was smiling or

grimacing, which was why she was glad he couldn't see her face. She was so nervous she couldn't help but frown at herself. What should she say? What should she do? She could barely hear her own thoughts above the thrumming behind her ribs. She felt sick to her stomach but in a good way.

They rowed in silence for a while.

Camilla thought about something to say, anything at all, but her mind was rendered blank. The faint scent of sunblock on Logan's skin entranced her, stealing her focus.

"You think you can handle it now?" he asked, at last.

Camilla nodded, and he let go of her. She rowed the best she could, trying hard to impress him. He never taught those girls from school to kayak—not that she knew of, at least—so she wasn't about to make him regret it. Her biceps and forearms seared like never before, but she ignored it. How Logan could do this every day for hours, she'd never understand.

The current suddenly strengthened, and she battled to keep the kayak in a straight line. She raised her head to puff at her hair, but something flashed before her eyes—like a lightning bolt or the sun when it reflects off glass—and the castle appeared on the water.

It happened so suddenly, so unexpectedly, and seemed so realistic that she let out a scream.

"Camilla, what is it?" Logan wanted to know, confused.

Camilla tried to stop the kayak from ramming into the limestone wall. She jabbed the oar into the water, and they toppled over. She plunged into the lake, headfirst. Water flushed her nose and mouth. She got trapped under the kayak, unable to swim to the surface. Weeds and algae entangled around her feet. She kicked and kicked, but only sank down deeper.

Camilla swallowed a mouthful of water.

It tasted of fish and seaweed.

"Logan!" she tried to scream, but her words emerged as bubbles. She stopped struggling, whirled around, and opened her eyes. She looked straight at the wall, which reached all the way to the bottom and stretched farther down the length of the lake than she ever saw from up top. It was more than just a castle, more than just an enormous wall.

It was a town.

A city.

Camilla blinked a couple of times, but the wall didn't fade. She reached out to touch it, to graze it with her fingers, when someone came up behind her and scooped her to the surface.

"Camilla!" Logan held on to her as she coughed and gasped for breath. She wrenched from his grip and turned, but the castle was gone. Nothing except plain old lake lay before her.

"Are you okay?" he asked. She still coughed, struggling to stay afloat.

Logan hauled her to the side of the lake, and they rolled over onto the shore together. They lay on their backs, their chests moving up and down. After a minute or so, Logan sat up.

"What happened to you out there?" he asked.

Camilla looked up at him, cupping her hand over her eyes to shield them from the sun. She thought about telling him the truth but realized he would only think she was crazy. She had tipped over the kayak and nearly drowned and all for a castle that wasn't even there.

When she didn't answer right away, he added, "You were doing great, but then you tipped us over." He rubbed his hands across his wet hair, making drops spatter across Camilla's face. "You were underwater for a really long time, and I couldn't find you . . ."

"I'm sorry," said Camilla, sitting upright. She coughed, and her lungs enflamed all the way into her throat. "I don't know what happened. I guess I'm a worse kayaker than you thought."

Logan laughed it off, but she sensed he didn't believe her. He nonetheless got up, held out his hand, and asked, "Do you think you'll be able to go in again? We'll have to swim to where we came from, and I still need to fetch my kayak in the middle of the lake."

"Yeah, I'm fine." Camilla took his hand, surprised at how easily he pulled her to her feet. Her shirt clung to her chest and, she realized her undergarments showed through the thin, white material. A gasp escaped her throat. She let go of his hand and crossed her arms over her chest.

Logan's eyes only briefly flicked down, but he immediately forced them back up to her face.

"Let's go," he said and turned.

They padded across the rocks to the water, though

only made it half the way before he heeled in his tracks. Logan held out his hand, stopping Camilla.

"What is it?" she asked. She leaned past him, curious as to what he saw. A fish? A piece of glass?

"I—I'm not really sure."

Camilla wasn't either. A little distance in front of them, floating on the lake, were two blobs that shimmered in the sun. They weren't so much shimmering as reflecting in the same way Logan's wetsuit did when wet. She began to tremble, and bile rushed up to her throat.

No.

It couldn't be.

Logan plugged his nose at the awful stench. He approached, slowly, hesitantly, dipped his foot into the water, and flipped over one of the blobs. When he did, Camilla let out a yelp.

"Gah!" Logan stammered, his face drained of any color. He avoided her gaze as he turned around, ran behind the nearest shrub, and vomited. He was still heaving when Camilla stepped towards him. He shouted at her, "Camilla, stay back!"

"Is it—are they—"

"Yes." Logan rose, still with a green tint to his skin. "It's the Morris brothers. And they're both dead."

CHAPTER ELEVEN
EXTINE

Extine took a swig of wine. The liquid guzzled down her throat—sour, tangy, slightly dry. At least the outside world excelled at making one thing: liquor. She placed the crystal glass on the table next to her throne and sank into the cushioning. The throne room was dark, the curtains drawn on both sides, with but a single line of torches blazing along the wall.

Even with such little light, she winced. She kept her eyes on the carpet, every now and then glancing at the portraits on the wall by the doors. The faces of her father and grandmother stared back at her, their eyes bright blue and their smiles ever as charming, as enchanting.

If only the two of them could see her right now. If only her father could see the trouble Pearl caused. She broke the law, sabotaged the line to the throne, and stole the family eyes.

The throne room doors creaked and opened on a screen. Two figures, shadows in the dark, slipped inside.

A ray of light cast down the carpet, right onto Extine's face—into her eyes—and she hissed. Their condition had worsened greatly over the past few days. Too much not to worry.

When she had woken up that morning to her chambermaid parting her bedroom curtains, her eyeballs properly seared. It was as if they were about to ignite, bubbling and sputtering in their sockets. Of course, the chambermaid had to go after seeing her like that. She couldn't risk stories spreading through the castle, not to mention the rest of the kingdom.

"Mom?" asked Remy, glancing about the throne room.

Milo made a line for the windows and grabbed the golden chord, ready to pull it.

"No!" Extine shouted. She leapt from her throne and charged across the room at him. She grabbed his hand and yanked it off the chord. Her vision darkened, her head became foggy, and she momentarily lost herself. When she came to, her nails were stabbing into his flesh.

Milo stiffened. His eyes widened, and the corners of his mouth curled down in pure distress.

Extine let go of him. She retreated several steps, working her jaw. She wiped her hands on her dress and rubbed her throbbing forehead. "I need more wine," she mumbled.

Remy followed her down the carpet to her throne. Extine grabbed the glass on the side table, tossed back her head, raised it to her mouth, and swallowed everything in a single go.

"Ah," she exhaled, squeezing her eyes at the warmth in her throat.

When she turned around, Remy stood before her. "Mom," she repeated. "What's going on in here?"

Extine swayed on her heels a little. She chuckled involuntarily, then twirled around so the ends of her dress fluttered through the air. Her head began to spin, and she stopped.

That outsider wine certainly worked fast.

"What does it," she hiccupped, "look like?" she asked, collapsing onto her throne. "I'm drinking my pain away!"

Remy grunted. She snapped her fingers and Milo approached. He walked right up to Extine and took the glass, along with the jug on the table, away. She extended her arm in an attempt to stop him, but she was too slow, too limp. She sat back with a furrowed bottom lip.

"You're the Queen of Escana, the one responsible for everyone's safety. You can't do this, Mom."

"Do what? Have a little fun every now and then?"

Remy crossed her arms. "This is not fun. This is suicide." She paused. "Anyway, while you're still sober enough to talk, do you mind telling us why they found the two kayakers in the lake?"

"Dead," added Milo.

Extine let her head hang to the side. The walls wobbled around her, as did her father's portrait. His brows knitted together, and his lips pursed. Typical father, always disapproving.

Even in death.

"Mom," Remy repeated, and she snapped back.

"Oh, the kayakers," still hiccupping, "right." Extine thought about denying it all, but her mouth wouldn't obey. Instead, she giggled and said, "Am I an absolute genius, or what? Now they'll never be able to tell anyone about what they may or may not have seen here."

"Genius my ass!" hissed Remy through gritted teeth. She put her hand over her eyes and muttered under her breath. When she removed her hand, she wore a similar frown as her grandfather in his portrait. "Do you know how this might affect the plan?"

"I did what had to be done," said Extine. She slurred her words, and her eyes crossed over one another, but she stayed somber, serious. She was still their mother, and she was still their queen. "What makes you think you can walk in here and confront me, anyway?"

Remy parted her lips to say something.

"*Ah!*" Extine doubled over. Her eyes sang in their sockets, just like the other day only much, much worse. She clawed at the armrests of her throne, waiting for the earth to shake again, but nothing happened. A bitterness flushed her mouth, and she heaved, coughed, gagged.

She felt it coming and fought to suppress it, swallow it, hold it back, but . . . she threw up on the carpet.

Milo ran towards her. He fell on his knees in front of her, holding back her hair as her stomach emptied itself of the porridge she had eaten for breakfast and nearly an entire bottle of wine. She still heaved, even when nothing came out. How humiliating, how mortifying.

She never threw up.

"Here," said Milo, handing Extine his handkerchief to clean her mouth. She accepted it, and he got up to fetch a jug of water on another table by the door. He handed her the entire jug, and she drank without hesitation. "Mom, are you okay? You look awful."

"Thanks for the compliment, honey," said Extine, wiping her mouth. She returned the jug and handkerchief, which he hesitantly took between his fingers, and sat back. She closed her eyes. They were tender, not burning anymore, but sensitive as ever.

When she opened her eyes and looked around, Remy stood exactly where she did moments ago, still with crossed arms. Even after everything, she didn't move nor did she react.

"Remy," Extine began, but she was cut off.

"We found Pearl's child if that's of any interest to you."

"You did? When?"

"On Monday."

Extine frowned. "That was two days ago."

"Indeed, it was. Perhaps you'd have known sooner if you didn't hide in dark corners all the time."

"What do you want from me, Remy?"

"A little help would be nice."

"Help? With what?"

"We've got all this *homework*—whatever that is—and the royal tutor knows nothing about anything!"

"Can't you just ask your father?"

Remy scoffed. "Ha! I haven't trained all week because

of him. He keeps disappearing off to who knows where. Some parents you two are." She exhaled. "It's a girl, by the way."

"Pearl's child? A girl?" Extine pictured Pearl when she was eighteen—her hazel waves and emerald eyes. Her daughter's ought to be blue, as the Allessien eyes always were. Blue eyes and hazel waves. The perfect face for a thief to hide behind. "What's her name?"

"Camilla."

Extine bopped her head. "Camilla. I see. Did you make nice with her? Does she trust you yet?"

"Not yet," said Remy. She and Milo exchanged an unsure glance then she scratched her chin. "On the first day, we might've . . . kind of . . . accidentally lost control of ourselves . . ."

"What did you do?"

"We were just asking her a couple questions and such, when she, uh, used her power on us."

"No! She knows how to use the eyes' power?" Extine got up off the floor. She trudged to her throne and flopped onto it. She hunched over, and her back curved with the cushioning.

"Actually, she doesn't seem to know anything at all." Remy pulled up her nose at her brother, who was down on his knees wiping up Extine's vomit. He seemed to have fetched a bucket and sponge while they were speaking. "You know we have people for that, right?"

"Wine stains if not cleaned right away, Remy. Besides, I'd much rather dirty my hands than ruin an antique like this," said Milo. He wiped his forehead and continued to clean.

Remy rolled her eyes at him. She spoke on, "Anyway, Camilla knows absolutely nothing."

"Nothing?"

Remy shook her head. "Not even the name of her own father. She said he died when she was born."

"I doubt that's true," noted Extine, rapping her nails on the armrests. "Pearl's cunning that way. She knows better than to tell her daughter anything and would much rather lie."

"What a wretch."

"Mm . . ." Extine paused. "She wasn't always, though. We used to be close until she upped and left one night." She shifted in her seat, so her head rested on her left hand, then went on, "But none of that matters now. I can't believe you lost control. You'd better fix this, Remy."

"We already did."

Extine raised her chin.

"At least, I think we fixed things. We apologized, and she didn't scold us or anything, so I reckon it'll only be a matter of time until we can lure her here," Remy explained.

Extine peeled herself off her throne. She stepped across Milo and waddled over to Remy, who took a step back when she tried to hold on to her for support. Instead, she used a pillar.

"Good. You must earn her trust at any cost." Extine waited for her eyes to focus and her balance to stabilize, before she let go of the pillar. "Do you know where she is right now?"

"We don't know where she lives yet, but I guess she ought to be at the police station right now."

"Huh? What would she be doing at a police station?"

"That's entirely on you, *my queen*." Remy pretended to curtsey. "Camilla discovered the kayakers in the lake. Well, she and some guy she was with—also a kayaker."

"*A guy?*" Extine's voice pitched. She thought back to when she herself was eighteen and had just gotten her eyes. Finn came to mind. "Do you think she has him under her control?"

Remy nodded. "Looks that way to me."

Extine's stomach twisted. If this was true, and Camilla already had a guy under her control, it meant her eyes were much stronger than they anticipated. It would prove much more difficult to lure her to Escana, and even more so to take her power from her.

"Get to the guy," she said.

"What?"

"If Camilla likes him enough to put him under her control, we must get to the guy to get to her. He'll serve as our way in, and we'll use him as bait." Extine thought about it for a moment, then asked, "Remy, how sure are you she doesn't know about anything?"

Remy sounded uncertain as she said, "Well, if she does know something, she has a great poker face." She adjusted her ponytail, pulled at the choker around her neck, and shrugged.

"Find out whether she knows or not. And soon. I

won't be bested by an eighteen-year-old thief, do you understand? This is my, uh, our kingdom, and it has to stay that way."

Remy nodded.

"Now go! Leave me be!"

Milo finished scrubbing the carpet. He gathered the sponge and bucket, stood, bowed, and headed for the door. Remy went after him but before she left, she paused in the doorway.

"Oh, there's another thing I forgot to mention."

"What is it?"

"Camilla's surname. It's Ward."

"Ward?" Extine rolled the word off her tongue. "You think it's the father's surname?"

"I don't know." Remy licked her lips, then spoke on, "But Milo contacted the Escanian births, marriages, and deaths building, and there's no one in Escana with that surname."

"Camilla's father is an outsider, then?"

"No, that's the thing. I think Pearl made up the surname after Camilla was born," Remy suggested. When Extine raised an eyebrow, she explained, "Camilla has a necklace."

"A necklace?" Extine didn't even try to hide her disappointment. She sighed and retreated to her throne. The cushions sank under her weight, letting out a similar whoosh as her sigh. "What does a necklace have to do with anything? I swear, Remy, if this is your attempt at stalling—"

"The necklace had the Escanian crest on it."

Silence.

"When I asked her about it, Camilla said it was her father's. Like I said, she didn't know his name," Remy narrowed her eyes, "but luckily, we don't have to. It can only mean one thing."

Extine pursed her lips in delight. "Indeed," she said. "Pearl's secret lover is someone in Escana."

CHAPTER TWELVE
CAMILLA

"Thank you again for your statement, Miss Ward, and I apologize for the inconvenience." Detective Marshall opened the door to the interrogation room, and Camilla stepped out into the corridor.

After she and Logan had discovered the Morris brothers' lifeless bodies at the lake, they caught the attention of a man on a search boat who called the police. All she wanted to do was go home and rest, but Detective Marshall forbade her from doing so. Since she and Logan found the boys together, both their statements were necessary.

They were promptly escorted to the police station, where they were asked to tell their stories. Logan, still in his wetsuit, had offered to go first. An officer had given him a hoodie to cover up, though it sat somewhat snug around his shoulders and chest.

Before he went in, he had asked, "Camilla, will you be okay?"

"Sure," she had replied.

"See you in a bit, then." Logan had left with the officer, and Camilla had taken a seat in the waiting room.

At the time, she really did think she was fine. She had flipped through some magazines, eavesdropped on a few conversations, and even used the facilities. It was only when she ran out of things to do that her mind got the better of her, and her thoughts began to roam.

She had recalled the stench, the reek of rotting flesh. How Logan had hurled behind the bushes and how he had forbidden her from coming closer. While she had obeyed, she still managed to get a glimpse of their blue-grey skin, lifeless eyes, and blood-stained mouths.

Camilla had never been more relieved than when Logan came out and the officer called her name.

"Still okay?" Logan had asked again.

"Still okay."

Half an hour and many questions later, Camilla was free to go. She walked down the corridor to the waiting room, off-balance and slightly less okay than she had led on. Her mind replayed the sight at the lake—the lifeless blobs that had bobbed in the water.

Her stomach lurched.

It was one thing to see a corpse in movies and pictures but an entirely different thing to actually encounter. Camilla suppressed a gag. Even though her mouth had been filled with bile the entire time, she had not once thrown up.

Logan, on the other hand, had thrown up twice at the

lake, once in a dustbin in the interrogation room, and possibly again in the bathroom after he got out.

Camilla hesitated before she entered the waiting room. She saw her mother's car in the parking lot through the window and knew absolute hell was about to break loose.

She breathed in and rounded the corner.

"Are you okay?" asked Logan, bombarding her before she had a proper gaze about the waiting room. He wrapped his hands around her upper arms and pulled her towards him.

"Yea, I'm fine," she said, absently glancing past him. "And you already asked me that three times."

The waiting room buzzed with people, much more than when she went in. Every few seconds the telephone rang and a set of sirens went off outside. People were slouching in their chairs, ladies clutching onto their purses, and boys with circles around their eyes.

But no Pearl.

"I know, I know, and that's only because I feel absolutely horrible! You should never have seen that," Logan rambled, scratching his chin. A shade of stubble had sprouted throughout the day. "I'm really sorry, Camilla. I just wanted to spend some time with—"

"Camilla!" cried a voice.

Pearl came out of the bathroom. Her hands were wet, but she pushed Logan aside and grabbed Camilla's face. She kissed her on the forehead and nose, then pinched her cheeks.

"Mom . . ." Camilla groaned.

"Oh, darling, I was so worried!" Pearl let go of her cheeks. She paused a second, then turned to address Logan. "Very nice to see you again, Mr. Wheeler." But it didn't sound that way.

"Nice to see you too, Ms. Allessien." Logan stuck out his hand, but Pearl simply wrapped her arms around Camilla again, smooched her on the cheek, and beckoned her to the door.

"Thanks for taking such good care of my girl. And sorry to take off like this, but we simply must get home. It's nearly nine o'clock already, and I'm sure you both have loads to do."

"Mom, please . . . can you give me a second?" Camilla pleaded. She wrenched herself loose then returned to Logan. He really did look sorry. "Listen, don't worry about today."

"But—"

Camilla spoke over him. "You taught me to kayak, and then you saved me from drowning. Sure, we found a couple of bodies along the shore"—she gulped as she said that—"and your kayak might still be out there, along with my bag, but it was a good day otherwise."

Logan grinned ever so slightly. The expression looked strange on him, unnatural almost. He barely had enough time to say, "I guess so . . ." before Pearl yanked Camilla away again.

"See you tomorrow!" she called from the door. He waved at her, and she felt a little better. Just a little. The feeling didn't last, however, as she was promptly shoved into the Chevy.

Pearl walked around it and got in. She shut the door and her demeanor drastically changed. "What on this great earth were you thinking, Camilla?"

"Mom, I—"

"What were you doing back at the lake in the first place? Not only did I warn you to stay away from there, but I thought you knew better than this! I'm extremely disappointed in you."

The Chevy roared to life, and Pearl backed out of the parking lot. She turned left onto the street then drove straight. The car groaned as she stepped on the gas, the gears clattering and the interior rattling. Her face was shadowed, lit only by the streetlights, though it proved enough to emphasize the frown between her brows and the scowl around her lips.

Camilla always thought Pearl looked young for a mother of a high school student, but now, with the red, green, and yellow traffic lights illuminating her face, the number of wrinkles around her eyes and forehead astounded her. There were few around her mouth, though. Little proof of laughter.

"I'm sorry, Mom."

No reaction.

"I just wanted to get away," Camilla continued, afraid to tell Pearl why she really went there: to draw, to see the castle again. Except that didn't work out either. She had seen the castle but couldn't sketch it. And, as a bonus, she now had another picture stuck in her mind.

The picture of two deceased kayakers.

THE PICCADILLY NOVELS—*continued.*

Hide and Seek. By WILKIE COLLINS.
Illustrated by Sir JOHN GILBERT and J. MAHONEY.

The Dead Secret. By WILKIE COLLINS.
Illustrated by Sir JOHN GILBERT and H. FURNISS.

Queen of Hearts. By WILKIE COLLINS.
Illustrated by Sir J. GILBERT and A. CONCANEN.

My Miscellanies. By WILKIE COLLINS.
With Steel Portrait, and Illustrations by A. CONCANEN.

The Woman in White. By WILKIE COLLINS.
Illustrated by Sir J. GILBERT and F. A. FRASER.

The Moonstone. By WILKIE COLLINS.
Illustrated by G. DU MAURIER and F. A. FRASER.

Man and Wife. By WILKIE COLLINS.
Illustrated by WILLIAM SMALL.

Poor Miss Finch. By WILKIE COLLINS.
Illustrated by G. DU MAURIER and EDWARD HUGHES.

Miss or Mrs.? By WILKIE COLLINS.
Illustrated by S. L. FILDES and HENRY WOODS.

The New Magdalen. By WILKIE COLLINS.
Illustrated by G. DU MAURIER and C. S. RANDS.

The Frozen Deep. By WILKIE COLLINS.
Illustrated by G. DU MAURIER and J. MAHONEY.

The Law and the Lady. By WILKIE COLLINS.
Illustrated by S. L. FILDES and SYDNEY HALL.

The Two Destinies. By WILKIE COLLINS.

*** Also a **POPULAR EDITION of WILKIE COLLINS'S NOVELS**, post 8vo, illustrated boards, 2s. each.

Felicia. By M. BETHAM-EDWARDS.
With a Frontispiece by W. BOWLES.
"A noble novel. Its teaching is elevated, its story is sympathetic, and the kind of feeling its perusal leaves behind is that more ordinarily derived from music or poetry than from prose fiction. Few works in modern fiction stand as high in our estimation as this."—SUNDAY TIMES.

Olympia. By R. E. FRANCILLON.

Under the Greenwood Tree. By THOMAS HARDY.

Fated to be Free. By JEAN INGELOW.

The Queen of Connaught. By HARRIETT JAY.

The Dark Colleen. By HARRIETT JAY.
"A novel which possesses the rare and valuable quality of novelty. . . . The scenery will be strange to most readers, and in many passages the aspects of Nature are very cleverly described. Moreover, the book is a study of a very curious and interesting state of society. A novel which no novel-reader should miss, and which people who generally shun novels may enjoy."—SATURDAY REVIEW.

"Away from what?" barked Pearl. They whizzed around a corner. "The safety of your own home?"

Camilla didn't reply, as her mother wouldn't possibly understand. Not even Camilla herself understood.

Not fully, anyway.

They drove from neighborhood to neighborhood, the houses shrinking from big to small to minute. Camilla and Pearl lived in the latter neighborhood, in a house with barely two bedrooms and a bathroom. There were three identical houses next to theirs, all of which were rented out to a drunk, two strippers, and the parking lot guard at the diner.

It might've proved small, and it might've come forth as grimy, but it was all Camilla ever knew.

Pearl turned right into their driveway. A single-story house with beige walls and a peeling door lay before them. She shut off the Chevy but didn't get out. It was dark outside, and Camilla only saw the framework of her mother's face: her chin and nose and forehead.

"Are you all right?" asked Pearl when the silence grew too much for them both. Her voice croaked.

"What?" asked Camilla, not sure whether she had heard correctly.

"What you did was very irresponsible and wrong . . . but I'm still your mother, I still love you, and I still care about you." Pearl took the keys out of the ignition. "So, are you all right?"

Camilla stared out in front of her. The pitch-black darkness proved a canvas for her thoughts, for her memories. Every time she blinked, she saw one of the two

Morris brothers. A picture in full quality. She spoke through the lump in her throat, "I—I saw two dead bodies today."

Silence.

"They were just floating there . . . lifeless . . ." Camilla shut her eyes and a tear rolled across her cheek. She quickly wiped it away, hoping her mother didn't see. She couldn't cry. Not now. Not about this. She didn't even know them. "Who would do such a thing?"

Pearl sat back with her hands on her lap. "I don't know. I can only imagine what you're feeling right now."

Camilla sniffed. She leaned against her mother's side, burying her head in the nook of her neck. Pearl smelled of fried food and ketchup, but Camilla didn't care. Right then, she needed to be comforted. She needed to feel safe and like everything would be all right.

And everything was all right. For a moment.

"I don't want you to see that Wheeler boy again." Pearl's words shattered that moment to pieces.

"What?" Camilla nearly choked on the word. She sat up. "But he's Logan! I've known him forever!"

"I know, darling. He's a great kid and an amazing athlete, but he's also a boy. A teenage boy."

Camilla cringed as she thought about where the conversation was headed. She and her mother never officially had *the talk*, but she had been told the gist of things throughout the years.

"Mom—"

"No, you have to hear this." Pearl stopped her from opening the car door. She rotated in her seat and took a breath before she went on. "You're a woman now, all grown up."

"He's just a friend!"

"Is he, Camilla?" Pearl challenged her. "Are you able to look me in the eyes while you say that?"

"It's too dark for me to see anything. I need to get some air." Camilla yanked away and got out of the car before her mother could stop her again. She rounded the Chevy, upped the steps to their front door, and took out the spare key under the moldy welcome mat.

Pearl paced up the driveway after her. "Camilla Ward! Don't you dare walk away from me!"

Camilla didn't obey. She entered the house and turned on the lights. One of them flickered before it went out, and another didn't even light up. She made for the kitchen and opened the cupboard that contained the spare lightbulbs, just to have it slammed in her face.

Pearl stood before her with watery eyes.

"You should listen when I tell you to stay away from Logan," she said. "Love is wonderful . . . until it isn't. You're way too young to have a child and have too much to lose."

Camilla threw her hands in the air like a shield. "Whoa! Mom! Who said anything about having a child?"

"I was exactly your age when I had you," said Pearl, properly in tears now. She briefly glanced at Camilla's necklace, then clutched at her own heart. "I lost every-thing because of that."

"Lucky for us I'm not you, then!" shouted Camilla. "And if that's really how you felt, why didn't you just give me up?" She watched as Pearl's face turned from sad to horrified.

"Camilla, I never meant—"

"You never mean anything. In fact, you never say anything either. When someone asked me the other day where you were born, I didn't even know! You're like a stranger to me!"

"Who asked you where I was born?" Pearl wanted to know.

Camilla scoffed. "See, there you go again, always changing the subject. You have no idea what it's like for me, Mom. I feel like a stranger in my own house—in my own town."

"Camilla—"

"Please. Until you're ready to really be honest with me, I'd prefer it if you stayed out of my life." Camilla rounded Pearl and made down the hallway to her bedroom.

"But . . . no! How am I supposed to stay out of your life when I know about all the dangers out there?" Pearl followed her from the kitchen, to the living room, to her bedroom. "Camilla, darling, just talk to me. Listen to me when I tell you that you and Logan have to—"

"Just shut up for once!" Camilla slammed the door in her mother's face. She waited with her hand on the knob, anticipating a reply, but Pearl didn't say anything. She actually did shut up.

Strange.

Usually, her mother would be banging on the door with her fists, demanding she let her in. She would be confiscating her phone and forbidding her from ever speaking to Logan again.

But Pearl did nothing like that.

In fact, she did nothing at all.

Camilla listened at the door. The tap in the kitchen had gone on, and dishes clattered into the sink. She rubbed her warm, tingly eyes and instantly knew what had happened. It was the same thing that had happened with Karen and with the booth attendant.

Camilla turned with her back against the door. She sank into a crouched position, wrapping her arms around her legs. There was a mirror opposite her. She could barely see herself in the dark, but for some reason, some unexplainable reason, her eyes seemed to. . .

Glow.

Bright blue, almost crystal-like. She resembled the type of monster that only showed its eyes when it lurked in a bush, ready to pounce, ready to kill.

The thought of death brought Camilla's thoughts back to the lake. She shuddered, thinking about what awful things must've happened to the Morris brothers since their disappearance. The medical examiner had said they were poisoned. Mandrake. A strong dose of it.

Camilla buried the image at the back of her mind. She replaced it with the castle—the structure that reached deep underwater—and the wall she had almost touched. She envisioned her fingers and how she was within grazing distance when Logan had pulled her away.

Perhaps it really was just an illusion. The final moment before she would've drowned.

A car passed by their house, and Camilla's room lit up. For some reason, and she wasn't sure what it was, she looked up at that exact moment. Her heart accelerated, her eyes widened, and her breath thinned. There, in the mirror, in the corner of her room, was a shadow.

A man.

Camilla screamed. She got up off the floor and fidgeted with the doorknob, but it was no use. She trembled too much to turn it. "Mom! Help!" she shouted, barely managing it.

Pearl barged into the room within seconds. She held a steak knife in her hand, ready to attack. "What is it?" she asked, flipping the light switch on the wall. The room filled with light.

"There's a—" Camilla spun around, but at once swallowed her words. There was no one there. Her window was raised, and her curtains swept aloft, revealing their front lawn.

Abandoned.

"A what?" asked Pearl. "What did you see?"

"N—Nothing." Camilla struggled to make sense of it. Of everything. A castle on the lake, a man in the woods, three hostile transfer students, two dead kayakers, and someone in her bedroom? Was it the same man? She checked under her bed, then flopped onto the mattress.

The moment her head hit her pillow, she burst into tears. Pearl dropped the knife on the carpet and ran towards her. She sat down next to her, holding her hand, rubbing her knuckles.

This only made Camilla cry harder.

"Darling, what's wrong?" asked Pearl. She didn't seem at all angry about before, as though she hardly remembered a thing. Her hands were wet from doing the dishes, and her fingertips were wrinkled. "I'm sorry I yelled at you earlier. I guess I can be a little overprotective."

Camilla wiped under her eyes.

"Mom, can I tell you something?" she asked.

Pearl nodded. "Of course. You can tell me anything. Anything at all. I'm always here for you."

"I know this might seem crazy," Camilla swallowed, not sure whether she should go on, "but I think there's something wrong with me. I think there's something wrong with my eyes."

"Y—Your eyes?" asked Pearl.

Camilla nodded, her vision still foggy. "Ever since my birthday . . . I don't know what's going on. And you, Mom . . . you said we'd talk about it. Do you know what's happening?"

A moment passed in which Pearl just sat there, speechless. Then, she flattened the duvet with her hands and said, "Cam, when a girl reaches a certain age, things start to change—"

"Ew, no!" Camilla shrieked, whipping a pillow out from under her and stuffing it in her mother's face. "Mom, stop avoiding it. I know there's something you're not telling me."

"I don't know what else to say to you, Cam. Whatever you think is going on with you, it's probably just shock. You just saw two corpses today. And with what had happened at the lake . . ." A pause in which Pearl got up. "Your eyes are fine. You're fine. Alright?"

Even though Camilla didn't believe her, she nodded and forced a smile. "Okay," she said, watching her mother reverse to the door. "And sorry about shouting."

"Shouting? Oh, don't worry about it." Pearl turned in the threshold. "Good night, darling."

"Good night."

Then, her mother shut the door. The moment it clicked shut, Camilla scrambled out of bed and latched her window shut. She caught a glimpse of herself in the reflection, her face all wonky and her features too dark to distinguish. What she could see, though, were her eyes.

And they were no longer glowing.

CHAPTER THIRTEEN
EXTINE

*E*xtine breathed in the cool evening air. It smelled of rain, but the sky was clear, glittering with stars. They danced in her presence, bowed before her, their queen. She listened to the Crystalvale clocktower beyond the trees: Nine ... Ten ... Eleven ... Twelve ...

Midnight on the dot.

Extine stepped into the moonlight. Her shadow fell across the ground in the courtyard, stretching all the way to the foot of the hedges, bending ninety degrees at her neck. This was what it had come to. She could only go out at night, in the dark, while everyone slept.

"Please, Your Majesty, have mercy!" pleaded the woman before her. She put her hands together as if she was praying and paced backward. She nearly tripped over a loose brick.

Extine mimicked the woman's every step. A part of her told her to yield, but another, slightly louder, part of her told her to press on—to do what was necessary for the kingdom. She had to remain queen. Yes. Sacrifices needed to be made for the sake of Escana.

"I'm telling the truth. I don't know who the father of Princess Pearl's baby is. I suspected the princess was pregnant, but I never knew for sure . . ." The woman extended her wrinkly hand to cover her face. She had sunspots across her nose and cheeks and forehead.

Extine huffed. She slapped the woman across the face, causing her to fall over on her side. She at once retracted her hand, which still tingled from the blow. She had just hit someone.

A woman.

A chambermaid to the royal family for forty years, to be precise.

Her name was Nina, and she had been Pearl's chambermaid once. She was Remy's now.

"You spent more time with Pearl than anyone else," Extine continued with her train of thought. She encircled Nina, walking slowly, adamantly, until inches away from stepping on her fingers. "You were more than her chambermaid. You were her friend and confidant."

"Your Majesty, I swear . . . I thought she might've lost the baby. I thought that's why she ran away—"

"Stop lying to me!" Extine hissed, fighting against raising her voice. The courtyard lay abandoned, and it best stayed that way. The last thing she needed was a pair of guards stumbling upon her, interrogating and torturing an old woman. A mother amongst the servants.

Nina sniffled.

"You knew everything about Pearl. You must have

some idea, some theory, as to who the father might be?" Extine paused with her hands behind her back, but went on before Nina answered, "You helped her hide the pregnancy, eh? I bet you helped her escape as well!"

"No!" Nina crawled across the ground. "I—I would never betray the crown. I swear on my life!"

Another slap across the cheek.

Nina fell on all fours. Her braid came loose, and her hair sprawled across her face, streaks of brown and gold and grey. She breathed heavily, her tears dripping on the concrete.

Extine just stood there for a moment, not exactly sure what she was doing or why she was doing it. Her eyes throbbed to the rhythm of her heartbeat, fast and loud.

Thump, thump, thump.

Extine wrapped her arms around herself. What had happened to her? She was never one for violence, except now it seemed the only way to get things done. The only way to prevail.

"Who's the father of Pearl's child?" she asked again, mostly to silence her buzzing, runaway mind.

"I—I don't know."

"Gah! I've had enough!" Extine raised her heel and was just about to stomp on the maid's fingers, when Finn emerged from the trees lining the courtyard, saw them, and called out to her.

"Extine! Stop that!"

Extine stumbled back. She tripped over the limestone bench behind her, just managing to grab onto it for support. It wobbled but held her weight. She heaved through an open mouth.

"Finn," she said heaving, "what are you doing here?"

No answer.

"Where have you been all this time?"

Finn approached. He pushed Extine back onto the bench, turned, and crouched down. He offered a hand to Nina, who merely looked at him with teary, reddish-pink eyes. "Here, let me help you," he said.

When after several seconds she hadn't reacted, he added, "Don't worry. I won't hurt you."

Nina placed her hand into his. He squeezed it, fleetingly smiled, then pulled her to her feet. She wobbled on her heels and wrapped both her hands around his waist, clinging to him with heavy eyelids and a saggy mouth. Her cheeks were red and swollen, almost blue.

"Where were you?" Extine repeated, more serious now.

Finn kept Nina on her feet, supporting her. "I was in town," he said. "It's quiet this time of night."

"Why were you in town?"

"You're seriously asking me that?"

"Yes, I am, Finn. The kingdom's unstable right now. Everyone has to be accounted for." Extine absently rubbed her fingers together, over and over. "If you don't want to tell me as your wife, then tell me as your queen. I'm only asking this once: why were you in town?"

"You murdered two boys, Extine!" Finn snapped. He took a moment to calm himself, his eyes flicking in the direction of the lake. "All of Crystalvale is alarmed. The borders are more unstable than ever. Do you really think luring people to the lake was our best move at this point?"

Extine thought of a reply, but she had nothing to say. Nothing to defend herself against his argument. Her mouth pulled into a knot. *He* was supposed to be in the wrong, not *her*.

"More importantly," Finn went on, whispering now, "what were you doing out here with Nina?" There was a level of judgement in his voice that made Extine want to growl at him.

"The father of Pearl's child is someone in Escana," she said.

"What?"

"Shocking, isn't it? It's a girl. Her name's Camilla. Remy, Milo, and the sorceress's daughter located her at the school. Not such a bad idea after all, eh? Except, there was an incident—"

"An incident?" snapped Finn.

Extine narrowed her eyes. "Yes, but that's not where I'm going with this. Remy told me Camilla owns a necklace with the Escanian crest on it. Her father's someone in the kingdom, Finn."

Finn's eyes moved from Extine to Nina. He was so shocked, so gobsmacked, that he nearly let go of her. He moved past Extine and set Nina down on the bench. She wheezed as he did this, but it was more a wheeze of old age rather than pain. He patted her on the back. "Just wait over here for a moment, all right?" he said, pulling Extine aside.

"Did Remy hurt Camilla?" he asked.

"What?" Extine blurted out.

"I mean, if she did, she might've used her power on her." Finn quickly changed the subject. "More importantly, did Remy actually see the necklace? You know, hold it in her hand?"

Extine nodded, still with narrowed eyes.

"It has the Escanian crest on it? Are you sure?"

"Yes," Extine insisted. "Why are you acting like this Finn? Is there something you're not telling me?"

Finn let go of her at once and stepped back. He shook his head, glancing down at the ground. "I'm only worked up. This is a serious accusation. There are hundreds of men in Escana, most of whom are honorable and loyal."

"One of them very clearly isn't."

Finn put his hands on his hips. He tossed back his head, turned in place, and emptied his chest. When he faced Extine again, he said, "What were you doing out here with Nina?"

Silence.

Extine pretended to dust off her dress. "My tale was still leading up to that, dear husband. Nina, over here," she pointed at the woman on the bench, "knows who the father is."

Finn choked, and Nina shook her head again.

"She was closer to Pearl than anyone else and kept all her secrets for her. I have to find out who the father is, Finn. I have to know who it was that betrayed Escana and stole my eyes!"

"And you're prepared to torture an innocent woman to do that?" Finn doubled back to Nina, who still sat there, sobbing, rubbing her face. She dabbed under her eyes with a handkerchief. "She's an old woman. What happened to you? You've never done this sort of thing."

Extine cursed under her breath. "I've never had to. When I still had my eyes, my power, and when I could still go out during the daytime. When I ruled this kingdom without any trouble," she swallowed, hard, "and when I still had *you*, Finn."

Finn's brows twitched. "W—What do you mean?"

"You never loved me."

Finn did nothing to contest. His forehead creased and his mouth worked, but he didn't deny it.

"You only married me because you were obliged to. You only thought you loved me because I persuaded you to with my eyes." Extine balled her hands into fists. "This chambermaid helped my sister hide her pregnancy for nine months . . . nine whole months, Finn!"

Finn gulped.

"And for that, she must pay." Extine drew a knife from her upper bodice and charged at Nina.

"Extine, no!" shouted Finn. He leapt in front of her, grabbing the sharp end of the blade.

Slice.

Blood oozed from the flat of his hand, but he held on to the knife, not letting go of it until Extine did.

Extine gasped. She dropped the knife, let out a shriek, and collapsed in a heap on the concrete. Her chest pumped up and down as if she was crying, and her entire body shook, but no tears filled her eyes. She squeezed them shut, trying to force it but nothing welled up.

Not even a single drop.

Extine looked down at her hands, at her dress. The white lace around the seam was stained with blood. Finn's blood. The sight of it dried up her mouth, crisped her eyes even more.

"Finn, I—I don't know what came over me." Extine glanced up, but Finn had his back to her.

"Nina," he said. "Go, now!"

Nina reached out to him, to his hand against his chest. "You're hurt. I must tend to your wound at once."

Finn motioned to the castle with his head. Its windows were pitch black, and the doors to the courtyard were open. "No, I'm fine," he said. "But please, you don't have to forgive the queen for what she did. But don't tell anyone about what happened here."

Nina stood up from the bench and bowed her head. "Thank you. Thank you so much, Captain Finn." Then, the old woman of sixty-something ran across the courtyard into the castle.

"Do you know what you just did?" asked Finn, slowly rotating. He loomed over Extine, blocking the moon from her view. His voice was thick, filled with disappointment.

"No. What?"

"You just destroyed your family's good name. I grew up in this castle. I knew your father, even after he had lost his sight. He would've been ashamed of you if he was alive today."

Extine kept her head down. Tears still refused to flow as she silently huffed.

Finn was, as always, right. On her eighteenth birthday,

her father had also lost his eyes. Lost his power. He, too, had been rendered blind, but, unlike her, he was proud. Not jealous or angry.

"I'm sorry," she whispered.

"You shouldn't apologize to me. You should apologize to Nina."

"No, not that. I'm sorry about your hand." Extine looked up at his palm. He held it against his chest to stop the bleeding. His entire hoodie was stained red, a growing circle of blood.

"It's those eyes of yours, Extine," he said. "There's dark magic inside of you, controlling you. It's swallowing every ounce of your goodness, leaving you with nothing but rottenness."

Extine expected him to turn on his heels and walk away, but he instead crouched to her level and raised her chin. He used his thumb to rub under her eyes, her swollen, shaded eyes.

"Leave it to me to find the father," he said, tenderly now. "And let me do it my way, the right way."

Extine nodded. She blinked a couple of times, each time more and more grateful to have Finn in her life— each time more and more afraid of losing him. That is, if she hadn't already. She looked closely at him, at the grey in his beard and the lines across his forehead. He had stood by her for eighteen years. He had kept her afloat, been her very best friend.

"Finn . . ."

Extine leaned forward in an attempt to kiss him. Their

lips were a paper's width apart when Finn pulled away at the last second. He sat up, looking beyond her.

Extine's world shattered to pieces. For a moment, she had thought she might've been wrong. She believed that he loved her, really loved her, and not because she persuaded him to.

Finn turned his head, knowing, perhaps fearing, that her previous question had been answered.

"Finn," said Extine, still on the ground. "Do you still love me?"

Finn stood in place like a statue, staring out across the courtyard. He looked much older from below—much older than he actually was. The bags under his eyes were twice as big, and the wrinkles around his mouth twice as deep. Extine swooned under her breath. Even with the added years, he was dreamy as ever.

"I married you, didn't I?" he said, shrugging a bit.

This was the answer Extine had feared the most. She struggled to her feet, slowly and dismally. Finn offered to help her up, but she dismissed his gesture. She didn't need him to stand.

"Like I said, you married me because of my eyes. Now that they're gone . . . do you still love me?"

Still no answer.

Finn merely stood there on his knees, straight faced. He didn't move, flinch, or twitch. He didn't even try to lie. The moment lengthened, but neither of them spoke. They listened to the fountain. To the bullfrogs around and inside of it and the crickets in the hedges.

What a fine summer's night.

Perfect to have one's heart broken.

Extine nodded to herself. She swallowed, for once glad she couldn't cry. Her eyes seared again, but, this time, it didn't hurt. She felt no need to scream and no need to double over or throw up. The ground didn't shake, and the barrier didn't flicker. Her eyes sizzled, but it felt . . .

Good.

Great, even.

"All right, find the father," she said. The strength in her voice surprised her.

"Do you promise?" asked Finn.

"Promise what?"

"That you won't intervene." Only now did Finn get to his feet. Blood ran down his forearm and onto his pants. He stepped towards Extine, trailing red splotches in his wake.

"I'm not promising anything." A pause in which her eyes flicked to his wounded hand. "Actually, I am. If you don't find Camilla's father by the end of this week, I promise . . ."

Bitterness filled her mouth, but she didn't care. Feelings of remorse, heartbreak, and disappointment flushed through her, filling her with strength. *To cut open more than just your hand.*

"Extine, things don't have to be this way," said Finn. "You just need help. You need to accept—"

"Accept what?" Extine forestalled him. "That I lost my husband? That my sister betrayed me?"

Finn parted his lips to say something, but the clock-tower struck one, and he closed them again.

154

Extine sighed. "I thought so."

"Where does this leave us?" Finn asked her.

"I don't know. But don't think because I birthed your children, you're exempt from my authority." She straightened her dress and pulled back her shoulders. She entered the castle with her head held high, her eyes burning in their sockets and a crack in her heart.

But a grin on her mouth.

CHAPTER FOURTEEN
CAMILLA

Camilla had never been much of an athlete. She had signed up for tennis when she was younger, having just watched Wimbledon for the first time, but barely attended two lessons. The athletes on TV made it look so easy and so much more fun to chase after a ball. She had tried field hockey a few years later in middle school, but that didn't work out either.

Now she was in high school, and despite knowing better than to torture herself, every student was obliged to take part in at least one physical activity. Chess technically classified as a sport, though the principal didn't quite agree. So, after much consideration—and a trip to her physician after a discus throw incident—Camilla had decided on track.

It was three o'clock on a Thursday afternoon—the obliged, weekly exercise slot. The Crystalvale High sports grounds crawled not only with students but teachers and coaches alike. They didn't take part, yet they more than eagerly patrolled the grounds for slackers.

"Come on, Miss Ward! Hustle!" one of the teachers shouted at Camilla, clapping his hands as she passed. He had a bigger-than-average belly and stood with a candy bar in his hand.

Quite the motivation.

"R—Right, sir!" Camilla replied. She was already out of breath and had hardly run around half of the track. She wore a grey tracksuit that matched the ominous clouds overhead and a pair of sneakers that no longer sported grip. A sharp pain stretched from the side of her stomach and into her right shoulder. She rubbed it, which only made it worse.

As she slowed, two girls jogged past her.

"Way to go, Keira! Keep it up, Maya!" shouted the teacher with his mouth full of a candy bar. He chewed, swallowed, took another bite, and added, "Miss Ward, you're slacking again!"

Camilla huffed. Not because she was out of breath, but because she was out of tolerance. Did they really have to go through this every Thursday? Every single time she ran past him?

"You could do with some exercise yourself," she mumbled, accidentally loud enough for Keira to hear.

"Nice one," she said, turning her head.

Camilla smiled out of shame, and Keira accelerated. She met up with Maya, who was already a quarter of the track ahead. As devoted marathoners for the school, they seemed more comfortable when running than when sleeping. They wore the standard Crystalvale High track uniform, though it was less of a uniform and more of a swimsuit.

Their tops were made ninety percent of sheer netting that stretched around their waists and upper bodies and ten percent of a thin, black film that left nothing to the imagination. Their shorts cut off under their bums, the school emblem printed across both cheeks.

They were the type of toned, with chiseled abs and calves, Camilla could only dream of being.

She wiped a sleeve across her forehead. Sweat rimmed her face, trickling down her neck and into her collar. Her scalp tingled from the heat, and the inside of her tracksuit stuck to her skin.

She glanced back to assure Mr. Candy Bar wasn't watching, then slowed down to catch her breath.

"Ah, Camilla Ward!" called an incoming voice.

Camilla winced.

"Just the girl I was looking for! Do you have a few seconds to answer some questions for me?"

Camilla made to run off, however, the person rounded her. It was Darren Wilde, head journalist of the school newspaper. He had electric pink hair and wore black square glasses with no actual lenses in them. He held up his notebook and pen, nearly poking her in the eye with it.

"Y—You want to ask me questions?" asked Camilla. She didn't think he knew her name, never mind that he was interested in her opinion. Darren nodded, and she asked, "What about?"

"Well, I heard along the grapevine you were with Logan Wheeler at the lake yesterday afternoon."

Camilla held her breath.

"Is that true?"

"Uh—"

"And is it also true that the two of you found the bodies of those kayakers together?" He adjusted his fake glasses and prepared his pen to write down her answer.

"I don't have anything to say." Camilla upped her pace to surpass Darren, but he doubled every step she took, staying in front of her the entire time. He scribbled down her words.

"What were the two of you doing at the lake together?" he pressed on. "And what was your reaction when you saw the kayakers? Did either of you puke? Did it smell bad at all?"

"Please, just leave me alone."

"Did it smell like sulphur like they say in the movies? Were the Morris brothers decomposed?"

"I don't want to answer any of this. It's too horrible to think about."

Darren disregarded her plea. He stepped in front of her, forcing her to stop. He lowered his head and peered over his glasses. "So, you're saying it did stink? And you did puke?"

Camilla squirmed, and he wrote something down.

"W—What did you just write? I didn't even say anything!" A new sort of heat flushed her face—a different type than when she was running or whenever she was with Logan.

"Are you and Logan Wheeler together?"

"T—Together?"

"Yes, together. A couple. Going out. Dating."

"What?" Camilla blurted out, and her mouth went dry. She rounded Darren and quickly walked away, but he kept up with her like an acrobat or a magnet attracted to anything remotely scandalous and juicy. She should've known he wasn't really interested in the kayakers.

"You sat together in the theatre the other day, right? During the emergency school assembly?"

"Yes, we did, but—"

"Excellent! So, the two of you *are* dating?" Darren widened his eyes, waiting for her to answer. He was just about to scribble something down when someone pushed him aside.

It was Remy, also dressed in a grey tracksuit. Milo and Fleur backed her up, both in the same attire.

"Didn't you hear her?" she snapped. "She said she didn't want to answer any of your questions!"

"Eh, who are you supposed to be?" asked Darren, taking off his glasses with a dramatic flick.

Remy showed her teeth at him. "Get lost already!"

"Fine." Darren jumped back. "Until next time, Camilla Ward," he said before he set off to the pavilions.

"What a loser," Remy growled, just loud enough for him to hear. He showed a crass finger at her.

"We ought to teach him a lesson," said Fleur. She tried her best to imitate Remy but failed horribly. Her mouth wasn't nearly as screwed and her cheeks not nearly as red. "Right, Milo?"

"Actually, I don't think he's all that bad," replied Milo. He scratched behind his head, lost in thought. "He was just doing his job. Persistence is sometimes the only way to get the scoop."

"So, what? You're a reporter now?" barked Remy.

Milo sighed.

The three transfer students settled in next to Camilla, and they speed-walked all together. Milo and Fleur stayed slightly to the back, while Remy kept in pace with her, stride by stride.

"Thanks for that," said Camilla, mostly out of politeness. She didn't want them to get the wrong idea: that she wanted to be friends with them or anything. Because she didn't.

"No biggie." Remy's walk quickened into a jog. She ran as if it was the least taxing thing in the world.

Camilla felt compelled to keep up with her. She filled her lungs with air, balled her hands into fists, and widened her strides. They had just set off, and she already wheezed.

Remy spoke on while she ran, "We meant it when we said we wanted to be friends with you. And besides, guys like that annoy me. Always sticking his nose where it doesn't belong."

Camilla fell back a little, unable to keep up with her. "D—Do you, uh, often jog like this?"

"Oh, yeah. My mom has me on a strict exercise plan." Remy shrugged. She looked askance at Camilla's sweaty, droopy, heaving face and chuckled. "But I take it you don't?"

Camilla shook her head.

"Let's rest a little, then." Remy slowed down. She put her hands in her pockets and whistled to herself.

They walked once around the field in silence until Camilla had caught her breath and could talk again. Remy must've waited for exactly that as she often glanced at her and smiled. Not a warm and friendly smile but something else, something unplaceable.

"You really should stand up for yourself more," she said.

"What?" asked Camilla, surprised.

"You just let that guy walk all over you, and look at him; he's got the limbs of a ribbon in the wind!"

Camilla laughed without the intention of doing so. She looked at Darren by the pavilion. As the conductor of the school band, he waved his hands through the air as they played.

"I'd say he looks more like one of those blow-up things at a car dealership," she said, but immediately bit her lip. What was she doing? Was she actually trying to impress them?

Remy punched her in the arm, and she flinched.

"See, I knew you'd get it!" And, for the first time, Remy sounded impressed. Her fist lingered a few seconds against Camilla's arm, almost with enough pressure to topple her over.

Camilla pulled away. Remy awkwardly rubbed her hands together. "So, the stories are true, aren't they? You found those two boys at the lake?"

"I, uh—"

"Oh, that's right. You don't want to talk about it." Remy walked faster. "It's fine, I understand."

"N—No," Camilla stuttered. "I just didn't want to talk to Darren about it. He would put it in the school paper, and, you know, say things about me and Lo—about me."

Camilla waited for them to comment on her slip of the tongue, but they didn't. She glanced sideways, crunching on her teeth. She could just smack herself for talking to them like this—especially after what they had done to her. But they seemed different somehow.

Nicer, almost.

"So?"

"*So?*"

"Did you see anything else at the lake? On or around the bodies, perhaps?"

"Something at the lake?" Camilla swallowed. *Only a castle surrounded by walls that reached for miles in every direction.* "No, nothing. And I didn't get a good look at the bodies either."

Remy seemed disappointed. "Oh, okay."

They rounded the track to the javelin pitch, where all the athletes were huddled under a green gazebo receiving a heated speech from their coach, a retired Olympic gold medalist.

"Hey, isn't that your boyfriend?" asked Fleur from the back.

Remy glanced sideways at her, but Camilla interjected, "Oh, no. Logan's not my boyfriend."

"But you like him, don't you?" Remy's eyes flared.

Camilla gnawed her bottom lip until she tasted blood.

She looked over to the huddle of athletes, spotting Logan at the far back with a javelin in his hand. He, like Keira and Maya, wore a Crystalvale High athletics uniform—although unlike them, he could pull it off. But Logan always went full-out at everything he did. Even looking good, it seemed.

When he kayaked, he won. When he ran, he won. When he tossed a javelin . . . well, he won. He was just sporty like that, the opposite of Camilla. She only ever did any proper exercise when she was forced to, be it by a teacher or the fact that she had to cycle everywhere.

Camilla felt the urge to lift her hood as they passed. Not only was she hanging out with the very people he found strange, but she was also wearing a tracksuit that resembled maternity wear. She attempted to pass unnoticed, yet Logan looked up and smiled at her. He studied her from top to bottom—her crimson face, sweaty uniform, and messy hair—and frowned.

It wasn't a pitiful frown but an amused one. An *I-can't-believe-you're-actually-jogging* one.

"I'll take that as a yes," said Remy, snapping Camilla back.

"What?" she asked, not entirely sure what they were talking about. "Me? In love with Logan?"

"No one said anything about being in love," commented Fleur.

Camilla warmed.

"See, this is what I'm talking about! You should stand up for yourself. Go and get what you want," Remy said.

"But not with him. You should stay away from that type of guy."

"That type?"

"The popular, talented ones," Milo clarified. "The type of guys that are addicted to the chase."

Remy agreed. "Logan's an athlete. He likes to win, and, right now, you're the ultimate prize."

"Ultimate prize?" asked Camilla.

That didn't sound too bad.

"Yeah, and so are a thousand other, much prettier, girls. He might seem interested in you now, but as soon as push comes to shove or as soon as you give him what he wants, he'll be gone."

"Now you sound just like my mother," Camilla muttered.

The transfer students exchanged a look. Remy stopped in her tracks, spun around, and cupped Camilla's shoulder with her hand. She squeezed, looking her straight in the eyes.

"Your mother warned you against him too?"

"Not him, specifically," answered Camilla, not knowing whether she should walk away or take the chance at being interrogated again. "She basically doesn't want me to date any guy, but I keep telling her, Logan's not like that. I've known him forever."

"Forever?"

"We met way back in kindergarten, then went on to the same primary school, middle school, and high school. We've just been friends for the most part. Until recently."

"Recently, you say?" Remy raised an eyebrow. She

nudged Camilla, winked at her, and smiled in a square-ish sort of way. "Well, why don't you invite him to our bonfire tonight?"

"Bonfire?"

"Yeah, by the lake. We thought since we're new in town, a bonfire would be a great way to make friends. There'll be lots of people, lots of drinks, and lots of opportunities to get with Mr. Kayak."

Mr. Kayak?

Camilla cringed at the sound of it. She looked from Remy to Fleur to Milo. They surrounded her again, only this time in public. She didn't know what to say or think or do. She barely knew them and had never gone to a party before. In fact, she had never even tasted alcohol.

"A bonfire? Tonight?"

They nodded their heads.

"I don't know—"

"Loosen up, Cam!" Remy whined, jumping up and down. With each jump, she yanked a bit on Camilla's shoulder. "Do you want this Logan guy to see you as more than a friend?"

Camilla merely stared at her.

"Do you want *him* to want *you* in the way *you* want *him*?"

More confusion.

More silence.

"Well?"

"Y—Yes," she stuttered. "I do."

"So, what better place to do that than at a bonfire?" Remy wrapped one arm around Camilla, and the two of them rotated so they faced the gazebo next to the javelin pitch.

The coach had finished his speech, and the athletes were lining up to prove what they were made of. Logan was second to front, and while the person ahead of him went through the motions, he rolled his shoulders and wrists. He had a seriousness about him that Camilla seldom saw. The only other time he narrowed his eyes like that was when he kayaked.

"Logan Wheeler," the coach called out his name, and he readied himself. He raised the javelin to his shoulder and ran down the pitch. His strides were quick and precise, akin to dancing.

When he got to a certain point, he drew back, decreased the length of his strides, and tossed. The javelin soared through the air like an arrow in the wind, spinning, spinning, spinning. It pinned straight up in the ground, farther than any of the others thus far.

"Nice one, Wheeler," commented the coach.

"Very nice indeed," Remy agreed.

Logan pumped his fists in the air. He returned to the gazebo and was met with several pats on the back. He high-fived a couple of guys, then embraced a girl—a blonde with fair skin and doll-like eyes—who made sure to hold on to his forearms when he pulled away.

Camilla felt a wring in her stomach, throat, and heart. *Who was that girl?* Logan laughed at something she said, and she laughed back, twirling her ponytail around her forefinger.

Camilla huffed. "What about the police curfew?" she asked, not taking her eyes off the gazebo.

"The police set up a curfew?" asked Fleur.

"What for?" added Milo.

"You don't know?"

Even Remy shook her head. "No, Camilla. What is it?"

Camilla broke away from Logan and the girl. "The two kayakers didn't drown. They were poisoned, which means murder. The police don't want anyone outside at night."

"D—Do they have any suspects?" asked Fleur. Remy cast her another look, and her panic vanished.

"No, not that I know of."

Remy chewed on this for a while.

Then, she said, "Never mind the curfew. With so many people there, I'm sure it's more than safe."

Fleur and Milo nodded in her aid.

"So, does this mean you're in?" asked Remy.

Camilla hesitated. She flapped the bottom of her sweatshirt, creating a breeze to cool herself down. With each waft, she caught a whiff of her deodorant. At least she didn't reek. She looked sideways at Logan and the girl, chatting now, still within too close proximity.

Yes, she had to do it.

The bonfire was her only option.

"If I can get past my mother, sure. She's been really protective lately, and I've never snuck out before."

"Where do you live?"

"Why?"

"We'll come and help you. Sneaking out is Milo's specialty. Plus, we've got a few tricks up our sleeves."

Remy and Milo exchanged a look in which they chuckled to themselves.

Camilla felt unsettled by this. She hesitated about giving them her address, but the idea of losing Logan before she even made an attempt at him silenced whatever doubts she had.

"32 Waterbrook Road."

"Great! Is nine all right?"

Camilla agreed.

"It's settled, then." Remy licked her lips. "Just don't forget to ask that cutie of yours to the bonfire."

"Especially before anyone else does," added Milo.

"Until tonight, Camilla Ward." This was the last thing Remy said before she, Milo, and Fleur walked off the track. They crossed the sports grounds to the watercoolers, where they cut to the front of the line. The supervising teacher scolded them, and Remy showed a hand at her.

Camilla rubbed her arms. Even though she was sweating, she had chills. There was only one word for the transfer students: Strange. Strange and frightening and crazy and carefree.

All right, four words.

Before anyone else does. She recalled Milo's words, only this time, it hit her much harder than before.

*E*xtine readjusted the scarf that draped over her head. She held the ends together with her one hand and supported herself with the other. Her heels sank into the soil and the bushes teemed with mosquitoes, but she couldn't get up. She had to stay hidden until Finn passed by.

After she had left him in the courtyard last night, she had locked herself in the throne room where she got to thinking. Finn had, once again, emerged from the outside world. He had supposedly patrolled Crystalvale, which might've been a viable excuse, had he not done it so secretively—and at the darkest hour of the night, nonetheless.

But ever since Camilla appeared in their lives, Finn had disappeared more times than she could count.

More times than she could accept.

She had spent the remainder of the night coming up with a plan—a way to find out exactly where Finn went and what he did there. When morning came, she grabbed one of her black satin scarves, wrapped it over her head, and hid in the bushes by the slit in the barrier.

She waited for Finn, ready to follow him wherever he went. Ready to catch him in the act.

Extine waited in the bushes for more than an hour and a half before, at last, Finn showed up. He wore a different hoodie, but the same purple baseball cap and lumberjack boots. He walked slowly, carefully, afraid someone might see him.

Finn halted, and Extine held her breath. His foot twisted in the soil, all the way in her direction. She squirmed but stayed put. *Did he know? No. Impossible.* She was cleverly hidden.

Finn let out a deep breath and walked on. He made through the trees on a slightly worn path.

Extine waited until he was a good distance off before she got up. She stretched her legs, dusted off her knees, and followed in his footsteps. She took care not to tread on any twigs or leaves and held up her skirt so it didn't catch on anything. Since she didn't own any pants, and Remy's were much too small for her, she had to make do with a dress.

Stupid outside attire.

Stupid outside everything.

Extine wiped a bead of sweat from the tip of her nose. The sun seared hot on her head, and she could hardly keep her eyes open from its rays, but she pushed on, battled ahead through the overgrowth. This was something she had to do, be that at the price of her suffering.

If Finn had known about Camilla all along . . . if he had kept it to himself for eighteen years . . .

Extine chose not to think about it. She kept the queen inside of her at bay, the sharp-clawed creature with a thirst for vengeance and craving for blood. But the creature wouldn't shut up.

He's a traitor.

Even worse than Pearl.

He deserves to die like those kayakers.

Extine wiped her forehead with the back of her palm and pulled down the scarf to cover her eyes. She hid behind the nearest tree and peered around it at Finn, now at the foot of a large rock—almost the size of a cave—in the ground. A man-sized crack divided it in half.

The split in the barrier.

Finn briefly scanned the forest around him then stepped into the opening. He vanished, and the forest was cast in silence. Not a bird chirped, nor a leaf rustled. Only twigs snapped on the ground as Extine slinked around the tree and squeezed through the crack after him.

She emerged to the sight of more forest, more trees and rocks and soil. Finn wove through the thicket ahead of her, almost as though he knew the area like the back of his hand.

How long had he been coming here?

Again, Extine chose not to think about it. She rushed after him all the way to a road, a highway. On the opposite side stood a worn, faded road sign which said, "Welcome to Crystalvale."

Her chest tightened. She had only left Escana once

before in her life and that was nearly twenty years ago. Her father wanted her to see why they hid the kingdom. He had taken her to the top of a mountain and had shown her the pollution, the destruction of nature. The way powerlines stretched for miles on end and sewage was dumped into rivers.

Back then, she had despised the outside. But it all looked so different now. The trees were whole, there were no giant, smoke-puffing vehicles, and one could hear the birds.

Finn crossed the road to the other side, and she quickly set off after him. It was all so strange. The road signs, the lines, the smoothness of the tar. The way another patch of overgrowth flanked the road. Unhindered. Unharmed. Except for some beer cans, of course.

A little way through the second set of trees, Finn entered the parking lot of a dining establishment. The Bunbun Diner, according to the pink-and-blue sign with flashing lights on the roof.

"So, this is where you go?" Extine said to herself. How disappointing. She had expected someplace much more exotic, more scandalous. "To get coffee and eat a slice of pie?"

Finn entered through the front door. He sat down by the window, and Extine dashed across the parking lot after him. He briefly glanced outside, and she hid behind a pickup truck. Her heart thumped in her throat. She waited a couple of seconds then peered out.

Finn was browsing the menu, wholly distracted. She got up and ran to the door but didn't enter just yet. She used the glass as a mirror while she readjusted the scarf over her head. She inhaled, exhaled, and pushed open the door. A bell chimed, startling her.

Finn sat in a booth at the back, almost by the restrooms. He had his cap pulled down and his face buried in the menu. A waitress came around to take his order: a waffle with ice cream and syrup. She wrote it down and reached for the menu, but he insisted on keeping it.

"Oh, okay," she said, slightly unnerved. She straightened her apron, slowly, delicately. Almost as though curtseying. "If anything else tickles your fancy, don't hesitate to call."

"Thank you," mumbled Finn.

Extine studied the waitress a bit closer. Finn refused to look at her and winced each time she spoke. She didn't understand this at first, but upon closer inspection, the pieces fell into place. Those hazel waves. Those olive-green eyes. That smile and voice and way of walking.

It was her.

It was Pearl.

"I'll be right out with your waffle," said her sister, then put away her notebook and strode to the kitchen.

Finn stared after her. He raised his cap and sighed so deeply that he sank in his seat. He placed the menu by the edge of the table and stared out at the parking lot, at the forest beyond it.

Extine squared her shoulders. She hesitated for a moment but approached the booth. How did it ever come to this? Of all the men in all of Escana, why did it have to be him? Her very own husband? Her heart bled and her mind buzzed, but she kept her composure.

"Well, what're you supposed to be dressed as, doll?"

Extine started. "What?" she blurted out.

A waitress stepped in front of her. She grabbed a menu from the basket by the door, ogling Extine's attire with screwed lips. "Is there a renaissance fair in town I don't know about?"

Extine cocked a brow. A renaissance fair? She followed the waitress's eyes down her body. From her frilly upper bodice to her puffy skirt and pointed shoes. Not exactly the standard outfit.

"Table for one?" the waitress went on when Extine didn't answer.

"Listen, uh," she paused to read the waitress's nametag, "Hannah, is it? I'm only here to meet someone."

"Oh, you are?"

"Yes, my husband. He's sitting right back there." Extine pointed to Finn's booth by the restroom.

Hannah seemed surprised by this. "Your husband? Okay. Your waitress, Pearl, should return in a second." She put away the menu and made over to another table to take their order.

Extine self-consciously pulled at the scarf around her head again. She crossed the diner and slid into the booth. Finn hardly even flinched, almost as if he had expected her to join him.

"I understand now," she said calmly. She crossed her hands on the table. "I understand it all now."

Finn toyed with a napkin, folding and refolding it,

twirling it around and flattening it on the placemat. Pearl passed by them, and he looked up but immediately lowered his head again.

"You're the father, aren't you?" Extine declared more than asked.

Still nothing.

"I can't believe how blind I was. All those years . . . I thought the two of you were just friends. Good friends." Extine swallowed. She thought back to their youth when Pearl and Finn had explored the castle together. When they had pretended it was haunted by ghosts.

"But she was the one you really loved. She was the one you always wanted to marry, not me."

"Extine—"

"You knew she was pregnant, didn't you?" Extine spoke on. "You helped her to escape that night." A pause. "And then you returned to Escana to marry me . . . like nothing had ever happened." She felt so close to tears, and yet her eyes were dry and crusty.

Extine waited for Finn to say something—to explain himself—but he just sat there with his cap over his eyes. Her shoulders tensed. "How long have you been coming here?"

"A couple of years," said Finn.

Extine nodded, although she didn't understand. How could this have been going on, right under her nose, for such a long time? She was the queen. She knew everything.

Saw everything.

"Have you ever spoken to her?" she asked. "You know, other than placing an order?"

"No, Extine. I would never betray you like that. I just check up on her, make sure she's safe."

"And Camilla?"

"I've never—" Finn choked on his words. He wiped under his eyes, though his cap sat too low for Extine to see whether or not he was tearing up. "I've never even met her before."

Extine knew she ought to feel bad for him—for her sister and her niece—but she didn't. It was as if her eyes were connected with her heart, her soul. When they scorched, her heart scorched. She felt no guilt, no sorrow, no sympathy.

Just anger.

"And our children?"

"What about them?"

"What are they to you?"

"Extine, I love our children with my entire heart. I love them equally as much as I love Camilla, and it saddens me to see their broken relationship. Camilla is Remy's sister," Finn tore his napkin in half, "and she hates her enough to want to steal her eyes from her."

"Pearl did the same to me, didn't she?"

Finn glanced up. He crumpled the two napkin halves then tightened his hands into fists, squeezing. "Pearl never wanted to get pregnant. We were terrified when we found out because we knew our child would never have the life she deserves. Camilla would've been killed, Extine. Pearl could never . . . I could never . . . she had to leave the kingdom."

Extine had nothing to say. She laid her head in her hands, trying to understand, to sympathize. If only she felt something, anything, but she couldn't get over it. Her sister and husband . . .

"You could never love Remy and Milo the way you love Camilla," she said after a moment of silence.

Finn was taken aback by this.

"You love Pearl too much. You love her so much that you'd break Escanian law for her. Camilla's the product of love, whereas Remy and Milo are the products of persuasion."

"Extine—"

But Extine could no longer sit there. She could no longer bathe in the humiliation of her obliviousness. She slid out of the booth upon which her scarf caught on a screw under the table, and she yanked on it. The scarf ripped, and she stumbled back, right into someone.

A waitress.

The waitress screamed. The plate in her hands flipped over, smearing Extine with waffle and ice cream. First, it was cold. Then came the heat. Golden syrup tangled up in her hair.

"Gosh!" gasped the waitress. "I'm so sorry!"

Extine turned, prepared to push past her to the door, but the moment their eyes locked, she couldn't move or breathe or think. It was Pearl. Her little sister, now a thirty-something-year-old woman. She had slight grey streaks in her hair and wrinkles around her eyes.

She had grown old before her time.

Pearl's mouth moved, but no words emerged. She barely managed an "Ex—" when Finn stood up, and she froze once again. The sight of Pearl's shock infuriated Extine.

Did she really think they would never find her?

"Pearl," Finn began, but that was about it. Pearl stumbled back and over the shards of broken plate.

Extine recognized the disappointment on his face. He had likely expected her to jump in his arms and kiss him, hug him, but she was so horrified, so terrified, she hardly looked at him.

"What are you doing here?" Pearl blurted out. "Where's Camilla? What have you done to her?"

"We haven't done anything to her," Finn tried to assure her. "And it's not what you think . . ."

Extine wanted to interject—to accuse Pearl of theft, treason, and adultery—when the other waitress, Hannah, turned up the television on the wall, distracting her. The news was on. A reporter sat behind a desk and the words "breaking news" flashed across the screen.

Hannah upped the volume a few clicks. The reporter said, ". . .the two campers who took the picture were reportedly fishing by Crystalvale Lake. They were indulging in some birdwatching when one of them spotted something on the water. Here's the picture they had shared on Instagram and, since then, has gone viral all over the country . . ."

The screen switched from the reporter to a picture of the lake. And there was something on it, over it.

"Is that a castle?" asked one of the diners.

"Magnificent!" said another.

"Creepy, if you ask me," commented Hannah.

Finn and Pearl gasped. Extine didn't. She couldn't gasp as she still couldn't breathe. It was the outline of Escana, slowly but surely becoming visible to the outside world. Matters were worse than she thought. Much worse. The power in her eyes wasn't enough anymore.

The picture of the lake vanished, and a short video clip replaced it. It started as a mere overview of the lake, but then something flickered on the water. The captor of the video jumped back, swore, and called for his friend. The flashing continued, as did their astonishment.

"What the hell is that, bruh?" asked the captor's friend, who was clearly high on something. Smoke puffed from his mouth, and he pointed at the lake with a pen-shaped device.

"It looks like a freakin' castle, man!"

The moment he said the word "castle" Extine started. She pushed past Pearl and made for the entrance. The ripped scarf dropped to her shoulders, but she didn't care. She had to return to Escana and fast. If the borders collapsed, she would've failed as queen.

"Extine!" shouted Finn and set after her.

The bell on the front door chimed three times: once for Extine, once for Finn, and once for—

"Finn! Extine!" cried Pearl. She stopped halfway across the parking lot, her hair whipping in the wind.

Finn surpassed Extine into the trees. "Extine, there's no time! We have to get back to Escana!"

"I—I'm right behind you!" replied Extine. Her scarf accidentally blew away, and she turned around to grab it. As she did, she couldn't help but catch sight of Pearl, her little sister.

"W—What happened to your eyes?" asked Pearl, getting a good look at Extine for the first time.

"What do you mean *what happened*? You know better than anyone. You did this to me," replied Extine.

"No, that wasn't me or Camilla. Father's eyes never looked like that when he lost his power."

Extine's limbs tensed.

Finn grabbed her by the arm. He pulled her into the forest, her head still turned and her eyes still focused on the one person she had known her entire life. The little sister she had forgotten about, cut out of her memory, and blamed for all her problems. Her darling little Pearl, the mother of the girl who stole the queen's eyes.

CHAPTER SIXTEEN
CAMILLA

The mandatory active session ended at five. Camilla quickly slipped out of her tracksuit and into that day's outfit: a tank top and flailing pants paired with pearly sandals. She stuffed the grey bundle into her backpack, ran to her bike, unchained it, and sped down the street.

If she wanted to ask Logan to the bonfire, now looked the perfect time to do it. Or, if not, the *only* time. When he was alone, and she wasn't dressed like an inmate at a women's prison.

Camilla spotted him up ahead, crossing the intersection. She raced after him, accidentally running a red light. Several cars honked in her wake, though it failed to bother her. A new type of courage possessed her—the will to do something for herself for a change.

Despite her mother's warning against seeing him again.

"Logan!" she shouted once she got close enough.

Logan nearly veered off the side of the road. He turned his head, pulled the brakes, and slowed down. He grinned, somewhat amused, perhaps confused by her.

"What the heck are you doing?" he asked. "Training for a cycling marathon or something?"

Camilla was so out of breath she could barely speak. Her tongue stuck to the roof of her mouth, and it felt as though she might throw up. She took a moment to catch her breath.

To choose her words.

Logan's grin didn't fade. He asked, "If not, well . . . do you maybe wanna cycle home with me?"

"I, uh, yes. If you don't mind the company, that is?" Camilla studied his face and posture.

Ever as calm. Ever as poised.

He had asked her so casually. Why couldn't she do the same? Because she was sweaty, out of shape, and nervous, that's why. Because she was Camilla Ward, and he was Logan Wheeler.

"Of course, I don't mind," he said. "Besides, how can I say no to an Olympic track athlete like yourself?"

"Oh, please!" Camilla scoffed and rolled her eyes. "I barely made it around the field once without needing to lie down." She bit her lip, already regretting how easily she admitted her inferiority. She was supposed to impress him, not rub it in his face how unfit she was.

Get it together, Ward.

"I know. I saw."

Camilla gulped. She hesitated before she asked, "You were watching me out there?"

"Ha! How could I not? I mean, you—" Logan looked down and adjusted his grip on his bike's handles. He was just about to finish his sentence when he swerved onto the sidewalk on account of a parked car in the street. When they rejoined, his entire attitude had changed. "You were right there, passing by the javelin pitch. I couldn't *not* see you."

Camilla tried to hide her disappointment. Her mind flashed back to the javelin pitch. To Logan. She thought about his amazing throw and about the blonde who talked to him.

"That girl was totally into you, you know," she said before she could stop herself.

"What?"

"That blonde. At the javelin pitch."

Logan slouched. "Oh, her," he said. "Nah, we're just friends. Besides, she's not really my type." His eyes briefly flicked to Camilla, and she couldn't help but look the other way.

Silence.

"What, uh, exactly, is your type?" she asked after a while.

They crossed the street into the second neighborhood from the school—the fourth block from Logan's house. Time was running out and fast. She had to ask him to the bonfire. Now.

Except, it had seemed so much easier in her imagination. There was just something about Logan—about his mouth and eyes and smell—that intoxicated her, robbed her of any words.

"My type? No way I'm telling you that," said Logan. "You'd just have to keep guessing, I suppose." His chocolatey skin still glowed from the practice session and his shirt clung to his chest, shaping to his body underneath. He might as well have been wearing a wetsuit.

"So, it's a secret, eh?" Camilla laughed. "If you ask me, that blonde has got the wrong idea, then."

"Speaking of ideas, what were you doing with those transfer students? I thought you said they were weird, that you're a loner?" Logan turned serious. So serious, his pedaling slowed. Since they were coming up to his neighborhood, Camilla thought perhaps he slowed down because he wanted to spend more time with her. But he was likely just distracted.

"They rescued me from Darren and his thousand questions." Camilla considered expanding on this but recalled one specific question: are you and Logan Wheeler a couple? She spoke over it, "Besides, they're not really that bad. In fact, they invited us to a bonfire tonight."

"Us?"

Camilla nearly drove into a ditch. "Uh, that is, if you wanted to go? But if you had other plans or—"

"No," said Logan as he grabbed onto Camilla's right handle. They wobbled to a stop, and his hand slid closer to hers, finger by finger, until his palm covered her own, warming it.

"As in . . . no, you don't want to go or you don't have plans?"

Logan said in a soft, almost breathy, voice, "I don't have plans. And I'd really like to go with you."

Camilla only realized she was holding her breath when she was forced to gasp. She also realized, even though his hand was on top of hers, her palm wasn't clammy. One of her fingers involuntarily twitched and Logan let go, almost as though he had touched a hot iron.

"Wait. What about the police curfew?" he asked, and the spell broke. "We'd never get permission."

"I thought we'd, well, sneak out."

Logan frowned and not in an amused sort of way like when he had seen her at the track or when she had ambushed him from down the street. His frown cut deep between his brows.

"Sneak out?" he asked. "Camilla, this isn't like you."

"It'll be fine. Loads of people are going." Camilla tried to keep her tone light. She tried to convince not only Logan but herself as well. "But if you don't want to go, I understand—"

"At what time should I pick you up?"

Camilla wanted to leap with joy. She did leap, though, when a car honked at them from behind. Logan apologized to the man who turned out to be their crazy English teacher, Mr. Beaver.

The car stopped next to them, and the front window rolled down.

"Mr. Wheeler, Miss Ward," said Mr. Beaver, rubbing the ends of his moustache between his thumbs and forefingers. "It seems the two of you are quite inseparable these days. Do I smell *love* in the air? The sweet, sweet aroma of modern-day teenage courting?"

Logan coughed. "Oh no, sir. We're just. . ." He looked to Camilla for help, who merely blushed.

"That's what they all say! Now, if you'd be so kind as to remove yourselves from the center of the road, I'd like to get home sometime this evening."

Logan and Camilla dragged their bikes to the sidewalk.

"Thank you! Now you two be safe, all right? And don't go finding any more dead bodies, you hear?" Mr. Beaver rolled up the window, stepped on the gas, and sped off down the street.

"Weird," said Logan once he was gone.

Camilla rubbed her cheeks. "Very weird." She cleared her throat and added, "You know, Darren asked me that same question. Well, a similar one, but he also asked about . . ."

Logan raised his eyebrows, waiting for her to finish, but she never did. They cycled on, crossing the street into the third neighborhood from the school—*his* neighborhood.

"The bonfire starts at nine, but you don't have to pick me up," Camilla sort of shouted in the wind. It was so strong now, the treetops whipped, and her thighs hurt from pedaling. "It's gonna be difficult to sneak out, so how about I just meet you there?"

"Cool," replied Logan as they approached his driveway. Or rather the massive, gold-encrusted gate that surrounded his driveway. He looked uncertain for a moment, scratching the back of his head. "Are you sure you don't want me to ride all the way home with you?"

"No, no. It's all right." She wanted to say yes. To hang out with him some more and listen to his smooth, yet sometimes husky, voice for a couple more blocks. But she also didn't want him to see her house. He had, indeed, seen it multiple times—been inside for several playdates and projects over the years—but things were different now.

A fear had ignited inside of her.

What if he stopped liking her if he saw it again? What if he realized how different their lives were?

"Are you sure?" asked Logan as he got off his bike. Camilla stayed on hers, ready to cycle off, but he didn't push the button next to the gate right away. He stood there, his eyes glinting.

"I'm sure," said Camilla. "See you tonight?"

Logan nodded. He turned and was just about to press the button when he spun around again. "Wait, before I forget. I have to show you something." He set his bicycle against the gate, dug in his pocket for his phone, and unlocked it. He swiped around, searching for something.

Camilla didn't know what to expect. She got nervous when he walked up to her and even more so when he leaned in. She felt the warmth of his breath on her cheeks, her lips.

"Have you seen it yet?" he asked, turning the phone towards her.

Camilla blinked, trying hard to maintain her focus. "Seen what?" she asked, a tiny bit hoarse.

"The viral photo of the lake."

"Of the lake?'

"Yeah, look."

Camilla gasped when she saw the photo. She was so surprised, so stunned, she grabbed the phone from Logan's hand and zoomed in. It only occurred to her a couple seconds later that he was smiling at her. She looked up, guiltily, and handed him back his phone.

"I'm sorry about that," she apologized.

"It's fine." Logan offered her his phone again, though she didn't take it. "I saw it this afternoon and immediately thought of you. Doesn't it look a little like that castle you drew?"

Camilla swallowed hard. "Yes," she said. "It looks *exactly* like the castle from my drawing."

Seventeen

Extine

EXTINE AND FINN raced through the forest. They ran in front of a truck on the highway, interrupted a couple's picnic, and passed a lone camper at the side of the lake, setting up his tent. He greeted them with the tip of his hat, though neither of them so much as acknowledged him.

"You two here to see the castle on the lake?" he asked, twirling the mallet in his hand. He surveyed the lake behind him. "It's mostly gone now, but if you look closely enough . . ."

But Extine didn't have to look closely to see the towers and flags and marble bricks above the water. Her insides plummeted, and her head turned, turned, turned. She felt utterly sick.

"Extine, come on," ordered Finn, already halfway into the trees again.

"You two ain't staying, then?" the man asked, but Extine turned her back on him and ran off.

"How far is the entrance?" she asked, at last catching up to Finn. He had removed his sword and was hacking through the overgrowth. So much for stealth. "We have to get to the castle!"

"We're nearly there." Finn upped his pace. The thicket became less, and the forest cleared up, opening. He wove expertly through the trees.

Their feet rustled across the ground—the only sign of life, the only noise save for the howling wind.

Crunch. Crunch. Crunch.

Extine glanced behind them. The lake was getting farther and farther away, along with Escana, her home. Her instincts told her they were headed in the wrong direction, but she had no other choice than to trust Finn. He had, after all, moved to and from the outside multiple times.

"Are you sure this is the right way?" she asked. "It had seemed much closer to the lake earlier."

"Yes, I know where I'm going."

Extine nodded, though she wasn't quite convinced. A gloom hung over them—the forest's shadow—rendering their surroundings even more identical looking than before. She had been so stupid thinking she could spy on Finn. Thinking she could leave the kingdom for a couple of hours and everything would be fine when she returned.

In fact, it never occurred to her how she'd get back. At

the time, she had been so determined to catch Finn—to find out where he went—that she never once questioned her plan.

At last, the cave-like stone appeared from in between the trees, and Finn slowed to a walk.

The overgrowth whacked at them from all sides, beckoning them towards it. But the opening seemed narrower from this side, and darker too. Extine watched as Finn slipped inside.

As lean as he was, he barely fit.

"Wow," she said, studying the crack in the side of the rock. She walked around it, tracing her hand along the cold, brittle stone. "I still can't believe Escana is on the other side of this."

"Yes, it's amazing what Allessien eyes, combined with a little sorcery, can do. Now, are you coming?"

Extine waited for Finn to extend his hand, but he didn't. She looked behind them again, and when she turned back around, Finn was no longer there. She heard his body chafe against the walls of the rock and his heels on the ground as he made deeper inside.

"Here we go again," she said, placing her hands on either side of the opening. Its edges were coarse and sharp, sure to rip her dress. She held her breath and slid inside, afraid she might get stuck or asphyxiate. Death by suffocation was hardly a queenly way to die.

"Extine!" shouted Finn from the other side. "Hurry!" She shut her eyes and shimmied through.

Two steps and a large draw of breath later, Extine emerged on the other side of the courtyard. The sky seemed much brighter in Escana, so she draped her scarf over her eyes.

"We don't have much time," said Finn, bounding across the courtyard to the castle. He removed his hoodie to reveal his Captain's uniform underneath and tossed it in the hedges.

"Mom! Dad!"

Remy and Milo ran down the steps by the courtyard doors. They were still dressed in their outside attire, but Remy had her training bow with her and Milo his longsword.

"Kids!" exclaimed Finn.

Remy dropped her bow at the bottom of the stairs. She marched right at them, at Extine. Milo hesitated before he followed. He briefly paused, picked up her bow, and walked on.

"Where the hell were you two?" she shouted, yanking the scarf right off Extine's face. She tossed it on the ground and stomped on it with her heel. "We've been looking damn near everywhere for you! And not just us, there's an entire line of people outside the gates!"

"Have you seen it?" asked Milo, astoundingly calmer than his sister. He held out his phone—a part of his disguise—which displayed the photograph they had seen on the news.

Finn barely looked at the photo. His brows furrowed, and he rubbed his forehead with his fingers.

Extine cursed aloud. "Get that horrid thing out of my sight!" She whacked the phone from Milo's hand.

"Mom, what's going on?" Remy asked.

Trying to tune her out, Extine shut her eyes as her daughter rambled on. "You never include me in anything important!"

It hurt too much to listen.

To think and talk and breathe.

None of this was her fault. It was Pearl's. It was Camilla's. The two of them had caused this.

"Mom, are you even listening to me?" snapped Remy.

Extine held out her hand, still with her eyes closed. "Sorceress Juniper. Where is she now?"

"In the foyer with Fleur, but—"

Extine pushed Remy aside and walked off. She climbed the steps to the courtyard doors and marched down the corridor. Finn grabbed her from behind, but she yanked away and entered the foyer. Sorceress Juniper and Fleur were clasping their cloaks, preparing to depart.

"Leaving, are we?" asked Extine.

"The borders are about to collapse," said the sorceress, matter-of-factly. "We have to flee at once."

"No, you can't. You have to fix this." Extine spoke without hesitation. She—and the kingdom—couldn't afford hesitation anymore. She hadn't seen a lot of the outside world, but she had seen enough to know that Escana had to stay hidden for as long as possible.

For its safety.

For its purity.

For her father.

"Your Majesty, there's nothing more I can do."

"Give me more power." Extine did her best to widen her eyes. She stood up straight with balled fists and gritted teeth. Remy and Milo ran up to her, but she shouted, "Stay back!"

Sorceress Juniper continued to fasten her cloak. She snapped her fingers. "We're going, Fleur."

"No! I'm your queen, and my word is law! Now, Sorceress Juniper. I said, give me more power."

The sorceress didn't seem at all pleased. Her hands dropped to her sides, and she whirled around.

"Your Majesty," she said, tilting her head. "We both know what little time we have left. Not only for the kingdom, but also for Your Majesty's life. As I said, dark magic is a poison."

Only Milo gasped.

Sorceress Juniper spoke on. "I did the best I could the first time, and I'm afraid if I grant Your Majesty any more power—even so much as a drop—death might be the likely outcome."

"*Death?*" sneered Remy.

"Extine, think about what you're doing!" added Finn.

Extine raised her hand at them. She swayed on her heels a little, mustering every ounce of energy she had left to stand upright. The moment lengthened, and as it did, her eyelids grew heavier. The foyer spun in circles, twisting and contorting before her eyes.

"I can't give Your Majesty any more power," Sorceress Juniper repeated a final time. "But that doesn't mean all is lost. There might be just enough time left to finish the plan."

Extine thought about it.

"Unless," the sorceress began.

"Unless what?"

"Unless Your Majesty offers the throne to the rightful heir."

"No!" shouted Extine and Remy at once. It was Extine who spoke on. "We'll go through with the original plan, then. We'll take back Camilla's eyes and fix the kingdom."

Finn fell to his knees. His voice broke as he said, as he pleaded, "No, Extine, don't do this . . ."

"Shut up!" she snapped. "You have no right to beg or plead! I don't want another word from you!"

Remy and Milo approached to comfort their father. The looks on their faces showcased that of confusion, but Extine refused to tell them the truth about who he really was.

Not at that moment, anyway.

Extine motioned for them to come closer. "Children, how far along are you with the plan?"

"We should have Camilla here by the end of the night," reported Remy. Milo and Fleur nodded together. "Come tomorrow morning, her eyes will be mine. I'll save the kingdom for you, Mom. I'll live out my destiny, my duty to Escana, my kingdom and home." She crossed her arms over her chest and raised her chin, a proud soldier and future queen.

Extine almost felt bad for lying to her.

Almost.

"Go, then," she said. "And make me proud!"

Fleur turned to Sorceress Juniper, who sighed deeply. "Fine, you can accompany them. But just this final time, all right?" said Sorceress Juniper, and Fleur nodded. She unclasped her cloak and set after Remy and Milo to change into their outsider disguises.

The moment they were gone, it was as if something let go inside of Extine, and she no longer had the strength to stay upright. First, it was her legs, then her lower back, abdomen, shoulders, and neck. Her entire body gave in. She collapsed on the ground, her hands in fists.

Extine coughed, again and again. When she opened her eyes, a red splotch lay on the tiles beneath her.

Blood.

Sorceress Juniper raised Fleur's cloak and draped it over her shoulders. She traced a finger from Extine's spine to the top of her head, whispering a series of words —a magic spell.

Extine felt the pain leave her body, but only for a second. She screamed and convulsed again. No matter how hard Sorceress Juniper tried, none of her spells had a lasting effect.

"I'm afraid the dark magic's gone too far, grown too powerful to be curbed," she said. "The only thing I can do to relieve the pain is to remove the spell from Your Majesty's eyes."

Extine nearly considered it, as even childbirth had proved less painful. When the sorceress had first warned her about the pain—about the side effects—that day in the library, she never expected it to be so potent. She turned her hands over, almost hurling at the sight of them.

Every vein in her body was black.

Black and swollen. Her blood pulsed so closely to the surface she feared her skin might rupture.

"If you remove the spell," Extine said, swallowing the bile in her mouth. It threatened to rise again, but she could just about hold it down. "Will I be able to keep up the borders?"

Sorceress Juniper shook her head. "No. The only thing keeping up the borders is the power in Your Majesty's eyes. Once the spell is undone, Your Majesty will be blind and powerless."

"Then the spell—" Another convulsion, another cough of blood. "—stays. I'm the queen . . . I've served this kingdom for nearly twenty years . . . and I will protect it with my life."

"Very well," Sorceress Juniper agreed. She tried another spell to relieve the pain, alas in vain.

Extine scrambled to her knees. She might die soon, and if she did, she wouldn't have said goodbye to her children. Even after everything, and with only a grain of hope keeping her alive, she wanted Finn to promise her something: never to tell Remy and Milo the truth.

Ever.

"Finn," she said, turning her head as far back as she could. "I know things between us might not—"

Sorceress Juniper forestalled her, "Your Majesty, the Captain's not here. He left quite a while ago."

"After I collapsed?"

"After Your Majesty collapsed, yes."

A single tear skidded down Extine's cheek.

It burned like acid, like hot water fresh from the boiler. The old her—the whole her—would have winced, but she savored the pain, the burn of disappointment and heartbreak.

Extine didn't know why she expected him to be there. It was an impulse, something she had grown used to over the years. But she was about to take Camilla's, his daughter's, eyes. About to ruin Pearl's, the love of his life's, only happiness in the world.

Extine lay back down. The tiles were cold and hard yet comforting in a way. She shut her eyes and channeled her energy on the barriers, the kingdom's last saving grace.

"Is everything all right, Your Majesty?" asked the sorceress.

Extine nodded. "I'll have my eyes by the end of the night, and the kingdom will be mine again."

Not just the kingdom, but Finn, too. His love for her might not have been real before, but it will be.

Once she had made him forget Pearl and Camilla ever existed, she'd be the only woman in his life.

And Remy and Milo would be his only children.

CHAPTER SEVENTEEN
CAMILLA

*P*earl was all worked up that evening. She followed, encircled, stalked Camilla wherever she went, even outside to the bins when she took out the trash. They ate dinner at the dining table instead of in front of the TV, and she only allowed Camilla ten minutes to shower.

"What's going on, Mom?" Camilla asked as Pearl ushered her down the hallway to her bedroom. She had barely towel dried her hair, and her feet still tracked water across the tiles.

"You have to stay in your room."

"What?" asked Camilla, braking. But Pearl was too strong, and she was forced to walk on. "In my room? For how long? Can't I at least blow-dry my hair first? Mom, stop pushing me!"

Pearl relaxed a little. "I'm sorry, but something happened today. I have to make sure you stay safe."

"Safe? From what?"

Pearl held on to Camilla's bedroom door. She stepped aside, let Camilla enter, and took a key from her apron pocket. She popped it in the keyhole, then leaned against the doorframe.

Camilla gave a step towards the door. What was happening? How was she supposed to go to a bonfire with wet hair? She couldn't meet Logan looking like this. She had to do something. Anything. "Is this about what happened at the lake today? Mom, I've told you—"

"No, Camilla, it's not that."

"What is it, then?"

"All I can say is that I reunited with someone from my past." Pearl's eyes were red and glinting, and her lower lip trembled when she spoke. She rolled her thumbs and adjusted her collar.

Camilla frowned. "Are you in trouble?" she asked. "If you are. . . if this person threatened you in any way. . ."

"No, it's all on me. Something happened a long time ago. I broke some rules and then. . ." Pearl never finished her sentence. She wiped under her eyes, sniffed, and raised her chin. "The point is, Camilla, as your mother, I have to protect you. I can't lose you."

"Lose me?" asked Camilla with raised brows. She wove her arms through the air, nearly toppling over a lamp. "What are you planning to do, then? Lock me up in here? Forbid me from going to school ever again?" She sucked her tongue, afraid of her mother's answer.

Pearl reversed. She was out of the room now, and the light from the corridor lit her eyes. They burned with worry, with regret. She made to shut the door and Camilla hopped forward.

"Cam, please," Pearl warned, closing the door even more.

"Mom!"

"It's only for tonight. I know this might seem strange, and I know you'll hate me for this, but you'll only be safe behind a locked door. A door that I'll be guarding for the entire night."

Camilla was speechless. She just stood there, dumbfounded and stupefied, watching as her mother shut the door. Guarding it for the entire night? The only night in her life that she wanted to do something for herself and sneak out? How fantastic. How absolutely brilliant.

The key turned in the lock, and Pearl strolled to the kitchen.

Camilla grabbed at her still-dripping hair. "You can't do this to me!" she shouted, but the pipes in the kitchen rumbled and groaned, drowning out her voice. Water ran in the sink, and dishes clattered into it. Camilla waited until Pearl began to hum before she slipped out of her nightwear and into a flowery sundress and sequined flats.

She squeezed the final drops of water from her hair, tossed her head upside down, and began to scrunch.

It was no use.

How all those girls on TV styled their hair this way, she had no idea. She flicked her hair from left to right and back to front, trying to manage at least a decent amount of volume.

Still nothing.

Camilla groaned and fell back on her bed. Perhaps she shouldn't go. Perhaps she should stay home, in her room, with her mother guarding the door. The thought of it frustrated her more.

Her phone buzzed on the bedside table, so she rolled over, unlocked it, and opened the message. It was from Logan: *"On my way to the lake. Better hurry. Can't wait to see you."*

Camilla dropped her phone next to her. She put her face in her pillow and let out a squeal. Could it be true? She picked up her phone and reread the message. Again and again and again.

She couldn't believe it.

But it was real.

Logan said he couldn't wait to see her. He wanted her to hurry. He wanted to spend time with her.

Camilla lay back and pressed her phone to her chest. She closed her eyes and dreamt about how many times he had changed his shirt for her. Twice? Three times? She allowed herself a final glance at the message, but her eyes caught the time, and she leapt off the bed.

8:58 p.m.

The transfer students were bound to arrive at any moment, and she had barely any makeup on. She ran to her dresser for a quick touch-up: some foundation, some mascara . . .

Some lipstick?

Camilla held up the bright red tube. She wavered a moment, debating whether she should put it on or not. She hardly ever wore color on her lips and whenever she did, it was always pink or peach. She wondered whether Logan might like the red. Would it be a good thing if he did? She brought the tube closer, so close it grazed her upper lip.

No.

No lipstick.

Camilla put down the tube. Just as she did, someone knocked on the window, loud and impatiently.

"Hey, open up!" Remy kept on knocking, even as Camilla walked across her bedroom and unlatched the window. They pushed it up together, and Remy tumbled inside. She wore pantyhose, a plaid skirt, a ripped shirt, and lipstick the color of burnt caramel.

"Sh, my mother might hear you!" Camilla warned. But the humming in the kitchen continued.

Milo and Fleur scrambled in after Remy.

They straightened out and looked about her bedroom at the hundreds of sketches plastered on the walls and ceiling. There were pencils and sketchbooks scattered across the carpet and pastel crayons on the windowsill—some of which had melted in the sun.

"So, this is where she lives," commented Milo as though Camilla wasn't in the room with them. She made to tidy up a little, but Remy grabbed her by the arm and pulled her back.

"Your mother?" she said, recalling Camilla's warning. Her nails dug deep into her flesh. "She's here?"

Camilla gestured to the door. "Outside. In the kitchen."

"Oh," said Remy, considering this for a moment. She let go of Camilla and toured the room. Her hand traced along the desk. She picked up one of the sketches and held it to the light.

Milo and Fleur gasped when they saw it.

"Did you draw this?" asked Remy.

"Yes, but it's not finished—"

"It's a castle. The same castle from all those pictures on the news. Did you copy it off from there?"

Camilla thought before she answered. She could lie and say she did, but she could also tell the truth and risk being laughed at by the three most peculiar people she had ever met.

"No," she said, and almost regretted it. "I kind of . . . well, I saw the castle a few days ago."

The transfer students all turned towards her. Their eyes shared in the same fire, burning, blistering, lashing at Camilla. Remy gnawed on her teeth. She wheezed slightly.

At last, Fleur stepped forward and spoke. "You saw it?" she asked, her voice somewhat softer, somewhat less threatening than when the others spoke. "With your own eyes?"

"I know it sounds silly—impossible, really. I must've just been daydreaming when I saw it." Camilla shook her head. She made to grab the sketch from Remy, but she yanked it away and held it above her head, out of her reach. "Please, just give it back so we can head out."

But Remy didn't budge.

She made her hand into a fist, puncturing the paper. She asked, "Did you see the castle again?"

"No, I only saw it once . . ." Camilla replied, more frustrated now. She looked to the door and back. They had to go. Now. Her mother might check on her soon. "Actually, I saw it again when I was at the lake with Logan. I went underwater and saw the walls go in every direction."

"Did you touch it?" asked Milo. Remy handed him the sketch, and he studied it with narrowed eyes.

"Did you?" Remy repeated, more aggressively.

"No. I didn't touch it."

"Why?"

"Please, can we go now?" Camilla hopped in place. "It's already after nine and my mother—"

A key wiggled in the lock.

Camilla froze. She shut her eyes as the door flung open, revealing Pearl in the doorway. She had a glass of milk in her hand and was midsentence when she looked up and gasped. She dropped the glass. It didn't break but rolled across the carpet, a streak of milk in its wake.

"Camilla," she said, looking from Fleur to Milo to Remy upon whose face she momentarily paused. She began to say something, stutter something. "Ext—no, it can't be."

"Mom, I just wanted to go to a bonfire," Camilla explained, but her mother hardly even looked at her.

Pearl surged forward. She pressed her hand to Remy's chest, pushing her back several steps. "You!" she shouted at her. "She sent you, didn't she? She wants you to take my daughter from me!"

Remy looked sideways at Camilla. "Eh," she said, "Mrs. Ward, I presume? I know what this looks like, but we're really just here to pick up your daughter for a bonfire at the lake."

Milo and Fleur nodded, but Pearl wouldn't have it. "Lies!" she screamed, even louder than before.

"Mom!" Camilla cut between Remy and Pearl. Her hand was still on Remy's chest, though no longer as forcedly.

"Camilla, get away from here. Whoever she said she is, she's lying. They're all lying." Pearl outright growled in Remy's face. "They're not your friends . . . They're here to hurt you."

"Tell her she's wrong," whispered Remy in Camilla's ear. When Camilla didn't listen, she pressed up against her and repeated, "Tell her you're going to the bonfire whether she likes it or not."

Camilla chewed her bottom lip. Her mother's teeth clattered, and her knees wobbled. She was scared out of her mind—but also seething, akin to that day at the lake and at the police station. Things couldn't go on like this. She was too paranoid, too overprotective.

And it had to end.

"Tell her," Remy insisted.

"What does she want you to tell me, Camilla?" asked Pearl, almost as though she already knew.

As though she was testing her.

"You're wrong," Camilla spoke too softly and had to repeat herself. *"You're wrong about them. They're not dangerous."* As the words spilled from her mouth, her eyes began to tingle, and Pearl's face straightened. Her trembling stilled, and her hand fell limply to her side.

"I'm wrong," mumbled Pearl. "They're not liars. They're your friends. They're not dangerous."

Camilla frowned at her mother's change of opinion. She looked around at Remy, who nodded at her. She had a wickedness to her eyes—a hunger, a fascination, a satisfaction.

"Go on," she pressed.

"And I, uh, I'm going to the bonfire with them," Camilla repeated every word exactly as Remy said it. Confidence built inside of her. She was standing up for herself, doing what *she* wanted to do. "Yes, that's right. I'm going! And I'm going to see Logan there!"

Pearl nodded as she spoke, still with no reaction.

Camilla took a step forward, towering over her mother. She wanted to say something else, demand something else, but noticed no response in her eyes or around her mouth.

"What's wrong with her?" she asked, turning to the transfer students. "She's not usually like this."

Remy jumped. "It's probably nothing. Come on. We have to go." She gestured for Milo and Fleur to leave through the window then turned to Camilla. "Tell her to go downstairs," she added.

"What?"

"Tell her to sit and watch TV or something."

"Tell her?" Camilla questioned. "She's my mom. I can't just tell her." She waved in front of Pearl's face.

No reaction.

"Just do it!" shouted Remy, already halfway out the window. She snorted and leapt down onto the grass. "Come on!"

Camilla turned to her mother. "Mom?" she said, and

Pearl craned her neck. Her eyes were open, and she blinked, but they were distant and bleak, blurry almost.

"Mom, are you okay? I'm so sorry. If you're mad, you can ground me when I get back."

Silence.

"Camilla!" cried Remy from outside the window.

Camilla's shoulders tensed. She couldn't believe what she was about to do. She didn't even think it would work, but her lips parted, and she said, "Go downstairs and watch TV."

More silence.

"Please, Mom."

Camilla partially expected Pearl to erupt into screams again—to grab her by the arm as she turned and made for the window—but she didn't. Instead, she circled around and left the way she came. She kicked the empty glass across the floor and sloshed through the milk.

No reaction.

Camilla paused in the window frame. Her mother never left a mess and never yielded in an argument. Something was wrong. Something strange and unexplainable. Something that even she didn't know how to control. She touched her left eye, still tingling.

"Camilla!" Remy shouted a third time. "What's taking you so long? You're not having second thoughts, are you?" She stood in the street under a lamppost, her hands in the air.

Camilla slipped outside, taking care that her dress didn't catch on anything. Her soles touched the ground, and she balanced herself. She caught a glimpse of her reflection in the window and flinched. For a moment, and just a moment, she thought her eyes were . . .

Glowing again.

It was like the night she had seen herself in the mirror. The night she had seen a man in her room.

"Is everything taken care of?" asked Remy from behind her. She reached out and grabbed Camilla's wrist. Her nails punctured her flesh as she dragged her across the lawn to the street.

"Yeah," mumbled Camilla.

They walked a few more steps in silence, Milo and Fleur trailing in their wake.

"Remy, do my eyes look like they're glowing to you?"

Remy stopped at once. Her grip tightened, but she spoke calmly. "They look normal to me. Why?"

"N—No reason," Camilla replied. She filled her chest with air and allowed herself to be swept into the night.

To the lake.

To Logan.

CHAPTER EIGHTEEN
CAMILLA

amilla's hair had completely dried when they arrived at the lake. A cool breeze whipped through the air, rippling the water into tiny waves. A massive bonfire lapped at the stars, and a sea of faces sat and danced and partied around it.

"Whoa," she breathed. Someone pushed by her from behind, a bottle of beer in his hand and a cigarette clenched between his teeth. "I thought you said this was a small party?"

She coughed from the smoke.

"It is," sang Remy. "Just stay here for a second, okay?" She mouthed several instructions to Milo, patted Camilla on the shoulder, and disappeared into the swarm of partiers.

"All right, then." Camilla clasped her hands together. She turned her back on Milo and Fleur, both of whom were swaying to the music that blared from a car in the parking lot. It was loud, crass, and lively. Not at all to her liking. Did she make a mistake in coming?

A mosquito buzzed around her head, and she swatted at it. Bugs, smoke, alcohol, and music.

Definitely not what she expected.

The thought of her poor mother, all alone at home, tumbled her stomach upside down. She had just stood there. Emotionless. Still. She had gone from absolute rage to total compliance in a matter of seconds. In a matter of words.

It was all so strange. Too strange.

Camilla made way for a couple of guys carrying a keg. Some of the orange drink spilled onto her dress, and she wiped at it. She thought back to when Pearl had entered her room. When she had charged at Remy as if she knew her, accusing her of being dangerous and bad. Of wanting to take Camilla away from her.

Remy didn't seem to know anything. Then again, she did tell Camilla exactly what to say.

And it had worked.

The current song ended, and Camilla's thoughts stilled. She turned around, but Milo and Fleur were gone. She spotted them on a log by the fire, sort of holding hands, sort of cuddling. She held up her wristwatch, but it was too dark to see the time. She turned it to the light.

9:30 p.m.

Nearly fifteen minutes had gone, and there was still no sign of Logan. Perhaps he didn't come after all. Perhaps he did, and was in the center of the crowd, swooned over by more girls.

The thought of the blonde girl by the javelin pitch woke Camilla up to reality. Who was she trying to fool? She could never be anything like that. She emptied her chest and turned around, ready to head home to an undoubtedly livid Pearl.

"Camilla!"

She spun around with such vigor, she nearly toppled over. She couldn't help but smile at his voice, at his face by the fire, and the way he walked towards her, a drink in each hand.

"I was just looking for you," said Logan. His eyes flicked across her body, across her hair and dress and sandals. He smiled crookedly. "Wow. I've never seen you in a full-on dress before."

Camilla blushed. She smoothed out her skirt. "I, uh," she stammered, lowering her head and twisting her heel into the ground, "just thought I'd try something different tonight."

"Well, I like it."

"Thanks." Her blush amplified. She hoped he wouldn't notice in the dark, but he clearly did, as he chuckled to himself and held out a cup. She hesitated before she took it. Whatever it was, it bubbled and fizzed and smelled terribly funny. Sour and bitter at the same time.

"Do you drink beer?" asked Logan.

"Beer?" she blurted out.

Logan withdrew the cup, all of a sudden hesitant. "Of course, I should've asked you first." He looked down at the beer then made to turn around. "Do you want me to—"

"No, no," Camilla forestalled him. She grabbed the cup

and took a sip, fighting not to contort her face as she swallowed. So bitter. So terrible. "I just never drank it before."

Logan cocked a brow at her. "And? How does it taste?" He took a sip from his cup.

"Eh, good."

"Good? Yeah?" Logan challenged her, clearly not convinced. He nonetheless allowed her to suffer in silence. "Now that our drinks are sorted, let's find a seat by the fire, shall we?"

Camilla winced as his hand slipped into hers. He led her through the crowd to another log next to Milo and Fleur. It was small, and they had to squeeze up against each other.

"Is this all right?" he asked with his entire leg pressed against hers, from thigh to knee to ankle.

Camilla tried to calm her breathing. She listened to Logan's, steady and deep, the exact opposite.

"Yep," was all she managed.

"Did you actually sneak out, then?" he went on. Their faces were so close, their cheeks nearly touched. He smelled of aftershave. Quite intoxicating—mind numbing.

"Kind of," said Camilla.

"Kind of?"

"My mother caught me"—Logan's eyes widened—"just as I was heading out, and she was really upset for a moment, but then . . ." Camilla swallowed her words, unsure of how to finish her sentence. She looked at Milo and Fleur, who ogled them from the side.

"And then?"

"No, no, no, no, no!" Remy interrupted. She had two cups in her hands, similar to the ones Logan had brought. "Are you actually drinking beer? You've got to be joking!"

Logan peered inside his cup. "What's wrong with beer?"

"It's cheap, tacky, and tastes utterly horrible!" Remy confiscated their cups. She handed them two news ones—a drink not quite as fizzy and a lot less bitter-smelling than beer.

"Drink this, it's much better," she said.

"What is it?" asked Camilla.

Logan seconded this with a snort. He swirled the drink around, watching it turn from red to brown by the firelight.

"It's my own special concoction. I've made it at every party I've ever thrown, and it's so good, people keep coming back for more." Remy sounded rather proud. She flicked her finger at them, ordering them to have a taste. "Don't be shy. Tell me what you think."

Camilla looked at Logan, who shrugged and drank first. His lips pursed, and the veins in his neck popped. He shook his head and let out a roar. "Woah, this stuff's strong!"

Remy giggled. "I never said it wasn't."

Milo and Fleur made space for her on the log, and she flopped down with one leg over the other. Music still blared from the parking lot, and people still danced all around, but in that moment—the moment in which Remy watched Logan drink—they might as well have been alone.

Camilla shuddered.

"Why aren't you drinking?" Remy asked her.

"I'm not really a big drinker," said Camilla, but she brought the cup to her lips anyway. The drink merely lapped against her lips, although Camilla contorted her face and pretended to have had the wind knocked out of her.

"Nice, eh?" Remy seemed to have bought it.

"Strong, yes."

Logan elbowed Camilla. She looked up at him, nearly colliding her nose with his chin. He winked at her, calling her bluff. She wanted to wink back but instead settled for a grin.

"What's in this stuff anyway?" asked Logan, perhaps trying to change the subject or perhaps just curious. He dipped his finger in his cup, whiffed it, and popped it in his mouth.

"It's a family secret," said Milo, quickly, and Remy frowned at him. "What? It really is a secret!"

"He was speaking to me, dimwit."

Logan narrowed his eyes. "I take it the two of you are brother and sister, then?"

"Unfortunately," said Remy before Milo could get a word in.

"And you?" Logan continued, motioning to Fleur, who hadn't once taken her eyes off Camilla.

"I'm a friend," was all she said.

Logan nodded and took another sip. He tilted his head back and emptied it, then put it on the ground. His hand returned to his lap, but instead of staying there, it slid to the side, so his fingers grazed Camilla's thigh. Warmth flowed from his fingertips and into her skin.

Camilla couldn't help but smile.

"Do you want more, Logan?" Remy offered.

Logan shook his head, but she got up and grabbed his cup off the ground. She looked at his lap for a moment—at his hand on Camilla's thigh—and clenched her teeth.

Camilla didn't understand this.

Did she *like* Logan?

"Come on, it's a party!" she cried, smiling again. She reached for Logan's hand and pulled him to his feet. "You must have another drink! You don't want to upset the hosts, do you?"

Logan wavered. He looked to Camilla and back then said, "Oh, all right. One more couldn't hurt."

"Great!" Remy dragged Logan off. She talked the entire time, although they were soon too far away for Camilla to hear what about. She crossed her ankles and smoothed out her dress.

Once again, she was stuck with Milo and Fleur. Neither of them had anything to say, unlike Remy, who rarely shut up. They forced Camilla into a three-minute staring competition, after which Fleur finally broke the silence by asking, "Are you enjoying the bonfire?"

Camilla shrugged. "It's okay."

"Not much of a partier, are you?"

Camilla shook her head.

Fleur smiled at her. "Don't worry, we're not either. It's mostly Remy who enjoys these things."

"You throw a lot of parties, then?"

"Quite a lot," admitted Milo. "But they're never really as laid back. How are you enjoying the lake?"

Camilla shifted in her seat. She looked over to where Remy and Logan had disappeared, hoping they were on their way back already. But they were nowhere in sight.

"Do you see any, eh, castles?" Fleur dared to ask.

Camilla had anticipated this question. Once Milo had asked her about the lake, she knew it was coming. She was surprised, however, by their seriousness. Did they believe her?

"Nope, no castles."

They both seemed disappointed. They exchanged a look and Milo said, "Listen, since none of us really like being here, how about we go somewhere a little quieter?"

"Quiet? Like where?" Camilla asked.

"We don't have a castle on the lake or anything, but we rent a cabin nearby." Milo motioned to somewhere behind them. Into the forest. "Do you want to hang out with us there?"'

Camilla tensed. A cabin? In the woods? With strangers who cornered her and demanded answers to questions she didn't know of?

"Thanks for the offer, but it's not as bad here. I think I'll hang out with Logan a little while longer."

"That guy?" asked Fleur.

"Are you sure?" added Milo.

"Yeah, why?"

They twisted in their seats, parting a little so Camilla

had a view of the shore. Milo pointed at two people by the water, two silhouettes so close they almost passed for a single person.

They were hugging. No, they were making out.

Camilla's first instinct was to look away. She didn't understand why they'd even show her such a thing and wondered how it had anything to do with Logan. She was ready to ask when the bonfire sputtered and the bodies, the faces, the features of the couple lit up.

It was Logan and Remy, locking lips.

"What?" Camilla gasped as she stood up. Her jaw worked, but she had nothing to say to that.

"A pity, eh?" shrugged Milo, and Fleur agreed. "I think you should get away. Let's go to the cabin."

Camilla's mind shouted, *No, I'm not going anywhere with you!* But the sound of her shattering heart tuned it out. She knew she had to go home, had to face her mother's wrath, but her lips moved before she could stop them. "Let's go. I've got no reason to stick around here."

Milo grinned. He stood and approached Camilla then hooked his arm around her neck and beckoned her away. They passed by Remy and Logan, and Camilla turned her head.

She had no right to be mad at either of them. Logan was allowed to flirt with whomever he wanted. Kiss whomever he wanted. They weren't a couple and likely never would be.

"You shouldn't see this, Camilla," said Milo, surprisingly loud. It was as if he wanted them to hear, to notice.

Logan pulled away from Remy. His mouth fell open, and his brows collapsed into a frown. He touched his lips, stained with Remy's lipstick. Blackish-brown. He removed his hand from her waist, looked up, and called out, "Camilla, wait! You can't go home yet!"

Camilla burst into tears.

"Cam!" Logan ran towards her, but Milo and Fleur pulled her back. Another step forward.

Another yank backward.

"You don't have to listen to this," said Milo, and pulled Camilla away. He kept on walking this time, holding her by the shoulders so she couldn't turn around. Logan called after Camilla, and tears tumbled down her cheeks, but she didn't look back and she didn't resist.

Remy also set after them.

"Logan!" she cried.

Milo raised his hand, and his sister stopped just short of the parking lot. Logan caught up to them, grabbing Camilla by the arm. He tried to whirl her around, but Fleur swatted him away.

"Leave her alone, you buffoon!"

"Camilla, please. I—"

Camilla whirled around on her own.

"It's fine, Logan," she said sniffing. "It really, really is. Enjoy the rest of the bonfire with your friends." She wrenched free from Milo's grip and walked alongside them into the trees.

Part of her expected Logan to follow her, but he didn't.

"Are you okay?" asked Fleur.

Camilla nodded. She stopped and glanced back. Remy had her hand on Logan's shoulder, comforting him. He didn't resist or yank away. And that was what hurt the most.

CHAPTER NINETEEN
CAMILLA

*T*he forest was cold and damp and dark. Camilla rubbed her arms. Mosquito bites painted her skin, itching and prickling, but she refused to scratch. She was panting, though the wind drowned it out. She wasn't used to this sort of hiking nor was she dressed for it.

"Is the cabin close by?" she asked, scouring the surrounding trees despite the blinding darkness of the night. "We've been walking for quite a while now—"

"Yeah, yeah. We're close," Milo insisted. His mood had changed greatly since they left Remy and Logan at the bonfire. He had gone from happy-go-lucky to serious and annoyed.

To outright rude.

Camilla nodded, though didn't say anything in reply. Her lashes crunched every time she blinked from dried-up tears in the corners of her eyes. She wondered whether she had made the right decision to go with them and whether she should've just gone home to her mother.

At least Milo and Fleur seemed harmless enough. They were Remy's lackeys, her entourage. Neither of them talked much, which allowed Camilla to think, to process everything. Logan had been so nice to her over the past few weeks. He had gone out of his way to spend time with her and expressed an interest in her drawings. Was he just being polite?

Or was she just another girl blinded by his charms?

"Are you angry with Remy right now?" asked Fleur. She parted a shrub and held it aside for Camilla to pass.

"No, not really." Camilla scratched above her left eyebrow. Another pesky mosquito bite. "I mean, how can I be, when I have no right to?" She traced her fingers along a tree trunk.

"And that guy? Are you mad at him?"

"Logan?" Camilla inhaled deeply. She still smelled him on her. Pine and mint and the scent of beer that was last on his breath. A pain shot through her heart. "No, not angry . . ."

Silence.

"Heartbroken is more like it."

Milo slowed down. Camilla caught him glancing across his shoulder at which he immediately turned back and upped his pace. He trotted through the forest with the elegance of an elephant. Twigs snapped, leaves crunched, and pebbles skidded across the ground.

"You deserve better," said Fleur. "Someone that

wouldn't lead you on, only to break your heart." Her gaze swerved to Milo and back, and the corners of her lips curved up.

Camilla hesitated before she asked, "Are you two—"

"No," Milo said. "We're not."

Fleur sighed. "We're just friends. Even if we wanted to, Milo's parents would never allow it."

"Is it because—"

"I'm a different race?" Fleur chimed in. "No, it's not that. Things work differently in Escana."

Camilla nodded, even though she knew Fleur couldn't see her. "It's kind of like that for me and Logan."

"In what way?"

"Well, you see, his father owns most of the town, and me . . . I'm the girl who sees castles on the lake." Her voice broke. She sniffed again, and fresh tears pooled in her eyes. An owl hooted in the trees somewhere, snapping her back. She quickly wiped her eyes dry.

"You really like him, don't you?" asked Fleur.

"I do." Camilla sobbed all over again. She didn't shake like before, but she also couldn't stop it. The image of Logan and Remy replayed in her mind over and over: Logan couldn't wait to see her. He had winked at her, and they had just gone to get drinks.

"Enough!" snapped Milo. He reached into his pocket and pulled out a silk handkerchief. He chucked it at her, and she barely caught it in the dark. "He doesn't like you, Camilla."

Camilla gasped.

"If he liked you, he wouldn't have kissed Remy. He would've asked you on a date already."

"Milo!" Fleur sneered.

Camilla dabbed under her eyes. "No, Fleur, he's right. I should just get over him, we're clearly wrong for each other." She opened the handkerchief, ready to blow her nose when the clouds parted, and the moon lit the forest. There was a picture on the handkerchief.

A crest.

"W—Where did you get this?" she asked.

Milo frowned. "The handkerchief? It's mine. I have twenty others like it, so you can blow all you want."

"No, it's not that." Camilla held it up. "This crest. The one on my necklace looks just like it."

Milo glanced at Fleur, who simply crossed her arms.

"Why is that?" Camilla pressed.

"Milo, don't," said Fleur through gritted teeth.

"Why not? She wants to know, doesn't she?" Milo licked his lips. He ran a hand through his hair, letting his fringe fall before his eyes. He likely wished Remy was there to take over. "That there is the Escanian crest."

Fleur choked. "Eh, Milo . . ."

But he spoke on. "Our town is just old-fashioned that way. My mother is the mayor of Escana, hence the hand-kerchief." He clapped his hands when he finished, startling some birds.

"The Escanian crest?" Camilla repeated.

"Yep."

"Why would your mother, the mayor, send you to a different school? Isn't that a bit hypocritical? She's supposed to denote your town." Camilla couldn't decide whether to believe him.

But he didn't seem to care whether she did.

He set off again, speaking as he walked. "Like I said, Escana's somewhat old-fashioned. Its schools are slightly lacking, and my mother wanted us to have a decent education."

"Oh." Camilla took another look at the handkerchief. "But why would the Escanian crest be on my necklace?" She thought about it, then gasped. "Yes, that's it! It's my father!"

"What about him?"

"He must be from Escana."

This time, both Fleur and Milo choked.

"Yes, he must've been born and raised there! Can you believe it? That I'd meet people from my father's home-town just days after my mother gave me this necklace?"

"Quite the timing," said Fleur under her breath.

Camilla rubbed the necklace with her thumb. She hadn't taken it off since her birthday, not even when she showered. She thought about Escana, a tiny town in the middle of nowhere. Her father's home, her heritage. Then it hit her: he might still have family there.

"Do you think I can visit it sometime?"

"What?" asked Milo.

"Escana."

Silence.

"Camilla wants to visit Escana, Milo." Fleur spoke through gritted teeth. She parted another shrub but didn't hold it back this time. It whacked Camilla in the side, scratching her arm.

"That could be arranged," said Milo. "But first, if I could only . . ." He stopped and looked around, scratching his head. He traced through the air with his finger, thinking deeply.

"Don't tell me we're lost?" Fleur hissed.

Camilla held her arm to the moonlight. It wasn't bleeding, but the branch had left a scratch. She rubbed it, triggering mosquito bites all the way from her shoulder, down to her wrist.

Lost, hurt, and itching.

It couldn't get any worse.

"We're not lost," Milo insisted. He peered past a tree. "We're just temporarily misplaced."

Fleur scoffed and crossed her arms. "We have to get to Esc—uh, the cabin before it's too late." She reached into her pocket and removed her phone. "See, it's after ten already!"

"You had a phone on you this entire time?" Camilla blurted out.

"Yeah, why?"

"You could've just turned on the flash! I mean, we've been walking around in the dark, tripping over things and getting lost, for nothing?" Camilla waited for Fleur to respond—to slap her hand against her forehead and confess her stupidity—but she never did.

Not even Milo said anything.

"Hello! Turn on your flash already!"

"Flash?" asked Fleur. She flipped her phone upside down, holding it with the tips of her fingers.

"Do you not have phones in Escana? Just give it to me." Camilla took a step forward, reaching for the phone. She couldn't see the ground, and her foot hooked around a root.

She tripped.

"Watch it!" Milo reacted just quick enough to catch her by the elbow. At the same time, Fleur discovered her phone's flash. Their surroundings lit up, trees and shrubs and roots and soil.

"Thank you," Camilla breathed. She looked up, right at Milo. He wore a leather jacket, a t-shirt, and a holster type of thing with a . . . blade? She straightened and wrenched away.

Milo adjusted his jacket.

"Are you okay?" asked Fleur. She wielded her phone through the air. "This flash thing is amazing!"

Camilla's mouth went dry. She looked at them, not as friends, but as transfer students, as strangers. They had arrived out of nowhere and dressed differently than anyone else.

And Fleur didn't know what a flash was . . .

"Milo," Camilla began, licking her lips. She took a step back. "W—Why do you have a sword?"

Milo clutched at his chest, at his holster.

Fleur let the phone hang.

They exchanged one of their many, many glances and approached Camilla at the same time.

"Camilla," said Fleur. "It's not what you think."

"What am I thinking?" Camilla retreated a few more steps nearly tripping over another root. "That you don't have a cabin . . . that you're not transfer students at all . . ."

Milo cocked his head.

"That you only brought me out here to cut me up . . ." Camilla swallowed as she said that last bit.

"Camilla, you can't be serious."

"That's enough, Fleur." Milo stomped on the ground. His jacket fell off his shoulders, revealing a thin, pointed sword with a patterned grip. It was holstered to his chest, short enough to be hidden under a jacket, but long enough to severely hurt a person.

"Milo—"

"I said that's enough! We don't have time for games anymore. We're taking her back to Escana, even if it requires force." He drew his sword with a single swift movement.

Camilla shrieked. "Hey, what's going on? You're all crazy!" She turned around and ran.

Milo and Fleur set after her. Fleur wasn't as fast, but Milo caught up to her within seconds. He tripped her, and she fell against the base of a tree. She rubbed her head, looking up at Milo, at his red-hot face. The sword in his hand glinted off the moonlight.

"Just stop fighting already," he said.

Camilla grabbed a branch off the ground and whacked at Milo. It splintered, forcing him back.

"Stay away!" she shouted.

Milo didn't move.

"I don't know who you are or what I've done to you

but leave me be!" Camilla scrambled to her feet. She reversed past the tree, turned around, and came face to face with Fleur.

"We don't have to hurt you." Fleur reached for her wrists, but Camilla kicked her in the shins.

"Ah!"

"I'm not going anywhere! Leave me alone!" Her voice pitched, and her eyes became alive. They tingled and throbbed, the way one's skin did when scratching an itch.

Fleur gave a step back. Her body tensed, and her fingers twitched, but she didn't dare make a move.

Camilla rubbed her eyes, again and again. She looked back at Milo, who stood exactly where she had left him, cemented, frozen. Fleur hissed something between her teeth, but Camilla couldn't make out what she said. She rounded her and set off, looking back one last time.

"Freaks!" she shouted.

No reaction.

Neither of them even tried to stop her. Like that day in the music room, they merely stared after her, veins throbbing in their necks. Camilla blinked a couple of times, and the buzzing in her eyes stilled. She ran through the forest in no particular direction.

Something attracted her, led her away from the dark and towards the light. The light of Crystalvale.

Camilla only slowed once she saw the town sign beside the highway. A car whizzed by, and she crossed to the other side. The Bunbun Diner was a short walk from there, and her home a few blocks farther. Sweat clammed against the sides of her face, and her head throbbed from her fall. Her body told her to stop, to rest, but she refused to do so.

She had to get home. To her mother. To the one person who might have the slightest clue as to what was going on.

CHAPTER TWENTY
CAMILLA

*C*amilla ran and ran until she couldn't. Her knees buckled and tears clouded her eyesight, but she held out and pressed on. It was strange, the pain heartbreak caused. Oh, how stupid she had been to trust strangers.

Pearl had been right about Remy. About all of them, including Logan. He wasn't who she thought he was, and perhaps that wasn't his fault. She had made him into something else. Someone else. He had been sweet, gentle, and kind, but in the end, he was what he was.

A popular guy. One who could get whichever girl he wanted. Only it turned out to be Remy instead of her. The girl with the ring through her nose and whose brother carried a sword.

The thought of it urged her back into a sprint.

The clocktower struck eleven, and darkness cloaked suburban Crystalvale. Camilla followed the streetlights, the image in her head from years and years of cycling home from school. She arrived at her house, still with the lights on. Shadows moved beyond the drawn curtains.

Shadows?

Plural?

Camilla ran up the driveway to the front door. Her heart pulsed at the back of her head. The door was unlocked, open on the screen. Pearl never left anything open.

Not a cupboard nor the fridge.

"Mom?" Camilla called. She didn't enter right away, but waited for her mother to answer.

She didn't.

Camilla swallowed whatever fear lodged in her throat and opened the door. It creaked on its hinges, and she cringed. Someone had gotten inside without her mother's consent. She could feel it in the air, see it by the way everything was exactly as it had been when she was banished to her room: the dishes, the dirty clothing, the still-on oven.

Camilla dashed to the kitchen and yanked it open. Smoke tumbled outside, filling her lungs. She coughed, grabbed a tea towel from a hook on the wall, and took out the hot tray.

Chocolate chip cookies.

Her favorite.

Camilla put the tray on the counter. She dropped the tea towel on the burnt mess, turned off the oven, and opened a window. Her eyes reflected in the glass. They didn't glow this time, but they were red and puffy and streaked with tears. She reached to wipe under her eyes, but something moved behind her in the window, and she spun.

Camilla screamed. It was him. The man she had seen in her room, in the forest. He was tall with broad shoulders, had brown hair with white streaks on the sides, and wore a hoodie and jeans. He raised his hands, retreating behind the island in the center of the kitchen.

"Who are you?" Camilla asked. She yanked open the nearest drawer and took out a steak knife. The man stepped back when she wielded it at him, still with his hands up.

"Camilla," he said. "Calm down, please."

Camilla's eyes darted to the coffee table by the door. Her mother's phone lay on it, along with her apron and keys. "H—How do you know my name? What have you done to my mom?"

The man took a precautious step forward.

"Camilla—"

"Don't you dare take another step! I'll call the police!"

"As you wish," the man agreed. He licked his lips. "I know what this looks like, believe me, but it's not what you think it. Lower the knife, and hear me out."

"No. There'll be no talking." Camilla grabbed another knife from the drawer. She pointed it at him, at his face. "I —I'll throw this at you if I have to. I'm serious. Leave our house!"

"What did you do to your mom?"

Camilla was taken aback by this. So much so, she momentarily lowered her weapons. She immediately raised them again. "What are you talking about? I didn't do anything to her. You did!"

"I'm not here to hurt you," the man persisted.

Camilla narrowed her eyes at him.

"Come. See. In the living room." The man turned around and walked off, even with two knives still pointed at him. He left the kitchen and turned the corner to the living room.

Camilla remained in place for a couple more seconds. Tears of horror, of heartbreak and fear, burned in her eyes, and her palms began to tremor. The knives were suddenly heavy. She waited for the man to return, to come back and summon her again, but he didn't. Was he with her mom? Was he using her as bait? Or was he . . . telling the truth?

She looked at the coffee table by the door again, at her mother's phone. She could grab it, lock the door behind her, run off, and call for help. Bob from across the street ought to be home.

But her mom.

She could be in serious danger.

With the knives still raised, Camilla walked past the island and stopped short of the corner. She waited, inhaled, and jumped around it, ready to stab the man if he attacked her.

But he wasn't there. He wasn't anywhere near Camilla, and not at all focused on whether or not she followed him. He stood by the TV, the light projecting on his back, looking down at Pearl on the couch. She just sat there, unresponsive. Camilla dropped the knives, and they clattered on the tiles.

"What's wrong with her?" she asked. "Is she still like this? I don't—I have no idea what—"

"You did this."

Camilla's eyes swerved onto the man. Her first instinct was to deny his accusation, to threaten him with calling the police again, but something about him intrigued her. He clearly knew her—and her mother—and definitely knew something about what was wrong with her.

"H—How do I fix it?" she asked.

The man gestured for her to approach. Camilla obeyed, walking as slowly and heedfully as she could.

"I told you, I'm not here to hurt you."

"That's what they all say."

The man smiled, and his cheeks flushed. He didn't move as she approached, nor when she stood right next to him, waving her hand before her mother's eyes.

No reaction.

"Do you know how to fix her?" she repeated.

The man nodded. He raised his hand, almost as if he wanted to touch Camilla's shoulder, but she winced and he withdrew. "It depends on you. Do *you* want to fix your mother?"

Camilla nodded.

"Well, what exactly did you do to make her like this in the first place?"

"Uh, I just told her." Camilla thought back to earlier that evening. "I said a whole bunch of things, and she just agreed. I told her to come downstairs and stay here until I get back."

"So, you're back. Tell her to react. Tell her to move, and she will." The man made it sound so simple, so normal.

Camilla cleared her throat. She looked her mother in the eyes, her dull, lifeless eyes, and said, "Mom, I'm so sorry. You were right . . . I should have stayed in my room." Camilla fell to her knees. She kept her gaze up and her eyes open. They tingled again, not as intensely, but just enough to lighten her sorrow and mend her heart a little.

A sort of elation filled her, and the words spilled from her mouth. "Come back to me, please."

Pearl blinked. She looked around the room, at Camilla by her lap, and at the man standing over them.

Camilla waited for her to scream, for her curl up and beg him to leave them alone, but instead, she did something so shocking, so surprising, that Camilla couldn't help but frown. Pearl got up, flew into his arms, and kissed him.

"Finn," she whispered with their foreheads together. "You came back. Why? What am I . . . What happened?" Pearl pulled away, but the man's arm stayed around her waist.

"She must've accidentally put you in a trance," the man replied when Camilla couldn't. "I came here to warn you, but found you on the couch like this. Camilla wasn't here, and—"

"Hold on," Camilla chimed in. She got up. "Who is this, Mom? And how could I have put you in a trance?"

Pearl's smile broadened, and she placed a hand on the man's chest. "Camilla, this is Finn." She bit her bottom lip. "He's . . . your father."

Camilla nearly swallowed her tongue. She had heard her mother call him by his name moments ago, but with everything that had happened, it flew right over her head. He's Finn. *The* Finn. Pearl reached for her hands, but Camilla pulled away and backtracked, right over the back of the couch.

"M—My father?" she stuttered.

Finn grinned.

"No, it can't be." Camilla raised her voice. "You told me he was dead. You told me he died in a car crash."

"I know, but—"

"You lied to me for eighteen years, Mom! You lied to me over and over!" Camilla was in tears now. This, in addition to what happened with Logan and the transfer students, made her bawl without control.

"And you," she added, turning to Finn. "Where were you all this time? Are you an addict? An alcoholic?"

Finn shrugged. "No, I'm a king. Sort of."

"What?" Camilla wanted to launch at him and hit him with every ounce of strength she had left. Her mother stood in the way, so she grabbed her hair instead.

"My wife is Extine Allessien, Queen of Escana. That technically makes me a king, doesn't it?" Finn tried to joke.

Pearl pushed away from him and approached Camilla,

who trembled too much to wrench away. She fell into her mother's arms, sniffing through the tears. Pearl held her against her, rocking her from side to side.

She whispered in her ear, "I know this is all confusing, but believe me, I wanted to tell you every day of your life. I hated lying to you, but I had no other choice."

"*We* had no other choice," Finn corrected her.

Camilla dried her tears on Pearl's shirt. She looked up at Finn, who tried his best to grin again, but the corners of his eyes didn't crease. She asked, "Are you—are you really a king?"

"I'm really married to a queen, yes. And no, I'm not an addict, and I'm not an alcoholic. I was betrothed to my wife, Extine, long before you were born, so your mother and I . . ."

"We could never be together." Pearl pulled Camilla to her feet. She used her thumb to dry her tears. "Darling, you look terrible. Have you been crying the entire night?"

Camilla shook her head and jumbled words spilled out of her. "It's nothing. It's just—I was with Logan—and then Remy came, and—the transfer students took me into the words—Milo, had a sword—"

"Remy?" Finn blurted out. "Milo? A sword?"

"Are they the people from your room?" asked Pearl, almost with the same expression of horror as Finn. She let go of Camilla and turned to him. "They're your children, aren't they?"

"They are, yes. I, well, I actually came to warn you about them."

Camilla raised her hands. "Wait, you're Remy and Milo's father? They're the Princess and Prince of Escana?"

"Yes, and you're their half sister."

"When I saw Remy earlier . . . I can't believe how much she looks like Extine," noted Pearl. She returned to Camilla. "Where are they now?"

"All three of them," added Finn.

Camilla swallowed "I left Milo and Fleur somewhere in the forest, and Remy at the bonfire. She kissed Logan, and I just had to get out of there."

"Remy kissed someone?" asked Finn.

"Logan Wheeler. Camilla's got a crush on him," Pearl explained, ignoring Camilla's sidewards glance.

"That boy's, he's in danger." Finn walked around the couch and grabbed Camilla. His eyes widened. "Did they ask you to go somewhere?"

"They asked me about a cabin, but Milo couldn't find it. They spoke about taking me to Escana."

"That's when you left?"

"Yes."

"That's good, right?" Pearl grabbed her chest. "We should hide her. Here, in the house, or we could go somewhere . . ."

Finn let go of Camilla and made a line for the window. He peered through a slit in the curtains, scanning the street. "No. Extine wants Camilla's eyes. She'll do anything for them. She killed those two kayakers."

"Extine did that?" Pearl gasped.

"Mom, how do you even know this Extine? And why does she want my eyes?" Camilla couldn't help herself from sounding like a whiny toddler. She hated being kept out of the loop, especially when she herself was involved.

"Extine's my sister."

"Sister?" Camilla contorted her face. "But that means . . . you're a princess, too?"

Pearl and Finn both shook their heads.

"Camilla, listen to me," Finn said. "We'll explain everything later, but right now, I need you to tell me about this Logan boy."

"What about him?"

"I think he's in danger." Finn and Pearl exchanged another look. "They're taking him to Escana."

"Our kingdom," Pearl added.

"Because Extine wants my eyes?"

"Exactly, although they used to be hers." Pearl sat down on the couch and gestured for Camilla to do the same. "Darling, I'm about to tell you the truth about your eyes, and I want you to listen very carefully . . ."

CHAPTER TWENTY-ONE
EXTINE

Extine paced down the length of the throne room. She had one hand on her head and the other on her lower back. Her pulse throbbed in her fingertips, and her ears rang. She could barely stand up straight, but she had to. She had to keep the borders from collapsing.

The plan played and replayed in her mind. She imagined what life would be like if she failed.

Without Finn.

Without Pearl.

Without Remy.

Extine stopped short of the wall. She pressed her head against the plush, velvety wallpaper. A groan escaped her lips. How had it come to this? She placed her hands on either side of her, leaning further into the wall. She pushed off, not away, but just far enough so she could raise her head to the painting above her. To King Lancelot Allessien's portrait.

"How did you do it, Father?" she asked. Her fingers curled, scratching at the wallpaper. "How were you able to lose your sight, your power, your title, and still be happy for me?"

King Lancelot merely stared past her to the back of the throne room. The portrait had been painted during the peak of his reign when he still had his sight. His eyes resembled sapphires by the torchlight, glowing and glittering. He had platinum hair, the same as Extine, but the rest of his face—his nose, mouth, and cheekbones—reminded her of Pearl.

"Would you have approved of this?" Extine went on. She let go of the wall and trailed down the carpet until she met her father's eyes, until he stared into her soul.

Still no answer.

"If you had been alive today . . . If you had been alive when Pearl ran away . . . She was always your favorite. I was just crowned because of my eyes." Extine spoke without thinking, without realizing the insanity of it all. "How am I supposed to move on? My husband had a child with my sister, and if that wasn't enough . . . How am I supposed to forgive them? Their child stole my eyes from me. She stole my Remy's birthright!"

Extine looked to her father's side, to the portrait next to his. It was of a fair young woman, an innocent girl, a newly crowned queen. She had a smooth face, untainted by wrinkles, and wore her hair loose, a sign of carelessness and ambition. A sign of recklessness.

The plaque beneath it read, "Queen Extine Allessien. 149th ruler of Escana. Firstborn to King Lancelot

Allessien. Long live the queen, for as long as she lives, our kingdom shall thrive."

"For as long as she lives, our kingdom shall thrive," Extine recited. "How disappointed you must be in me, Father. I have lived for those words for the past eighteen years, but—"

Extine set her arms by her sides. She marched to the wall, to her father's portrait, and placed her fingers to his lips. She traced along the outline of his face, of the portrait's frame, and down the wall to its left, until she reached her own portrait's lips.

"But now," she resumed, "I realize I've been going at it all wrong. I was too soft." She pierced her forefinger through the portrait's left eye. "I was too eager to please the people, too blinded by love to have hunted Pearl down." The portrait's right eye followed next.

"Camilla will never know the pain that accompanies the power . . . She'll never understand . . ." Extine stepped back. Her hand was still raised, her fingers trembling. She lowered it, admiring her renovated picture: the fair young woman, the newly crowned queen. Without any eyes.

"Camilla Ward doesn't deserve the throne. Actually, neither does Remy. I'm the only one fit to rule." Extine took a breath to calm herself. She dabbed her forehead with her sleeve and adjusted her dress.

The throne room doors burst open, bashing against the walls and shaking the line of paintings.

They fell, one by one. Only Extine's remained. The one without eyes.

Remy and Milo waddled inside. They were carrying someone by their hands and feet.

Extine's heart leapt with excitement. They had done it. They had found Camilla, drugged her with Sorceress Juniper's potion, and brought her here.

Her plan had worked.

She parted her lips in praise, but they turned the person sideways, and her spirits fell.

It wasn't Camilla in their arms, but a boy. A tall, relatively handsome, unconscious young man.

They let him fall on the carpet. Remy groaned as she stretched out her back, and Milo mumbled something about how heavy the boy was.

They turned to face Extine.

"That's not Camilla," she said.

"No, it's not," Remy acknowledged with a touch of furstration. She rolled the boy onto his back with his hand crossed over his chest. He drooled a little on the carpet. "Mother, meet Logan Wheeler."

Extine pulled her shoulders into her neck. "And who, if I may ask, is *Logan Wheeler*?" She whistled through her teeth, struggling to keep her temper. She had sent them out to find Camilla, not some boy.

"Logan is Camilla's boyfriend."

"He's not technically her boyfriend," Milo corrected her, but she gave him a stern look, and he stepped back with a shrug.

"Anyway, he's the one we think she's used her power on," Remy continued.

Extine rubbed her temples. "When I told you to get close to the boy, I didn't mean you should capture him!"

"I know, but you don't understand." Remy shifted from one leg to the other. "Things were going exactly as planned. We had drugged them both at the bonfire, but it didn't affect Camilla. I had to improvise."

"*This* is improvising?"

"Actually, this was what we had to do when even improvising failed. I took the boy aside and seduced him while Milo and Fleur were with Camilla. She saw us, got angry, and they offered to take her away. Honestly, I don't know what the two imbeciles did wrong after that."

Extine turned to Milo. He had a guilty grin on his face, and his shoulders hunched in embarrassment.

"Well? What happened?"

Milo sighed. "Fine. We were on our way to Escana when, well, I kind of . . . we got lost in the forest."

Remy threw her hands in the air.

"You got lost?" asked Extine. "How did Camilla get away, then?"

"She kind of, maybe saw my sword, and," Milo looked from Extine to Remy, both of whom were properly fuming, "used her power on us." He shrank a little when he finished, as if expecting a blow to the head.

"See, Mother?" said Remy. "It wasn't my fault. I found them without Camilla and had to do what I could to salvage the plan. She likes this guy, so I figured we could use him."

"Use him?"

"Yeah, as bait."

"Bait?"

Remy nodded.

"You fools!" Extine made her hands into fists. She half ran, half stumbled down the carpet towards her children, pushed past them, and scoffed at Logan on the ground. "We don't have time to lay bait!"

"Mother, just listen—"

"No," Extine cut Remy off. "This is it. We're at the end of the line. The kingdom's doomed without the Allessien eyes." She tried to raise her voice, but broke into bloody, gurgling coughs. She covered her mouth, bent over and clutched at her knees, staring down at Remy's boots.

She just stood there, watching her suffer. Not even Milo rushed in her aid.

Extine cleared the blood around her mouth. She set her face and rose. They might ignore their mother, but they wouldn't dare disrespect their queen. "Take him to the dungeons. Have the guard prepare the same poison he did for the kayakers. This boy is of no use to us."

"Right away," said Milo.

Remy didn't comply as easily. "That's it?" she asked.

"What is?"

"You're just going to shoot down my idea like it's nothing? Like *I'm* nothing?"

Extine approached Remy. They were the same height now, mostly because she could no longer stand up straight. She came so close, their noses nearly touched, but Remy didn't wince.

"You're absolutely right. You are nothing. I'm the queen, and my word is law. Do you understand?"

Remy's cheeks inflated.

"Do I have to repeat myself?"

"I heard you just fine," Remy grumbled. Her eyes flicked across Extine's face. "Just remember, I'll be queen soon. And the moment we reclaim Camilla's eyes, I'll be the kingdom's savior, and my word will be law."

They stood in silence for a moment.

Extine tilted her head to the side. The throne room doors were slightly open, and servants ran up and down the corridor past it, preparing to flee before the borders collapsed. No one, save for the royal family, Sorceress Juniper, and Fleur knew about her stolen eyes, about Camilla. The head chancellor had requested Extine make an announcement, but she refused.

This wasn't the kingdom's problem. They didn't have to know, not before she had put things right.

"Despite what you think, you are not fit to be queen," Extine said. She turned around and paced up the carpet to her throne. She had to sit down before she collapsed again. The room was dark before her eyes, not because someone had blown out the candles, but because of her eyes. Seconds passed, and her sight returned—her seventh blind spell in the past hour. It was happening more and more frequently.

Sorceress Juniper was right.

"What do you mean I'm not fit?" asked Remy.

"I've given you more than a week to capture Camilla, yet you bring me her boyfriend as an excuse. You act like you're superior to everyone else—like your brother is your personal footman." Extine put her legs on the ottoman in front of her. She sat back in her throne and added, "A queen should be able to control herself, but you, my dear, are much too hotheaded."

"And you're not?"

"Enough, Remy." Extine swallowed, closing her eyes for a moment. When she opened them, Remy stood in front of her with one leg on the ottoman.

"Take the boy to the dungeons," Extine repeated.

Milo reached for his feet, but Remy showed her hand at him and he paused.

"Don't, Milo. Not yet." She yanked the ottoman out from under Extine's feet, and stepped closer. Her eyes were narrowed as she said, "You're powerless, Mother, and you know that. You're the one who's not fit to serve, not me. Even with whatever dark magic you have in your eyes, you're going to die soon, and I'll be next in line for the throne."

"Even if I die, you'll never have the eyes."

Remy spun around, pointing at the wall where the portraits used to hang. "I deserve to be up there! It's my birthright, even if some outsider stole it from me!"

"You can't be queen without the eyes," Extine told her. She could hardly hear herself above the white noise in her ears, but she knew she had to keep her composure. The illusion of confidence and control, of power.

"Of course I'll have the eyes." Remy's voice pitched. "You said they'll be mine."

Extine scrunched her nose.

"They're going to be mine, aren't they?"

"Would you have given them to me?" Extine didn't allow her an answer. "I was never going to give you the eyes. My reign's not over yet."

"You—lied to me?" Remy wheezed.

"Lied, misled, call it what you want. But as long as I'm still alive, the Allessien eyes will be mine."

"I can't believe this. It's just typical." Remy drew a knife from her boot. "I hate you!"

She pointed it at Extine, who hardly flinched. The tip of her blade touched Extine's nose.

Remy trembled, squeezing the knife with both hands. Her cheeks flushed and she bared her teeth.

Seconds passed in which neither of them moved.

"Why haven't you killed me yet?" asked Extine.

Remy strengthened her grip on the blade. The leather-encased handle crunched between her fingers.

"You hesitated," Extine added. "One should never hesitate."

"You can't do this to me," hissed Remy. "You can't rob me of the eyes. Not again."

"I'm afraid I just did."

Remy's mouth widened, and her face reddened. Extine expected her to boil over, to snap and slice down, but instead, she squeezed her eyes and groaned, lowering the weapon. She dropped the knife on the tiles. Its clatter echoed through the throne room and off the walls.

The sound was sharp and harsh. Deafening, almost.

"How did you become this wicked?" asked Remy. Tears

burned in her eyes. She still towered over Extine, kneeling on her lap.

"If you experienced everything I have, my dear, knew everything I know, you'd have turned out the same." She thought of Pearl, Finn, and Camilla. People were nothing but poison. "Go already. Make yourselves useful and take the boy to the foyer. Tie him up under the grand staircase and send a fleet of guards to Camilla's house."

"The grand staircase? I thought—didn't you say the dungeons?" asked Milo, still with Logan by the door.

"I've changed my mind." Extine forced a wicked smile. "I think we should give Remy's plan a whirl after all. We've got nothing to lose, right?"

Remy snorted and got off Extine's lap. She kicked the knife across the throne room, then turned on her heels and made a line for the exit. She stepped over Logan, pushed past Milo, and yanked open the throne room doors. They bashed against the walls again, and this time, the final painting—the painting of young Extine— tumbled down.

"Oh, and Remy," Extine called, "fetch Sorceress Juniper. Tell her to meet me here. The two of us will be taking matters into our own hands from now on." Remy didn't answer back, but Extine knew she heard her.

She'd do exactly as she said, for she had no other choice, no alternate duty than to obey the queen's orders.

"Do you need help with that, dear?" Extine watched Milo drag Logan by his feet. "I could summon a servant?"

"No, I'm fine." Milo shook his head and left. He didn't even bother to close the doors behind him, nor did he apologize for his sister's behavior. Both her children had changed, even if not in the same way.

Finn was gone, their father, and now their mother too. Their family was destroyed.

Extine worried, not about this, but because she couldn't bring herself to care.

CHAPTER TWENTY-TWO
CAMILLA

"So, my eyes have the power to *persuade* people and hide things from them?" asked Camilla, recalling what her parents had just told her. She pulled at a piece of thread in the couch. "And because I'm the first-born of the next generation, I'm the heir to the throne? Of a kingdom hidden from the outside world? The one you both are supposed to come from?"

Pearl and Finn bobbed their heads.

"This is a joke, right?" Camilla yanked at the thread and it snapped. She let it fall to the floor.

"We're not joking, darling." Pearl squeezed Camilla's thigh and sighed. "I know all of this might be difficult to believe, but you're in great danger. Extine wants her power back."

Finn agreed. He blocked the TV, and his features darkened. Pearl leaned past him to switch it off, and his face came to light. His forehead cracked into a frown. "Even I'm not sure what she's capable of anymore."

"Honestly," Camilla said, shaking her head. "If she wants my power badly enough to take Logan prisoner, I say we give her what she wants. Let her be queen and leave me out of it. I haven't even finished school yet."

"We can't do that," said Pearl.

"Why? I don't want the power. In fact, I've grown sick and tired of everyone commenting on my eyes."

"Because," said Finn, more seriously now. "Once the power exits your body, you go blind."

Camilla coughed.

Pearl placed a warm hand on her cheek. "That's how you received the power. Once the next heir becomes of age, all of the previous heir's power diminishes, and he or she loses their sight. When you turned eighteen, all of Extine's power went to you, and she went—"

The words stilled in Pearl's mouth. She let go of Camilla's cheek, turned to Finn and asked, "But, when I saw the two of you at the diner . . . she wasn't blind."

Finn rolled his thumbs. "That's part of the problem. When she lost her power, Extine, uh, summoned a sorceress who used dark magic on her."

"Dark magic?" Pearl gasped and got to her feet. "And? Did it work? Did she get her power back?"

"If she did, we wouldn't be in this mess."

"Right."

Finn looked beyond them. "Extine's changed. Not just on the outside, but on the inside as well. She's more reckless, more impulsive. And her eyes have turned black around the edges. They're like coal."

"Oh, Extine . . . What have you done?" Pearl said to herself, shuddering.

Finn comforted her by cupping her left shoulder. His free hand reached for her chin. Neither of them blinked, and neither of them spoke. They leaned into each other.

"Hey, we're still in the middle of something," Camilla ran her hands through her hair, combing out the knots from roots to tips.

Finn cleared his throat. He removed his hand from Pearl's shoulder. "The point is, Camilla, you can't return the power unless you're prepared to go blind."

Pearl hummed in agreement. "We have to get you out of here. I've saved up money to fix the water heater, but we can use it to get away from here."

"No, we're not leaving."

"Camilla—"

"Just listen. I've been treated differently my entire life. I thought it was all in my mind, that I was crazy, that there was something wrong with me. Now I know where I come from. My father's alive, and he's not some drug addict that's been in and out of prison his entire life.

"There's this boy I really like, and a big chance he might actually like me back. He was captured because of me. Because I didn't realize what was going on. I can't abandon him. I don't want him to end up like those kayakers."

"What are you saying?" asked Finn and Pearl at the same time. They exchanged a look, but quickly turned away again, like they were shy.

The sight of her parents together, possibly still in love, only spurred Camilla on.

"I won't let Logan die. We have to save him."

Finn shook his finger at her, exactly like a father. "No, you can't. That's exactly what they want."

"I know you think you understand it all, Camilla, but you don't know Extine," warned Pearl.

Camilla crossed her arms. Nothing they could say was going to change her mind. For the first time in her life, she had a purpose, something meaningful to do. "Here's how things are going to work, okay? Either you come with me by your own choice, or I use my power to persuade you. It's up to the both of you, so you'd better make the right decision."

Finn gave in first. He unzipped his hoodie to reveal a holster with a sword similar to Milo's. "I was controlled by Extine for eighteen years," he said. "I'm finally free, and I'd really like to stay that way."

"Mom? What do you say?"

Pearl looked from Camilla to Finn. She furrowed her brows and shrugged. "Well, all right. I guess it'd be good to see the old place again." Her tone at once turned somber. "Camilla, I just have to warn you about one thing. Just like Finn was under Extine's persuasion all those years, it might be possible that you've done the same thing to Logan."

Camilla didn't know what to say. She didn't want to confirm it, but she also couldn't deny it.

Might it be true? Did she persuade Logan into liking her without realizing it?

"No," she said. "Logan and I, we're . . ." What exactly? She recalled how easily Remy had seduced him.

Even if he was drugged or put under a spell, it still hurt all the same.

Camilla swallowed whatever uncertainty welled in her throat. She wanted to assure her parents that what she and Logan shared was real, when––

Thump, thump, thump.

Someone bashed on the front door.

"Open up in the name of Queen Extine Allessien of Escana! Surrender to us, and no one shall be harmed!"

"Guards," declared Finn as the bashing grew louder. "Extine must've sent them."

Camilla heaved. Everything suddenly became real. Her eyes. Her family. Logan's capture. "W—What do we do? Can't I put them in a trance?"

"No, we have to go. Now!" Finn ushered them down the hallway to Camilla's bedroom. He shut the door behind them, walked across the room, pushed up the window, and checked outside. When the coast was deemed clear, he ordered them to clamber out.

"It was you, wasn't it?" asked Camilla out of nowhere. Finn raised an eyebrow, and she explained, "That night. my mom and I fought, and I ran to my room. You were in here with me."

Finn nodded. "Camilla, I'm really sorry I scared you—"

"There's no time," Pearl interrupted.

Finn locked Camilla's bedroom door. He dragged her bed in front of it and tipped over her dresser to obstruct the way.

Pearl pushed Camilla out the window. The fall wasn't far, but it hurt all the same. She plummeted on the lawn, flat on her back and without any breath.

Pearl jumped out after her.

Finn ran to the window, climbed outside, and shut it behind him. With his sword clutched between his teeth and his hoodie hung around his elbows, he dove onto the ground, landing beside Camilla and Pearl.

"Come," he said. "I've bought us some time, but we have to get out of here." He held his sword in front of him, leading them to the street.

Camilla looked to their driveway. The fleet of guards had broken down their front door. Anger bubbled inside of her, a desire to confront them for destroying her home.

"Camilla!" Pearl hissed, and Camilla followed.

They ran in the direction of the lake, although Finn soon swerved away from it. They crossed the highway and entered the forest, heading the same way Milo and Fleur had taken Camilla. The sounds of civilization diminished, replaced by the songs of owls and beetles. "Where are we going?" she asked when she could no longer hold it in. "Isn't the kingdom on the lake?"

"It is," Finn replied without stopping. He sounded hardly out of breath, whereas she and Pearl huffed in his wake. For the first time, Camilla was grateful she had chosen track as a sport. She might've passed out already if she hadn't. "But the entrance to Escana is this way."

Minutes passed, and when Camilla finally ran out of fuel, they stopped. She crouched, steadying herself against a tree. She heaved and coughed, fighting for breath. How queenly of her. How absolutely elegant.

Once she had gathered enough saliva to at least swallow, she rose and looked around.

They were in the middle of somewhere and nowhere, deep inside the forest. A tall rock towered in front of them.

"Is this it?" she asked, squinting in the dark.

"Yep."

A crow screeched somewhere in the trees. The wind shook the branches, showering them in leaves. Camilla surveyed the ground. Footprints led from the trees to a narrow opening in the rock. She didn't understand this at first, but the moment she realized, she gulped.

"Ladies first," sang Finn, bowing at her.

"What about you, Mom?" asked Camilla.

"Fine, I'll go," Pearl yielded. She walked up to the rock, turned on her side, and shimmied into the opening. Once her entire body had disappeared, Finn glanced at Camilla.

"W—What if I don't fit?" she asked.

"I fit."

Camilla had no comeback. Finn was, indeed, much larger, broader, and taller than her. He had a chiseled jaw, high cheekbones, and silvery scruff—everything she had always imagined her father to look like. A manly man, like Logan.

Finn beckoned Camilla to the opening in the rock. He showed her how to enter and guide herself through, then stepped aside. Camilla glanced at him a final time. He grinned at her. "Go on, it's fine."

Camilla held her breath and shut her eyes as she entered, shimmying as quickly as possible.

Halfway through, light spilled onto her face. She opened her eyes and moved towards it, exiting into a whole new world she never knew existed. The first thing she saw was the castle on the lake. It was real.

"Beautiful, isn't it?" Pearl placed a hand on Camilla's back.

"Amazing." She focused on keeping her mouth from dropping open. "Mom, why did you crumple my drawing?"

Pearl hesitated. "I guess I was, well, scared." She rubbed her elbow.

"How could you be scared of such a beautiful thing?"

"Sometimes the most beautiful things are the most dangerous." Pearl stared up at the castle, at its towers and windows and balconies. "I didn't know if I'd be able to protect you."

"Perhaps I don't need your protection."

Pearl's eyes watered.

"Don't worry, mom, I'll always need you," Camilla added and squeezed her mother's hand. "But as support. Backup, you know." She let go of Pearl's hand and wandered across the grass to the courtyard. They were within the castle walls, but beyond it, up the slope, lay a stretch of buildings, houses, and shops. The castle shimmered under the almost pinkish-purple moonlight. Lanterns surrounded the courtyard, a stone square bedazzled with statues of soldiers on horses.

An arrangement of pillars led to the castle steps, around each of which twirled a grapevine.

"This way," announced Finn, breaking the spell. He wielded his sword and motioned for them to follow. "Nobody knows we're here, but Extine might have taken precautions."

Pearl grabbed Camilla's hand again. Without letting go, they followed Finn up the steps to the open crystal door. He gestured for them to wait as he peered around it, then showed his thumb at them. They entered the castle into a corridor with black-and-white steps. The curtains were drawn, and torches lined the wall, withering in the breeze from outside.

"Stay close to me."

Camilla attempted to silence her stride, but it was difficult as her sandals had a raised heel. Voices echoed from around the corner, and Finn stopped.

He placed a finger in front of his mouth, but Camilla couldn't help her shoe from scraping against the tiles.

"Ye heard that?" asked the first voice. He approached the corner, rattling with every step.

"All I'm hearing is that armor of yours," replied the second voice. "I can't believe you're actually wearing it. Unless we're at war with the outsiders like they say, I doubt you'll need it."

The first voice scoffed. "Ha! Don't come cryin' to me when ye're killed. I don't trust anythin' that goes on anymore. Last I heard, the queen captured a third outsider, another boy."

"Either she's looking for someone specific, or she's got some strange fetish. Is the boy still alive?"

"Well, no one's been tasked with disposin' his body yet, so I suppose so. I won't be surprised if he's dead tomorrow." The guards snickered, and their footsteps trailed off.

One of them said something else, but their voices clashed with their clattering armor.

"They're headed to the gates," said Finn. He waited a moment before he set off down the corridor again.

"Where are we going?" whispered Pearl.

"To the dungeons." Finn slowed as they approached the corner. He peered around it, and when it proved safe, they moved on. "I think that's where Extine would've taken him."

Camilla hiccupped. "The dungeons?" The thought of Logan in a dark, wet cell twisted her stomach and tied her throat in knots. She thought about every movie she had ever seen, about people locked up in chains, forced to eat stale bread and drink water from the same bucket they defecated in.

Logan must be terrified. If not terrified, angered and confused. And it was all because of her.

It was her fault he was in there.

"Do you think those guards are right?" she dared to ask. "She wouldn't have killed him already, would she?"

No answer.

They were about to turn another corner when Finn held out his arm and stopped them again. Camilla blew into her cheeks, afraid to so much as exhale. Pearl squeezed her hand.

"I think someone's coming," declared Finn.

"Then you'd better hide," said a voice behind them, and Camilla yelped. It was the shrillness, the bitterness of the voice that gave away its owner.

"Remy," said Finn.

"Dad?" Remy uncrossed her arms. She looked the three of them over, one by one, and like that day in the theatre, she paused a on Camilla. She pulled up her nose and asked, "What are you doing sneaking around in the dark? And why are you doing it with these two?"

Finn scrambled for an answer.

"Are you helping them?"

Pearl pushed Camilla behind her. "He is," she said. "Hello again, Remy. I'm Pearl, your aunt. I would say I'm pleased to officially meet you, but I'm afraid our circumstances are of a different tenor."

"The feeling's mutual, believe me."

"What did you do with Camilla's friend?"

Remy shrugged. "Tossed him in the dungeons. I can take you there if you'd like?"

Camilla stepped out from behind Pearl. She turned to Finn, who looked like he was about to throw up. She placed a hand to his chest. "No, Dad. We can't trust her."

"*Dad?*" spat Remy.

Finn turned a shade paler.

"Wait. You're Camilla's father? You're the one who broke the law and stole Mother's eyes?"

Still no answer.

Camilla half expected Remy to burst into flames and

call for the guards, but instead, to everyone's surprise, she burst out laughing.

She laughed so hard tears rolled down her cheeks.

"What's so funny?" snapped Camilla.

"That witch deserves it. All of it." Remy wiped under her eyes. Some mascara came off on her finger, but she didn't seem to care. "She betrayed me. She promised me your eyes but went back on her word. It's only fitting she should lose her husband along with her children."

"Remy!" snapped Finn.

"What? Am I wrong, Dad?"

Finn couldn't answer.

"I thought so." Remy surpassed them and turned the corner. She called out, "Are you coming, or what?" When they hesitated, she added, "If we don't hurry, your boyfriend might die."

CHAPTER TWENTY-THREE
CAMILLA

Camilla had her reservations about Remy's sudden cooperation, but she nonetheless followed her through the castle. She really did seem angry with Extine, and she wouldn't dare doublecross her own father, would she?

They rounded a corner into a much narrower, much darker corridor. It looked abandoned at first, but upon closer inspection, she noticed a thick wooden door at the end, guarded by two armored soldiers. The moment they noticed them incoming, they crossed their spears.

"I thought all the guards had gone to the walls?" asked Pearl.

"Extine must really want to keep folks out of there." Finn licked his lips, glanced at Camilla, and added, "Or keep someone inside."

"Logan," she breathed and fled forward, but Remy pushed her back against the wall. All air was forced from her lungs, and she wheezed.

"Stay behind me. Let me handle this, all right?" Remy ordered, much too confidently. She raised her chin and marched down the corridor to the guards.

They straightened. "Evening, Your Highness," they said, tilting their heads. One of them noticed Finn behind her. "Evening, Captain."

"Is something the matter?" the other guard asked.

"No, everything's fine." Remy took a step forward and touched the guard's wrist, tracing it with her finger. "Well, now that you ask . . ." She bit her bottom lip. "Could you possibly make way for us?"

The guard cleared his throat. "I—I'm afraid we're not p—permitted to, Your Highness."

Remy's smile faded, and she yanked away. "As the crown princess, I order you to let us pass!"

The second guard interjected, "As he said, it's simply not possible. Her Majesty Extine gave us orders to deny access to anyone except the queen herself."

"What about me?" asked Finn. He brandished the Captain's badge on his sash. "I'm your commanding officer. I hereby relieve you of your duties."

"No one except for the queen herself," the guards repeated. "Our greatest apologies, Captain."

Remy stomped her foot. "Listen, you buffoons! I'm the firstborn and heir to the throne. Make way."

Still nothing.

"Camilla," hissed Remy. "You know what to do."

"Hold on," Pearl chimed in. "Camilla mustn't use her power for personal gain. You should know that."

Camilla slinked out from behind Pearl. "Logan's in

there," she said as respectfully, yet sternly as possible. "I'm doing this for him, not myself." And before Pearl could pose any objection, she turned to the guards.

Remy and Finn stepped aside.

"Camilla, are you sure about this?" asked Finn.

Camilla nodded. She swallowed a final time, then spoke in the best Remy impersonation she could manage. "Do it. Do what the princess said, and let us pass. *Right now.*"

The guards did nothing—said nothing. They just stood there, frozen without reacting.

Camilla waited for them to burst into laughter. Seconds passed, and when they still didn't move, she shrugged. She must not have been as in control of her power as she thought.

"Right away, Miss," said one of the guards, and she spun back around. "Sorry for the inconvenience."

The guards uncrossed their spears. One of them flipped through a ring of keys. He popped the correct one in the lock, twisted it twice, and opened the door.

"You did it," Remy muttered.

The second guard held open the door for them. The stairway to the dungeons was dark, lit only by a line of nearly burnt-out torches. A dankness filled the corridor, the smell of wet towels and mothballs.

"Thank you," said Camilla as they entered.

"Reel it in, Miss Goody Two-Shoes," Remy snorted.

They padded down the steep flight of stairs. Remy removed a torch from the wall and held it above her head.

A chamber awaited at the bottom of the stairs, lined with cells. Logan was nowhere to be seen.

"I don't understand," said Remy. She extended the torch, so it lit the cell to her right. Its interior consisted of a bunk bed, a bucket, and a tray of old food. Flies zoomed around it, and water dribbled down the walls from the ceiling. "He was supposed to be right here."

"This is where you wanted to keep him?" asked Camilla with disgust. How revolting, how absolutely merciless. She turned, frowning at her parents. "This is where you keep all of your prisoners?"

Pearl shrugged. Her lips parted to say something—to explain, perhaps—but Finn cut her off. "Logan might not have deserved it, but most of the people in here do. That man over there"—he pointed to a chained-up prisoner—"murdered three young girls." A pause before he continued, "And the one next to him, he set fire to his neighbor's fields. The poor farmer has nothing left to feed his family with. No crops and no money."

"Well, why did he do it?"

"Some dispute over a dried-up well, but my point is, these are bad people."

Camilla studied the grimy floors, bars and walls. "But, with living circumstances as horrible as these, how will any of the prisoners be rehabilitated?"

"Rehabilitated?" scoffed Remy. "I don't know how prisons work on the outside, but in here, everyone's executed. Thieves, murderers, traitors . . ." She glanced sideways at Pearl.

Camilla clapped her hand to her mouth. She surveyed

the scrawny men with beady eyes and pale faces. Some of them—she could tell by their long beards and skeletal bodies—had been in there for a long, long time. They wore nothing short from rags and had little to no water.

"This is wrong," she said.

"It's a good thing you're not queen, then," said Remy.

Finn held up his hand to quiet them. He looked at the ceiling, at the vents in the walls.

"What is it?" asked Camilla.

"Don't you hear that?" he asked.

Camilla shut her eyes and listened. Someone, a boy, was calling from somewhere in the castle.

"Help, anybody! Help me!"

"Where is that coming from?" asked Pearl. She strolled along the wall, stopping directly under one of the ventilators. "There, that one! It leads to the foyer, Finn, doesn't it?"

He nodded.

"It's him," Camilla said, recognizing his voice. She withheld herself from jumping and up and down with relief. "It's Logan! He's up there in the foyer!"

"He's still alive." Finn sighed in relief.

"Well, come on!" Camilla was the first of them to set off up the stairs again. As much as she wanted to fight for the prisoners' better treatment, she tuned out their cries, focusing instead on the one cry she couldn't bear to ignore. Logan was in trouble and needed her help.

She found them on the opposite end of the castle. Remy took them on a detour upstairs, and Camilla couldn't help but gawk at the pristine bedrooms, lounges, and view of Escana from the floor-to-ceiling windows in the corridor. Lights flickered for miles in every direction, almost blending together with those of Crystalvale, but separated by a line.

An invisible border.

Logan's cries briefly died down, but the moment they went downstairs, his voice dialed up again.

"Logan!" Camilla shouted.

"Camilla?" came Logan's voice.

"Logan, where are you?"

"Camilla! Get help!"

Pearl wrapped an arm around Camilla and held her hand to her mouth, dulling her cries. "Hush up, will you? You'll wake the entire castle."

"No worries," Remy assured her. "Everyone's out looking for her. My mother's somewhere with Sorceress Juniper. No one should hear anything."

Pearl didn't let go of Camilla. "Why would they just leave a prisoner unattended like that?"

But her question went unnoticed.

They arrived at the bottom of the stairs in the foyer. Paintings of the Escanian landscape extended down the walls, each valley and hill connecting with that of the next artwork. The front doors were made of murky crystal, and their feet sank into the carpet as they walked.

"Camilla!" shouted Logan a final time.

Camilla wrestled herself free. "Logan!"

His voice was right there, right behind her, under the staircase. She pushed past Remy and rounded the stair-case to the hollow underneath. It was dark and musky, but the scent of Logan's aftershave revealed his presence. Good old mint and pine. Camilla reached out and felt her way around. She found Logan was tied up against the wall.

"We need a light!" she cried.

Remy held the torch above her head.

Logan jerked when he saw her and bashed his head against the bottom of the stairs. Camilla held him still as she used Finn's knife to cut the ropes.

"You can't trust her!" shouted Logan the moment he was free. He pulled Camilla next to him.

"It's okay," she said, swallowing the doubt that welled in her throat. "She helped us find you."

Pearl and Finn joined Remy, and Logan relaxed. Camilla helped him up and out of the staircase's hollow. Once he stood, he grabbed Camilla's shoulders and looked her in the eyes. He spoke fast and vigorously as if she might run off at any moment. "Camilla, about what had happened at the lake," he swallowed. "That wasn't me . . . well, it was me . . . but it must've been that drink they gave me. I was fine one moment, and—"

"It's okay," said Camilla, stilling him. Her gaze lowered to his lips. His hands were still on her shoulders, squeezing them. She wanted to hug him, have him hold her and kiss her and tell her everything was going to be all right, but instead, she stepped back, away from him.

"We have to go," interrupted Remy.

Pearl agreed. "We have to get out of here, get a car, and drive someplace far away."

Finn looked as if he wanted to say something—to contest this—but Remy agreed for the both of them.

Naturally, she'd agree. With Camilla gone, she'd be first in line for the throne again.

"Come on, follow me," she said. "I know a shortcut."

Logan hesitated, but Camilla grabbed hold of his hand and interlaced her fingers with his. She tightened her grip, and he smiled at her. They might have stayed like this for a couple more minutes, but Finn and Pearl both turned around, scrutinizing them as only parents did.

Camilla blushed, and Logan let go of her hand.

Finn grabbed Logan by the shoulder and ushered him off while Pearl did the same with her. "Don't think I'm letting you out of my sight," she said.

"What's going on?" Logan finally asked. "Why would someone want to capture me? Where are we?"

"There's no time to explain," Pearl answered before Camilla could. If she did, she might have told him everything. About her parents, her aunt, the transfer students, and her eyes. Camilla swallowed. Her eyes.

Up to that moment, she had forgotten about what her mother warned her about. She snuck a glance at Logan, and his eyes flicked towards her, almost as if she had compelled him to. Sourness flushed her mouth.

All she could do was swallow it and move on.

The castle only darkened the farther they ran. The curtains were all drawn, leaving no moonlight to filter into the corridor. The torches on the walls hissed and smoked, having died quite some time ago. Their only light was Remy's torch, a lump of glowing coal on a stick.

"Remy, where are we going?" asked Pearl.

"This is not the way out," Finn said.

Remy heeled in her tracks. The torch sputtered, scattering ashes at them. Darkness enveloped them. She dropped the torch on the floor.

"It's funny, really," she said, hushed now.

"What is?" asked Finn.

Remy's voice trailed down the corridor in the dark. Pearl and Finn followed after it, but Camilla stayed with Logan. She reached for his hand, but he wasn't there.

"Logan?" she whispered.

"I'm right here." He grabbed her wrist and pulled her after her parents, after Remy.

"What's so funny?" Pearl repeated.

"The two of you grew up in this place, right?"

"Yeah?" said Finn.

"Well, it's funny how you only now realized we weren't on our way out. When we were already there."

Pearl huffed. "Where?"

"Here!" announced a woman with a strong voice. One by one, the torches on the wall lit up.

Camilla blinked vigorously.

They were in a room, a hall, a giant open area with a carpet down the middle and a throne at the end. Several potted plants were arranged throughout the room, all wilted and black—likely from a lack of sunlight.

A woman sat on the throne, dressed in a black gown. A veil hid her face.

"Extine," hissed Pearl.

Another woman stood next to Extine. She was the

spitting image of Fleur, with dark skin, golden eyes and curly markings across her face.

"Remy, why did you bring us here?" asked Finn.

Remy walked down the length of the carpet. She only spoke once she reached the throne. "I'm sorry, Dad. To be honest, I never signed up for a sister."

They all turned for the door, but the sorceress wove her hand, chanted several foreign words, and they banged shut.

"Extine, let us out!" Pearl demanded.

Extine rose to her feet. "Ah, my dearest sister. I'm afraid you're not going anywhere. Not until I've gotten back my eyes."

CHAPTER TWENTY-FOUR
EXTINE

"Oh, Extine," said Pearl, softly. She was in her waitress uniform, and her hair stood in several directions, but despite her dismal appearance, she spoke in a way that demeaned Extine, belittled her. A tone of disappointment. "What happened to you?"

"You did, Sister," replied Extine. She removed the veil, slowly, so she could relish Pearl's reaction. "You did this to me. You and your miscreant daughter."

Finn stepped in front of Pearl and Camilla. He held out his hand to protect them, to keep them from approaching her. The sight of it—of him, caring so much for a traitor and a thief—sickened Extine. She strutted down the carpet towards them, her eyes glued to Camilla.

That blue. That gloss.

Those were her eyes all right, the eyes of the firstborn child.

"Is this how it is now?" sang Extine. She stopped halfway down the carpet. "You abandoned us, your family of eighteen years, for a waitress and your illegitimate daughter?"

Remy scoffed in Extine's aid.

"Where's Milo?" asked Finn, looking about the throne room. "What exactly does he know?"

"Enough to keep him out of this," said Extine. "But once all of this is over, I'll make sure he knows exactly what type of man you are, Finn Rawd. He'll never look up to you again."

Finn gritted his teeth. His foot inched forward on the carpet, but he restrained himself, held himself back. "Remy, I know you're angry. I understand why you might hate me, but Pearl and I—we were together before your mother and I. Before we were even married."

"Do you still love her?" asked Remy with crossed arms.

Finn shut his eyes and inhaled deeply. "I can't lie to you, Remy." His hand reached for Pearl's, and they shared an askance glance. "I do still love her."

"And just like that, you're dead to me."

"I understand." Finn's eyes glazed with tears. He took Camilla's hand as well, and they faced Extine down the carpet. "We're not afraid of you. You have no more power." His eyes swerved to Sorceress Juniper. "And that witch can only perform unstable dark magic."

"No more power, eh?" Extine cocked her head at him. She let out a giggle and said, "Move aside, Captain! Let me take a good look at my niece. Or should I say my *step-daughter*?" She narrowed her eyes at him, and Finn's arms snapped against his sides.

Finn's face was painted with resistance. He inched to the side, little by little, each movement forced.

Extine's eyes no longer affected his mind and heart, but his body seemed more than willing to comply. Finn's inches became giant strides, and he reached the wall, still stiff as a board.

"That's better."

Extine resumed her walk down the carpet. Sorceress Juniper trailed closely behind her, followed by a hesitant Remy. She surveyed Camilla from top to bottom. She didn't look like a Camilla and certainly wasn't at all what Extine had imagined. She had expected long, platinum hair like herself, a slightly fuller figure, and someone not quite as . . .

Shy.

Camilla, instead, had light hazel tresses. She was tall, but not too tall, and skinny, but not lanky.

"What do you want from me?" Camilla demanded. Her voice pitched, but her face remained serious.

Extine couldn't help but laugh aloud. Such confidence. Such innocence. Such a stupid thing to ask. She clearly knew next to nothing about what was going on, and it was almost endearing.

"Isn't it obvious?" She paused, not just for dramatic effect but to steady herself. She gripped the netting of her dress and forced her face into a smirk. "I want your eyes, dear child."

Camilla took a step back, right into Logan. He grabbed her and pulled her behind him. His teeth showed—two rows of pearly whites, perfectly straight. Sporty, brave, committed, and handsome. He might have been a good fit for Remy if he wasn't aligned with the other side.

"Oh, sweet, sweet, Camilla," Extine cooed. Her smile at once faded. "He doesn't love you!"

Camilla swallowed hard but didn't at all seem surprised. Extine looked at Pearl, who just stood there chewing her lip. It was written across their faces, obvious and for everyone to see.

"You told her then, eh?" asked Extine.

When Pearl made no reply, she resumed, "He only thinks he loves you because your eyes persuaded him to. It's all because of your eyes; those pretty, pretty eyes." A pause. "It's just like with Finn. He never loved me! And he only married me because of my eyes!"

Remy took several steps forward. She stopped short of Extine. "Mom, is that really true?"

"I'm sorry you had to find out this way. If you want to blame someone," Extine pointed at Pearl, "blame her. If Pearl hadn't gone off and had a baby in secret, everything would have been fine. I would still have my eyes, and your father would still love me.

"I never planned on getting pregnant, Extine." Pearl leapt forward, one eye on Extine and the other on Sorceress Juniper. Her voice lowered. "And I never wanted to leave Escana."

Extine gnawed on her teeth.

"I only left because I had to. I knew that if I let my child live, you'd kill her. I left because Finn was supposed to marry you and because I knew I could never be happy while he was with you."

"So, what? You think what you did was selfless? Giving me the husband and giving me the throne?" Extine snorted. "You weren't being selfless. You were being self-ish!" She turned to Camilla, still hidden behind Logan. "You stole my eyes! You stole my husband! You don't deserve the Allessien power . . . you deserve a loveless life of blindness!"

"You'll never have my eyes!" shouted Camilla.

Extine winced at her sudden burst of confidence. Perhaps Camilla wasn't the pushover she made herself out to be. Either way, she still wasn't worthy of inheriting the Allessien eyes.

Of becoming Queen of Escana.

She placed her hands on her hips. "Oh, what a child you still are," she tutted. "I'm not asking, thief."

Extine clicked her fingers, and Sorceress Juniper reacted. She moved quickly down the carpet, like a feather in the breeze, launching at Camilla. And before Logan or Pearl or anyone could do anything, she put her hand over Camilla's eyes and plucked out her power.

It emerged as a ray of light—bright blue and beaming —that illuminated the entire throne room.

Extine shielded her eyes from it. She peeked a little through her fingers, basking in its magnificence. The great Allessien power. The power that had protected Escana for centuries, concealed it from the outside world. Her father's power. Her grandmother's power.

Her power.

Sorceress Juniper uncorked an empty vial and dropped the power inside. It somewhat resembled a jellyfish, squirming and lapping at the glass. She replaced the cork and retreated to Extine's side before either Pearl or Logan could grab a hold of it in her hand.

Extine licked her lips. She took another look at Camilla's eyes, now pale grey, almost white.

"W—What have you done to me?" she asked, looking all around her. A tiny shriek escaped her mouth, followed by a frantic panting. She stumbled into Logan, who clutched her by the wrists to balance her, to calm her. "I—I can't see anything. I've gone blind!"

Camilla fell to her knees. She kept her head down and her hands on the carpet, grabbing at it.

"Mom, where are you? Mom!"

Pearl fell next to her. She took her face in her hands and kissed her forehead, over and over. "There, there," she said, consoling her. "It's all right. I'm here. I'm right here with you."

Logan remained aloft.

"It's almost painful, really," said Extine after a while. "Watching someone's heart shatter." She turned sideways and clicked her fingers. "Finn, darling, I order you to watch this. Watch as your daughter's heart is ripped to shreds . . . just like you had done to mine."

Finn resisted against it, but his neck automatically craned. Tears pooled in his eyes as he watched Camilla sob into Pearl's neck. She felt around on the ground and touched under her eyes. She briefly looked his way but showed no response, no recognition.

Extine chuckled under her breath. She relished the shock on his face, the hurt between his brows.

"Extine," said Finn through gritted teeth. A tear spilled over onto his cheek, but he huffed, blowing it away. "Why are you doing this? Camilla's done nothing wrong."

Extine chose not to answer. While Camilla had done nothing wrong, she also hadn't done anything right. She didn't even try to defend herself against Sorceress Juniper, to protect her eyes. If the power was that important to her, she would have defended it with her life.

"And now, Camilla, you'll see that I was right. No person with the Allessien eyes can ever experience true love." Extine almost laughed. She waited for Logan to step over Camilla and leave after realizing that he had been under Camilla's persuasion the entire time.

But he didn't.

"Why aren't you leaving?" she snapped at him. "She's a fraud. A thief. Just leave already!"

Logan started. "C—Camilla," he stuttered. "Did she just —was that—how are you blind?" He turned and called out to Finn. "Why are you standing there? Come and help!"

When Finn didn't respond, Logan cursed aloud and fell to his knees. He grabbed Camilla's hands and squeezed them as he spoke into her ear, "Camilla, I don't know what's going on, and I don't know what that woman just did to you, but I'm here. I'm always here."

Camilla relaxed. She looked up at him with her blank, greyish eyes, and he jerked ever so slightly.

Extine rubbed her hands together. This was it. He was realizing what a wreck she was, what an absolute liability. Any moment now, he was going to let go of her hand and run off.

Any moment.

"Logan, please," Camilla said in between silent tears. "You mustn't see me like this. Just go"—Extine nodded—"before my power wears off on you. Before you realize what a loser I am."

"You better listen to her, Logan," Extine sang.

"What are you talking about? What power?" asked Logan, tightening his grip on her left hand. He took her right one as well. "And I already know what a loser you are, Camilla."

Disappointment filled her otherwise empty eyes.

"That's why I like you so much."

"Y—You like me?"

"*You like her?*" Extine repeated and, to her greatest horror, she watched as Logan leaned in and kissed Camilla. They stayed that way for several seconds, brandishing their love for each other, a love that wasn't supposed to exist. Extine frantically waved her hand at Sorceress Juniper. "Hand me that vial!"

Sorceress Juniper handed it over. "It's a quick sip, Your Majesty. A single swallow, in other words."

"I know what to do, you imbecile!" Extine uncorked the vial and brought it to her lips, but before she drank, she took another look at Logan and Camilla. He wiped his thumb under her eyes, and she smiled. Smiled, even when her power had just been taken from her.

Her sight.

It didn't make sense. Shouldn't be possible.

"Drink it," pressed the Sorceress. "Drink it now, Your Majesty. Before it evaporates from the vial."

Extine raised the bottle again, but this time, Pearl caught her eye. She was looking at Finn, mouthing her love to him, her apology for failing their daughter. Finn nodded back, likely saying it's okay, and that they had failed together. Even though they had been apart for eighteen years, they were a family. Their love was stronger than time, stronger than separation.

No, Extine thought to herself, *just drink already*. But she couldn't help herself. She turned her head to Remy, shut her eyes, and thought of Milo. Her children, the only ones she never had to persuade to love her. Like Pearl, she had failed them. She had failed to protect them from the truth, from heartbreak. Milo still didn't know, but he'd find out soon enough.

For the first time in days, her eyes welled up with tears. It didn't burn or tingle or hiss in any way. Her stomach didn't cramp, and there was no bitterness under her tongue.

"Why are you smiling?" she asked Camilla before she could stop herself.

Camilla raised her head. Even though she couldn't see a thing, she looked Extine straight in the eyes. "Why shouldn't I smile? I'm happy. For the first time in my life, I have both my parents, and I finally know why I always felt so different from everyone else. I have a guy whom I really, really like, and who actually likes me back. Even without my eyes."

"B—But what about the power? Aren't you wrecked without it?"

"No. I didn't know about the power for eighteen years of my life. I think I'll manage without it."

"So . . . you don't *want* it?"

"I don't need it."

Extine had nothing to say to this. Camilla had just lost her sight, her power. She was supposed to be a miserable wreck, not happy. She was supposed to be alone and rejected, not loved. She thought back to when her father had lost his sight. He too had smiled, had rejoiced in the fact that Extine would be crowned queen. He had been surrounded by family.

Surrounded by love.

Extine replaced the cork and lowered the bottle. She couldn't do it. She couldn't steal an innocent girl's eyes. Camilla was something, someone, she had always wanted to be: a true Allessien heir. She looked from Camilla to Pearl, and a tear trailed across her cheek.

Camilla was the spitting image of Pearl, both inside and out. They held on to each other, even amid crisis. Neither of them shouted, and neither of them cursed. She sniffed. Her younger sister was always more collected. More responsible and more attractive.

"This is not you, Extine," said Pearl, almost as though Extine had spoken her thoughts aloud.

Extine's first reaction was to sneer, but she managed to hold her tongue. She whispered, "I'm so sorry, Pearl." After that, the words just spilled out. "I'm sorry that you had to hide your pregnancy from me and that I was such a horrible sister you thought I'd—*kill* your baby. You deserved the crown just as much as I did. We're sisters, blood, and no law should tell us who may give birth first."

Extine approached Pearl, and they took hands. Sorceress Juniper muttered something behind them, but Extine ignored her. She handed over the vial with Camilla's power.

"Here," she said, folding Pearl's palm. "Camilla's the rightful heir, no matter how it came to be."

"Thank you," said Pearl. She turned and took Camilla's hand. She placed the vial upright in her palm, exactly as Extine did, and uncorked it for her. "Drink up, darling."

Camilla fiddled with the vial. She brought it to her mouth, parted her lips, and was just about to drink when Remy charged past Extine and grabbed it from her.

"No!" she shouted, raising it above her head. "It's not her birthright! It's not her power!"

"Remy, what are you doing?" asked Extine. She attempted to snatch back the vial, but Remy was too quick. She yanked it away and ran up the carpet to the throne, where no one could reach her. She clambered on top of it, standing with each foot on an armrest.

"I was supposed to be the firstborn!" she shouted, stomping her foot. She nearly lost her balance and dropped the vial but hopped down onto the cushioning just in time. "I'm the rightful queen! Escana will be mine!" And with that, Remy gulped down the power.

The power slid whole down Remy's throat, almost as though she had swallowed an oyster. She tilted her head back and shut her eyes. Her lips parted, letting out a satisfied, "Ah . . ."

Extine was at a loss for words. She, along with everyone else, just stood there, not quite registering what just happened. She felt helpless, useless. Her every limb had gone numb, and shock rippled across her skin. She was confused, but not nearly as much as Camilla.

"W—What happened?" she asked, extending her hands. Pearl wrapped an arm around her shoulders and pulled her in. Logan gently touched her elbow. "Where's the bottle?"

No answer.

"I need my eyes. I need to see again."

"Extine," said Finn from the other side of the throne room. He gave her the type of look that required no words. She nodded at him, and he was free to run to Pearl and Camilla's side.

Camilla felt around through the air.

Finn took her hands, kissed them, and held them against his chest. He leaned in and placed a peck on her forehead. "Camilla, are you okay?" He turned to Pearl. "Is anyone hurt?"

"No," said Pearl.

"Camilla?"

"I'm—I'm fine. I just don't know what's happening."

"I reclaimed my rightful title as heir to the throne, that's what happened," announced Remy, at last lowering her head and opening her eyes. They changed just then from their normal glassy blue to a blue the shade of the ocean and with the sheen of polished crystal.

Extine made to approach her, but Remy raised a finger and tutted. She moved her head from side to side.

"No, Mother," she said. "Don't even try to reason with me. And don't think about scolding me either. Your rotten eyes are no match for mine. At last, you'll see what I'm worth."

Extine set her jaw. It pained her to see the scowl on her daughter's face. Her malicious smile and the hatred, absolute repulsion in her eyes. It was the very face she had seen in the mirror for the last eighteen years. A face painted with bitterness. With hot, steaming jealousy.

This was all her fault. She had made Remy into a monster. No, even worse. Into herself.

A lump lodged in Extine's throat when she looked at Pearl and Camilla, tightly squeezed together.

Camilla stared sideways at the wall. Pearl every now and then pushed loose hair from her face and wiped under her eyes. She put a hand on her cheek and pulled her in even more.

"Don't worry, darling, we'll fix this," she whispered.

Extine pried her eyes open. She refused to blink, as the moment she did, tears might stream across her cheeks.

In a way, all of this was her fault.

If she had just understood the truth sooner, the truth about family and absolute love, she wouldn't have angered Remy, and she wouldn't have destroyed a young girl's life.

It hurt just looking at them, at their undoubted support for each other. She longed for a bond like theirs. An unbreakable love, even after eighteen years of lies.

"Remy," she said, much to her daughter's irritation.

"What did I just say?"

"I'm your mother. Let me speak." Extine stepped towards her but stopped when Remy leapt down from the throne and ran down the carpet. Her hands were by her sides, balled into fists, and her boots rattled as she walked. Remy stopped less than a hand-width away from her.

"Get it over with already!"

Extine swallowed. "I know I haven't always set a good example."

"That's an understatement."

"And I know I haven't always been there for you—"

"Let me stop you right there. I don't want to hear any excuses or amends. You betrayed me, remember? You told me I could have the eyes, and then you took them away from me."

"And I'm really, really sorry about that."

Remy's eyes flared. "Oh, I bet you are!" She pursed her lips and tossed her hands out in front of her. "But just look at you, you're atrocious! No wonder your sister got your husband!"

"Remy!" snapped Finn.

"Just shut up," Remy commanded.

The flare in her eyes amplified—almost into a glow—and Finn shut up. Remy grinned when he did. She dusted off her hands and placed them on her hips. Her lips parted, but her upper lip began to twitch. She winced, reaching for her cheeks, then the corners of her eyes.

"Wow," she breathed. "These babies have quite the kick to them."

Extine frowned. A kick? She never experienced a kick. Well, she did, but only with her current eyes—the ones Sorceress Juniper had given her. And that was more a stab than a kick.

"So, as I was saying," continued Remy. She pressed a finger against Extine's chest, inching it up to her neck, face, cheeks, then eyes. Extine winced at the tenderness of her skin. She tried not to express any pain, but Remy only pressed harder, upping the difficulty.

A tiny groan escaped her lips.

"It's only a matter of time until you lose your eyes, Mother. Presumably the rest of your body as well."

"Stop fooling around already," hissed Extine under her breath.

"At last, something we can agree upon." Remy pushed Extine aside and approached Camilla. She stopped several paces off, staring at her with a mixture of pity and contentment.

"What's going on?" asked Camilla. "Why is everyone so quiet? Did something happen?"

Remy snickered. "It's funny if you think about it."

"What is?" asked Pearl in Camilla's place.

"I'm afraid only Camilla would understand. Step aside, Auntie!" Remy flicked her wrist, and Pearl let go of Camilla. "I was wary of you after that day in the music room."

Camilla looked up. Her eyes had a white gleam to them, a waxiness. A redness from all the crying.

"I thought you might be a difficult one, and, for a while, you really were." Remy gave two steps towards her. "But, in the end, you were weak. You ran when someone else kissed your crush and hesitated when you could have gotten your powers back. You could've controlled me like you had controlled those guards! You could've protected yourself."

Silence.

Remy grabbed Camilla's chin and yanked her closer. "The problem is I can't control you when you're blind, which means I'll have to find some other way to make you suffer."

"Suffer? For what?" Logan asked.

Remy suddenly smiled. "Yes . . . of course!" She smoothed back her hair and fluttered her lashes. "I'll have your boy toy for myself. After all, who'd want to go out with a blind girl?"

"I don't care if Camilla's blind. I'll always adore her for who she is."

"Oh, silly outsider, it's no longer your choice." Remy widened her eyes and raised her voice. "You love me. You feel nothing for Camilla except for pity."

"I—I—"

"You love me, and you feel nothing for Camilla."

"*I love you, Remy,*" said Logan, entranced.

Camilla wrapped her hands around his arm. She shouted into his ear, "Logan, don't look at her!"

"Come. Stand next to me." Remy motioned to her side. She made a triangle with her elbow for him to hook into and smiled. It wasn't a sincere smile nor was it one of seduction.

It was of pure contentment.

"Logan?"

"It's too late, Camilla Ward."

"I feel nothing but pity for Camilla." Logan left Camila's side. He showed no more resistance, no reservations.

The Allessien eyes were so powerful, his choice almost seemed willing. But Extine knew the truth better than anyone. The only thing was, from the outside, it seemed less triumphant. She never really noticed, never really saw, the cruelty in ripping two loved ones apart.

Just like she had done with Pearl and Finn.

"Logan, no!" shouted Camilla.

Remy held out her hands to receive Logan. He raised his, ready to take hers, when she balled them into fists and drew in her arms. She scrunched her face, squeezed her eyes, and doubled over, groaning in pain. Logan lowered his hands, no longer under her control.

"Ah!" shrieked Remy. The ground trembled, and the windows shook. The flask of water on the table next to the throne toppled over. "W—What's happening? What is this pain?"

Extine had no idea.

"Didn't this happen to you the other day?" asked Finn, but he was cut off by another of Remy's yelps.

"Yes, but that was because of the dark magic. Remy's eyes are real. It's not supposed to be like this."

"Make it stop!" shouted Remy, clutching the sides of her head. She got on all fours and crawled to Sorceress Juniper's feet. The sorceress merely looked down at her, at her suffering.

"Don't just stand there! Help me!"

"Help Your Highness do what?"

"Take my eyes out! Take them out, now!" Remy grabbed Sorceress Juniper around the ankles and pulled herself to her feet. "This pain . . . it's too much! You have to take the power out!"

Sorceress Juniper placed her palm over Remy's eyes, and just like she had done with Camilla, she plucked out the power and put it in another vial. She corked it, and Remy collapsed to her knees again. Sweat dribbled down her temples, and her entire body quivered.

The ground stilled, and the windows ceased their rattling. The toppled flask of water rolled off the table.

Crash.

"What on earth was that?" asked Pearl.

Sorceress Juniper shrugged. "I'm not sure. The power of the Allessien eyes is still quite the mystery. My best guess is that only the true heir possesses the capacity to carry the eyes' power."

Remy wiped across her eyes. She looked around, blinking vigorously. A wail even louder than before escaped her lips. She shouted, "My sight. I can't see anything!"

"That's the price of power, my dear." Sorceress Juniper stepped away from Remy and held out the bottle to Extine who frowned. "Does Your Majesty still want the power?"

"But—won't the same thing happen to me?"

"I don't think so," said the sorceress. "After all, Your Majesty possessed the power once before."

Extine took the bottle from Sorceress Juniper. She held it in her hand, finally, after weeks of waiting, of planning and suffering. It was hers for the taking, as easily as a single gulp. The vial was warm, emanating with power. She looked up at Camilla, at her waxed-over eyes.

Extine rubbed the cork with her thumb. She thought about when Remy had controlled Logan and the sickness she had felt in her gut. Nearly two decades had passed since she was crowned. Nearly two decades of being queen. All of that had come to an end, and whether she liked it or not, it was time for her to pass on the duty to someone else.

"No," she said. "Give it to the rightful heir."

Pearl rubbed Camilla's arms. She ushered her forward and lifted her palm so Extine could place the vial in her hand again. This time, Camilla didn't hesitate. She uncorked it, brought it to her mouth, and swallowed before anyone could snatch it from her again.

A deep breath escaped her lips, followed by an even deeper inhale. Like Remy, she raised her chin and shut her eyes. When she looked down again, Extine was met with bright blue.

Brighter than Remy's.

"I can see again," Camilla laughed. Her eyes burned with tears. She dropped the vial and wrapped both arms around Extine. She whispered in her ear, "Thank you so much."

"For what?"

"For making the right choice."

Extine pulled away. She had chills from their hug, not because it was bad, but because it was incredible. No one had hugged her—really hugged her—ever since her parents had died and her sister had run away. Not even Remy or Milo had hugged her like that.

"Don't ask me why I did it," joked Extine.

Pearl stepped forward and placed a hand on her shoulder. "You're a good person, that's why."

Extine briefly forgot all about what had happened. She forgot about the day she had lost her eyes and the day she had called upon Sorceress Juniper for dark magic. She forgot about the kayakers that penetrated the border and how she had disposed of them. She forgot about how she had tortured that chambermaid and how Finn had broken her heart.

All she felt was peace. Peace and joy and contentment. And she didn't use any power to feel that way.

The moment was short-lived, however, as Remy's sobbing amplified, and she called out, "Mom! Where are you? Mom!" She crawled around on her knees, a trail of tears in her wake.

"Please don't cry, Remy," said Extine. "That's my favorite carpet. We don't want it ruined by tears."

"That's not funny. I'm blind!"

Extine extended a hand at Remy who took it and got to her feet. She pulled her into a hug and let her cry into her neck. She placed her chin on her head and breathed in her hair. It smelled of the little girl she so often played hide and seek with outside.

"It's going to be okay," she assured her, but Remy only cried harder.

"What happens now?" asked Camilla.

Extine held on to Remy. She turned to Camilla and bowed her head. Pearl and Finn and Sorceress Juniper all did the same. Logan seemed confused for a second but quickly caught on.

"Now," said Extine, and she couldn't believe the rest of her sentence, "you will be crowned queen."

"Me? Queen?" asked Camilla. Her entire face grew so hot, beads of sweat surrounded her temples. "No way. I can't do it. I just turned eighteen this week!"

Pearl wiped a strand of hair from Camilla's face. "You're more than ready. You only need your eyes."

Camilla pulled away from her. She stumbled back into Logan, who wrapped his hands around her shoulders. His palms were coarse, but they had a warmth to them that soothed her.

"You can't refuse," said Extine.

Sorceress Juniper agreed. "Escana must be ruled by the bearer of the Allessien family eyes. Whether Your Majesty wants to or not, it's the way things have been for centuries."

Remy waved in front of her. "If she doesn't want to, she doesn't have to." She still held on to Extine but stood fully upright now. "Let me do it. I'll be queen, and she'll be at my command."

Camilla scoffed. Even after everything that had just happened, Remy was as power hungry as ever.

"Your command?" she asked. She had never looked a blind person in the eyes before and struggled to do so now. She kept searching for a sign of recognition, but there wasn't any.

"No." Extine cut off their conversation. "Camilla must be queen. It's her duty as the firstborn."

"My duty?" Camilla choked. "A few minutes ago, you were prepared to tear my life apart for the title!"

"I know, and I've come to my senses. Camilla, as the current queen, I order you to accept the title." Extine stomped her foot on the carpet, and at the same time, the throne room doors burst open.

Milo stood in the doorway. His hair, clothes, and shoes were soaked, and his chest pumped up and down. Camilla's breath snagged when she saw him. She recalled the incident in the forest when he had threatened her with a sword. He was less scary now, but still . . .

"Milo!" exclaimed Extine, almost as if she hadn't seen him for weeks. "Honey, are you all right?"

Milo countered her question with one of his own. He asked, "What happened here?" His eyes swerved across everyone in the throne room. He paused a moment on Logan and Camilla and completely stopped on Remy. "Sister . . . your eyes . . . are you blind?"

"What? What do you want, idiot?" snapped Remy, and he swallowed the rest of his inquiries.

Extine interjected, less hostile, "Milo, is something wrong?"

"Oh, right. Mom, Dad, you have to come outside this instant! The borders are breaking apart. And people, outsiders, have gathered around the lake. They can see Escana!" Milo made to say something else—perhaps comment on the peculiar position he had found them in—but Sorceress Juniper darted past him followed by Extine and Pearl and Finn.

"Milo, are you still there?" asked Remy, inching forward. Camilla stepped aside for her to pass.

"I am."

"Don't just stand there, then! Take me outside! And don't you dare let me walk into anything!" Remy found his ear and flicked it. She grabbed his arm and followed him into the corridor.

Camilla and Logan were the only ones left.

They stood there in silence, listening to the pattering of rain against the windows and Remy's shrieks as she tipped over a set of armor. Camilla hadn't noticed the rain until now, especially not with everything going on. The wind howled, tossing the trees against the castle.

"I think we should go," suggested Logan. His voice cut through the otherwise silent throne room.

"Do we have to?"

"You're what, the queen now?" he asked, raising an eyebrow. He visibly tried to hold it back but smiled anyway. "As crazy as all of this might be, it looks quite serious to your family."

"My crazy, twisted family."

"Are you kidding? This is all, well, impossible. Magic eyes? A kingdom on the lake? Your family's so cool. Somewhat deranged and murderous, but cool." Logan held out his hand.

Camilla looked at it and then at him—at his mouth and nose and eyes. She sighed but took his hand anyway. He squeezed it, and the next moment, he hauled her down the corridor.

They arrived in the foyer to open the front doors. It led out onto the wall—a sort of walkway to the gates and then to the rest of Escana. Leaves whirled inside, along with everything else light enough to be carried by the wind. It was dark and storming, but what remained of the moon reflected off the lake, lighting the concerned faces of everyone outside.

Camilla approached. Two guards pushed past her, running in aid of Extine, their queen. They asked her whether she was all right, and she said something to them, then pointed at Camilla. They were upon her at once. She shook her head at them, asking them to leave.

They didn't.

"Your Majesty," they said as if they had known her forever. Raindrops ran across their lips as they spoke, often spraying onto her face. "The borders need to be fixed; they're collapsing."

One of the guards pointed at the sky—a glass-like dome that encased the kingdom. It had a crack through it and constantly withered, disappearing and reappearing.

Camilla looked past the dome across the lake. She saw the line of pavilions, the police strip, and the ticket booth. They were on the lake, exactly where she had seen it all along. There were people on the shore, not too many, but enough to quicken her heartbeat. They took pictures and recordings, a thousand flashes in the dark.

"Your Majesty, we don't have much time." The guards ushered her to the edge of the wall.

Camilla spat water from her mouth and flicked back a wet strand of hair. Her dress stuck to her body and chills rolled across her skin, but she hardly even noticed. She looked through the rain for Pearl and Extine. They saw her first and rushed up to her, both speaking at once.

"This is much worse than I thought," said Pearl.

"You have to fix the borders, Camilla, before the kingdom is revealed," Extine agreed with her.

Camilla's head throbbed, but Extine just went on, "It's all up to you. You're the one with the eyes."

"W—What must I do?" Camilla looked around again, this time for Logan who wove through the guards towards her, and for Finn who was explaining everything to the staff.

Remy and Milo were at the edge of the wall. Milo held onto Remy, protecting her, and Remy just stared out in front of her, likely listening to the chaos, trying to form a picture of it all.

"Camilla! Focus!" Pearl snapped her fingers at her. Her apron whipped in the wind and water gushed across her cheekbones, pooling in the hollow of her clavicle. She reached out and cupped Camilla's cheeks. "Still your mind. Tell the world to look past Escana. Tell them to forget it." She squeezed slightly, allowing water to drip into Camilla's mouth.

"I don't think I can," said Camilla. She turned and looked out across the lake—the dark mass of water that stretched before her, the only thing that separated Escana from Crystalvale. "How do I still my mind? How do I tell the world to forget about a place this magnificent?"

"You can do it. I know you can."

Camilla begged to differ. She opened her mouth regardless of the rain and inhaled the fresh evening air. She had to catch her breath, recollect herself. Her heart leapt in her chest, in her throat. Everyone's voices echoed in her head, their desperate pleas for help. She kept thinking of the people across the kingdom all in a panic, all depending on her to rescue them.

The pressure was too much. Their expectations were too high. Her fingers tapped, tapped, tapped against the jagged bricks of the wall. Her toes curled in her shoes, and her throat closed up. She coughed a little, then a little more. Panic crept up into her mind.

"Camilla," said a voice, and everything around her stilled.

Logan stood right next to her, pressed up against her with his shoulder. She looked to her side, at his soaked shirt and face and hair. She tilted her head, meeting his eyes, his soul.

"Still your mind," he said.

"I—I don't know how."

"Quite a bummer, isn't it? Not knowing something." Logan smiled, although it seemed strained. "Listen, I might not exactly know what's going on here, but I do know you're much stronger than you think you are, Camilla. Even when you're on the track, I know you can run faster than you allow yourself to." He nudged her, brushing his fingers against hers.

"This is not the same as running, Logan."

"Isn't it?"

The sky lit up with lightning. Seconds passed, and thunder broke in the distance, rolling across the lake.

"You once told me you wanted to be seen for who you are. And this is you, so let us see what you can do."

Camilla smiled back at him. She had wanted to thank him for the encouragement, apologize for dragging him into this but never got the chance. It played like a movie before her eyes: how she parted her lips to speak and how Logan leaned in, placing his mouth to hers.

They had kissed a while ago in the throne room, but she had been too in a daze to even notice it.

To relish it.

Now, not only could she see him, but she could give herself over to him, allow him to comfort her. Logan's hands slid around her waist, and he pulled her closer—so close she could feel his heartbeat in her own chest.

Thump. Thump. Thump.

Slow, steady, confident.

The stubble around his mouth scratched at her skin, but she embraced it, savored his touch.

Camilla forgot about the chaos, the enormous weight that rested upon her shoulders. She tuned out everyone around her and allowed herself to be lightened, her mind to be stilled.

The clouds stopped rumbling, and the rain ceased. The waves became still, and the borders stopped flickering. The people across the lake stopped taking pictures, and a melody of confused groans swept through the evening air. Everyone behind her broke into a cheer.

"You did it," said Logan as he pulled away. He pressed his forehead against hers, moving his hands up to her cheeks.

"Only because of you." Camilla chewed her lip. She pecked Logan one more time then turned away. Her mother stood in front of her, and she blushed. "Mom, is the kingdom safe now?"

Pearl nodded. "It is," she said. "And you saved it."

The crowd kept on cheering. Camilla curtseyed, considering it the customary thing to do. She reached for Logan's fingers, and he grabbed her entire hand, raising it in the air.

"All hail Queen Camilla!" he shouted.

More cheers.

"You've done well, Your Majesty," said Extine. She curtseyed, but Camilla pulled her into a hug. They stayed this way for a moment, upon which someone tapped Extine's shoulder.

It was Sorceress Juniper. "Your Majesty," she said. "Need I remind you, your eyes are still poisoning you."

Extine touched the dark circles that reached danger-ously far down her cheeks and to her inner neck. The whites of her eyes were cherry red, and dark veins colored her hands and feet.

"I'm ready," she said.

Sorceress Juniper nodded. "Are you certain, Your Majesty?"

"Remove the spell," she confirmed. "I don't want to live with this horrible pain anymore."

Sorceress Juniper almost grinned. She removed an amulet from her pocket, held it in her left palm, whispered something into it, then flashed it over Extine's eyes, face, and body.

Extine gasped for breath.

The darkness under her eyes disappeared, as well as the veins and creases and redness. She blinked, and her eyes changed from black to blue to grey. She sighed, acknowledging the inevitable. She was blind now, just like Rem.

"Are you okay, Extine?" asked Pearl.

"It was bound to happen, right?" she said, reaching for her sister's arm. "Even with Remy as the heir, I'd still have lost my sight. It's the price of power, a price that cannot be overlooked."

Pearl squeezed the water from Extine's hair. She pulled Extine into her, and it was as if they had never parted.

"Thank you for sparing my daughter," said Pearl, her voice muffled. "You made a great sacrifice, even after we'd caused you so much pain. If there's anything I can do, just say."

Extine shook her head. "No, you don't have to do

anything. Just forgive Remy for what she did. She's still a child, really. And the whole thing's on me. If only she still had her sight."

Pearl thought for a moment. Her face then lit up, and she said, "I'll do more than just forgive her."

"What do you mean?" asked Extine and Camilla in unison.

"Are you talking about me?" asked Remy.

Milo brought her over, leading her down the length of the wall. She seemed calmer now, more relaxed. Her mascara ran in lines down her face, and her hair lay flat against her head.

Pearl turned to Sorceress Juniper, who was wringing water from her dress. Her voice trembled as she said, "Can you transfer one person's sight to another?"

"What?" Camilla blurted out. "Mom, you can't possibly––"

Pearl spoke over Camilla, rephrasing her question, "Can you transfer my sight over to Remy?"

"Pearl, you don't have to do this," added Extine.

"Can you do it or can't you, Sorceress?" Pearl ignored them.

"Don't do it," Remy contested. "I can't expect you to make such a sacrifice. I––I don't deserve it."

"Sorceress?" Pearl insisted.

Sorceress Juniper cocked her head. "Well, I've never done it before . . . but I guess it's possible."

"Great, then let's do it. Quickly."

"Mom!" snapped Camilla.

"Pearl!" Extine added. "Why are you doing this?"

Extine grabbed Pearl's wrist. "You can't give up your sight like it's nothing."

"You did. For my daughter. It's only fitting I do the same."

"That was different," Extine beheld.

But Pearl pulled away and turned to Sorceress Juniper. "Remy made a mistake, but she doesn't deserve to be blinded for it. She's still young and can do a whole lot with her life."

She shut her eyes.

Sorceress Juniper cupped them, then plucked out her sight—a white, withering wisp between her fingers. Pearl gasped for breath, and Camilla let out a squeal. Her stomach gurgled, and she nearly hurled when Sorceress Juniper popped her mother's sight into Remy.

"There," said the sorceress, wiping her hands on her dress. She pried open Remy's eyes, one by one, and checked out her pupils. "Your sight should return in a couple of seconds."

"Thank you," whispered Remy to no one in particular.

"Mom!" Camilla ran to her mother's side. She pulled her face towards her and gasped. It was horrible, terrible. She was blind. "What have you done?"

"Nothing that I wouldn't do again."

Remy placed her palms over her eyes. She shivered a little, then removed her hands and looked around. For the first time since Camilla had met her, she laughed, really laughed.

"I can see," she gasped. Milo hugged her from the side, but she pulled away and turned to Pearl and Camilla. She kneeled before them, her head down. "Thank you. I don't deserve this—"

"No, you don't," Camilla agreed with her.

"Camilla." Pearl reached out to her. Her fingers crept up her neck and cheeks to her mouth. She placed them over her lips, hushing her. She smiled, even though her gaze was askew.

"But, Mom," Camilla began, although Pearl hushed her again.

"Everyone makes sacrifices. I sacrificed my life for you by coming here to recuse Logan. Extine sacrificed her eyes, her daughter's birthright, for you. I've already seen everything I wanted to. You've grown up before my eyes, achieved the most amazing things already."

Camilla wrapped her hand around her mother's finger. She kissed it and removed it from her lips.

Pearl continued, "You've become the woman I always dreamt you would. Strong and independent."

Camilla blinked away the tears, but it was no use. They slid down her cheeks, wetting Pearl's finger. She pursed her lips, tasting their saltiness, their bitter sorrow.

"I know this is not what you imagined for your life, but like Extine, like me, you too must make a sacrifice."

Camilla turned her head sideways. She avoided Pearl's gaze, even though she couldn't see a thing. She glanced at Logan through the corner of her eye, at the outline of his body in the sun on the horizon. What will happen to him, to them, their relationship? She thought deeply, watching bright orange rays reflect off the lake, scattering across the wall.

The night had passed, the most terrible, horrific—yet most fantastic—night of her entire life.

Camilla studied their reflections in the lake. A whole lot of people, once strangers, now family. The water lay still and serene. They were a perfect picture, a painting fit for the foyer.

If only her mother could see it.

"Sacrifice?" she said to herself.

Camilla turned her back to everyone and faced the lake. The outsiders had gone now, and the shore lay abandoned, a grazing spot for geese and ducks. The morning breeze sailed across her, over her, through her. She breathed it in, chilling her throat and lungs.

Pearl wouldn't ever gain her sight back, just like she, Camilla, wouldn't ever gain her freedom back. But a whole lot of people had made a whole lot of sacrifices: Finn wrecked his family, Extine gave up her power, and her mother . . . They all did it for her, to protect her.

Their losses couldn't go to waste.

"I'll do it," said Camilla, and everyone on the wall became quiet. "I'll do my duty and serve as queen."

CHAPTER TWENTY-SEVEN
CAMILLA

"What a crazy night, eh?" asked Logan, squeezing Camilla's hand. Their fingers were interlocked, their arms swinging back and forth as they strolled across the shore, basking in the sun.

"Really crazy," agreed Camilla.

Logan slowed down, then completely stopped. "Let me get this straight. Your mother is a princess from a kingdom on the lake, hidden from the outside world by the power in your eyes?"

Camilla nodded.

"And your father is married to your aunt, the former queen?"

"Yep, sounds about right."

Logan cocked a brow at her. His mouth stretched into a grin. "You realize that means your half siblings are also your cousins, right? And your aunt is also your stepmother?"

"Can we please not go into the details?" Camilla

laughed, but her head still spun every time she thought about the past couple of days and everything that had happened.

Logan resumed walking. He twisted his arm, so Camilla was forced to walk right next to him, against him. Their shoulders chafed together, and their hips collided every few steps.

"Sorry about that," Camilla mumbled upon another such occasion. She glanced down at her bare feet, buried in the sand. She still had her sundress on, damp from the rain.

Logan dismissed her apology. "Don't you find it funny?"

"What?"

"All of this." Logan tossed his hands in the air, yanking along Camilla's arm. "That the girl who hardly ever seeks the spotlight turns out to be the heir to a hidden kingdom. It's quite ironic if you think about it."

Camilla let go of Logan. She stepped in front of him, facing him. "Do you think I'm in over my head?"

Logan seemed taken aback. "Camilla, I didn't mean it like that."

"I know. It's just, do you think I'll be able to do it? You know, run an entire kingdom by myself?"

Logan reached for Camilla's chin. He raised it and answered slowly, softly, "I think you'll make a great queen, Camilla Ward. And you're not alone. I'll be here for you, no matter what."

Camilla placed her left hand on Logan's cheek. She buried her chin in his palm and looked right into his eyes.

They were the deepest brown they'd ever been, glossing in the morning sunlight. He raised her chin even more, lowering his head and closing his eyes.

Camilla pulled away. Her eyes flicked to her feet again, and she wrapped both hands around Logan's, still holding her chin. She gently removed it, pressing it against his chest.

"What's wrong?" asked Logan frantically. "Did I do something?"

"No, no."

"What is it, then?"

Camilla swallowed. "The thing is, Logan . . . you won't be able to . . . you can't be there for me."

"What?"

"I've spoken to my aunt and her advisors, and . . . in order for me to efficiently protect the kingdom of Escana, my mother and I have to sever all bonds with the outside world."

Logan pushed away from her, shaking his head. "Wait, are you . . . what exactly are you saying, Camilla?"

"I'm saying," Camilla choked up mid-sentence, "that you have to forget about everything."

"Everything?"

Tears pooled in the corners of her eyes. She whispered, "About Escana. About my family."

She drew a shaky breath.

"About me."

Logan's brows contorted, and his cheeks turned crimson. He was angry, livid. He stepped in and grabbed

Camilla's wrists. "No. I won't forget you, Camilla, I can't forget you!"

"Logan—"

"You're going to use your power on me, aren't you?"

No answer.

Logan's jaw worked. He shook Camilla's wrists a couple more times then opened his hands and stepped back with his arms in the air. He placed them behind his head and groaned.

"I don't have a choice, Logan," said Camilla after a while. "There are laws I have to follow."

"I know."

Camilla was shocked at Logan's answer. He had gone from denial to acceptance in less than a second. He didn't look at her anymore and constantly kicked his foot in the sand. Her heart tightened with every one of his groans— every one of his angry huffs.

"Well?" asked Logan, straightening. His eyes were as red as his face. "Just do it already."

Camilla thought about apologizing to him a final time but decided it was better to just make him forget. More efficient, as the advisors would say. She cleared her throat of any scratchiness and said, "Last night never happened, Logan. You woke up on the shore this morning. You don't remember anything about Escana. About my family..."

She couldn't bring herself to say the final part.

Logan's frown faded, and his knees wobbled. "I woke up on the shore... I don't remember anything... " He paused, and Camilla thought about finishing it off, but he all of a sudden started awake, rubbing his eyes. "Camilla? It's morning? W—What happened?"

Camilla couldn't speak.

"I don't—Are we still at the lake?" gasped Logan. He turned around and walked across the dock.

Camilla hesitated but followed. As much as it broke her heart, she had to finish what she was sent to do.

Logan stopped by the edge of the dock and stared out across the lake. Camilla joined him but kept her distance. She followed his eyes to Escana, to the great wall in front of them. A pair of guards patrolled across it, and the sun sparkled off the purplish marble.

"What are you looking at?" she asked.

"Nothing in particular." Logan rubbed his forehead with his thumbs. "What happened last night?"

"Y—You don't remember anything?"

"Nothing," he said, and his rub turned to a scratch.

"I guess that must've been one strong drink Remy gave you," Camilla said, attempting a laugh.

"Yes. Definitely." Logan paused. He bit his lip and frowned. "What happened after I drank it?"

Camilla's chest filled with air. She let it out, slowly, heavily. She hated lying to him like this, but he couldn't know the truth. Or maybe . . . What if she told him, and kept it a secret from Extine and the advisors? No. Not only would that be unfair to herself, but also Logan.

He had to be set free.

"Actually," she said, and her eyes locked with his. They sizzled and tingled with power. "You were really out of control. You ran around, talking about castles on the water and kingdoms with power-hungry queens. Even when the bonfire ended, you danced in the rain until dawn."

"Right. Of course, I did." Logan was only entranced for a second before he blushed bright red and scratched behind his head. "Boy, I must've looked like a total idiot, eh?"

Camilla shrugged. "Not really."

"Hey, listen, Camilla?" Logan took his eyes off the lake and turned towards her, his arms crossed over his chest. She raised her eyebrows at him, hoping her eyes weren't still as watery as earlier. He licked his lips and said, "Did anything... else... happen last night?"

"Like what?"

Logan kept his eyes on her mouth. "Did we, uh, did I . . . never mind, I'm just being silly."

"No, no, tell me," Camilla insisted. She wanted to reach out and place her hand on his shoulder but withheld herself. She flexed her fingers. She should just get it over with already and go. The longer they spoke, the harder it became for her to do what she had to.

"Well, I have this vague memory of us... of you and me..."

"Doing what?"

"Did I kiss you last night?" Logan blurted out. His eyes widened, and his cheeks reddened even more. His hair was still on the damp side, and he smoothed it back against his head.

"You did," said Camilla with a weak smile.

"Really?"

"And... I liked it."

Logan uncrossed his arms. For a moment it seemed like he didn't know what to do with his hands, but his eyes flicked down, and he reached for Camilla's fingers. She quickly slipped her hand behind her back. He frowned when she did this, hurt shadowing his eyes.

"I'm sorry, Logan," she muttered. "I should never have said anything. I'm... well, it's hard for me to tell you this... much harder than I thought. I'm going away. Far away."

"What? For how long?" Logan demanded. Like before, he put his hands behind his head. He stared out across the lake again, his eyes on screens, and his jaw clenched.

"A while."

"How long of a while?"

Camilla spoke softly as she answered, "I don't know." She kept her head down, unable to look him in the eyes when she was lying to him. She wasn't going away for a while, and she did know for how long: forever. Her coronation was set for the next day, and the advisors had given her until then to depart from Logan and anyone else she might miss.

"Well, where are you going?"

Camilla only now looked up at him. He shielded the sun with his body, so she only saw his outline. His broad, six-foot, kayaking-sculpted outline. Her heart sped up a little.

"I've recently reconnected with some estranged family. My mother and I are going to live with them for a while." Camilla tried to act as convincingly as possible. She'd never lied as much as she had that morning.

"Estranged family, eh?" asked Logan. His expression softened. "All right, I understand. It's family." He smiled, but Camilla noticed something different this time, something hesitant.

"Logan," she said, and his smile faded entirely. She took a step towards him, the dock creaking under her feet —her mind warning her not to get too close. "I don't want you to wait for me."

Logan stiffened.

"I don't know what happened between us or what exactly this is, but I'm going to be gone for a long time." Tears pooled in her eyes. "And I want you to move on, live your life."

Logan wiped under her eyes with his thumb. He shook his head. "No, Camilla. I can't forget you."

"I don't want you to forget me," she said, basking in her cowardice. She just couldn't do it. She couldn't bring herself to wipe Logan's memories of her. "I just want you to let me go."

Camilla stepped back.

"You just have to," she whispered.

Logan said nothing.

Camilla continued, "This is really hard for me. And if there'd been any other way, any other option... all I can say is... maybe, maybe one day..." She looked away and swallowed. Maybe one day? Maybe what? They could be together? An outsider and an Escanian?

"Maybe one day?" Logan sounded less hopeful and more despondent. This time, instead of stepping away or approaching her with caution, he grabbed her wrists and pulled her close.

Their faces were within touching distance, their breaths clashing, warming up Camilla's cheeks. She wanted to frown, wanted to scold him and pull away, but she couldn't.

"Logan, please."

"I won't do anything if you don't want me to. So, tell me. Tell me you don't want me to kiss you."

"I feel like that's a trick statement."

"Tell me to let go of you, Camilla. Tell me!" Logan tightened his grip.

Camilla's breath caught in her throat. She should just tell him. It was as easy as a few words. But it wasn't easy. It wasn't easy at all. She relaxed a little, letting go of herself.

Logan took this as a sign of approval, of giving in to his charms. He leaned in, just like before, and, once again, Camilla only just managed to lower her face. Logan's lips pressed softly against her forehead. She expected him to pull away, to apologize and act awkwardly, but he lingered for a while. When he did pull away, he smiled softly and let go of her.

"Until we meet again, Camilla Ward," was all he said.

"Soon," Camilla replied. She stepped back, turned on her heels, and walked away down the dock. With each step, each clop against the wood, her heart pounded louder in her chest.

Logan remained in place. He didn't run after her, and he didn't call out to her. He respected her decision, and that made everything all the more difficult. All the more torturing.

Camilla stepped off the dock onto the shore. She made for the parking lot, and then for the trees, dying to look back. But she didn't. Even if she did, she wouldn't see Logan through the film of tears in her eyes. She blinked, and they surged down her cheeks.

"Soon," she repeated, "that's a promise."

THANK YOU FOR READING

Thank you for reading *The Girl Who Stole the Queen's Eyes.*

Please consider leaving a review wherever you purchased this book. Not only does it help an indie author and publisher make more books, but you'll also be helping other readers find their next favorite book.

OTHER ZENITH TITLES YOU MAY ENJOY

Queen of All by Anya Leigh Josephs

Casting Shadows by Dziyana Taylor

A Love Across Time by Genevieve Jane

The Facts and Legends of Callie Catwell by Sophia DeRise

Sea and Flame by Tallie Rose

ABOUT THE AUTHOR

MARILIZE LOXTON recently graduated with a Bachelor's in English Literature and Creative Writing from the North West University of South Africa. Having worn glasses since childhood, she was inspired by the idea of using eyes as a main theme in a fantasy story, particularly what it would be like to lose and regain sight.

Aside from *The Girl Who Stole the Queen's Eyes*, Marilize is working hard at signing with an agent and ultimately bringing her work to a larger audience. When she's not writing or reading, you might find her either in the kitchen baking up sweet treats, or in the bathroom with her dog, trying (probably failing) to get him toweled off after a bath.

ABOUT THE PUBLISHER

ZENITH is a YA/NA imprint of GenZ Publishing, launched in 2019 and growing more every day. We believe in the importance of reading and writing in shaping the future. As such, we focus on publishing debut, emerging, or underrepresented authors whose voices are ready to be heard.

Find out more and submit your story: www.zenithpublishing.org

www.ingramcontent.com/pod-product-compliance
Lightning Source LLC
Chambersburg PA
CBHW060513030726
47498CB00004B/934